THE INVISIBLE DOOR

Twisted Mystery at Ashmont Hall

J. Z. Richardson

TABLE OF CONTENTS

1 NEW ARRIVAL   P. 5
2 MEMBER OF THE FAMILY   P. 10
3 LOUISE   P. 16
4 A SURPRISE   P. 22
5 OUR LAMB IS BACK   P. 30
6 MYSTERIOUS MUSIC   P. 35
7 DISCOVERIES   P. 42
8 PUZZLES   P. 47
9 AN EARLY CALL   P. 53
10 CHURCH AND A GIRL   P. 59
11 SECRET PASSAGE   P. 64
12 THE NOTE   P. 69
13 FLIRTING   P. 76
14 EMERALD MAKES A CHANGE P. 81
15 LOUISE'S WARNING   P. 87
16 FIRST GLIMPSE   P. 92
17 KAY'S BOUDOIR   P. 96
18 REHEARSAL   P. 101
19 WADING THROUGH   P. 106
20 A NEW JOB   P. 110
21 ODD COUPLE   P. 115
22 THE SECOND PAGE   P. 119
23 SCANDAL   P. 124
24 AN ACCIDENTAL FIND   P. 129
25 ASHMONT COMPETES   P. 134
26 A SHOCKING CLAIM   P. 139
27 FAMOUS WEDDING   P. 143
28 THE LECTURE   P. 147
29 DISAPPOINTMENT   P. 152
30 KAY'S PLAN   P. 156
31 FORCED TO STAY   P. 161
32 DINNER PARTY   P. 168

33 THE KISS   P. 174
34 AVOIDANCE   P. 180
35 THE VIOLIN   P. 185
36 ILLNESS   P. 190
37 DANNY   P. 197
38 EVENING QUEST   P. 203
39 CRISIS   P. 209
40 EMERALD HAS PROOF   P. 214
41 THE BOX IS OPENED   P. 218
42 THE PEPPERMINT PONY   P. 221
43 SUN AND STORM   P. 226
44 ELECTRIC WORDS   P. 229
45 CRASH AND COMPANY   P. 233
46 HOME   P. 239
47 UNEXPECTED GUEST   P. 243
48 CHRISTMAS GIFTS   P. 247

1

NEW ARRIVAL

"**N**o. Make a fresh pot, Nora," said Kay to her sister, who had come in with a rattling tray. Kay waved her hand at it as if the motion could sweep the old tea from existence, by magic.

"But it's so late. Surely she'll be here in a few minutes."

"No sign of her yet. I've sent Saxon down the road to call me when she's coming. Supposed to be in a blue four-door. And I will not serve her stale tea. Ashmont Hall has a reputation to be upheld."

"Reputation or not — she's *family*. Or practically so, anyway. Shouldn't that be our first consideration?" asked Nora, with a characteristic tremble in her voice.

A pile of knitting in the chair near the fire moved, then coughed. Under the pile was a tiny, ancient lady. She spoke, in her tiny, ancient voice.

"Nora, when she gets here, tell me. This afghan for her isn't quite finished yet; I want it to be a surprise."

"No, Mother Ann — remember? You're not doing the afghan for Emerald Johnsey. It's to be for — "

"Sybilla. That's who we're waiting up for."

"Not Sybilla, Mother Ann," corrected Kay, two or three times until her grandmother understood. "Not Sybilla. We're expecting young Emerald Johnsey. Remember? Nick and Charlotte's daughter?"

Wind rattled the windows, then a flash of lightning tore through the room. For a few moments the diamond-shaped windowpanes cast their crisscrossed shadows over the antique furniture and walls, cutting them up neatly. "It's turning into quite a storm," said Nora nervously. She looked out the window. "This might be her now. I see a little car driving up."

Until Emerald warily turned left onto the driveway under the arbor, and her headlights swept across the mansion, she had looked forward to this moment. Six hours she had traveled with anticipation; the last two minutes suddenly turned tedious. The opposite of how a journey should be.

She couldn't help the feeling of guilt, clinging to her conscience like a stubborn cobweb; even though Dad had told her, insisted that she should move to North Carolina to live for a few months, to take a break from everything at home. She and Dad both were worn out. The day that Dad first mentioned it caught her completely off guard. They had just returned from an excruciating visit with Mother, and Emerald had sunk weary in the recliner.

"Look, I have an idea," Dad said. "What say you spend the next semester at Finley College? You can stay with the Keckleys, you know, at Ashmont."

Ashmont.

Ashmont Hall.

Instantly the words plucked from her memory the wonderfully rambling house, lush grounds, the whole atmosphere of otherworldly charm; but above all these — the "most exquisite woman in the world," as she remembered describing in her childhood diary: Kay Keckley.

"You mean with those ladies we used to visit a long time ago? Kay and — what was her name?"

"Why you should remember your own aunts!" chuckled Dad. "Don't you? I guess it has been a few years since we've been there. Kay and Nora, and their grandmother. I can't believe the old lady is still going strong."

Kay and Nora were sisters and very much alike. Nora was sweet, but Kay was the picture of elegance in Emerald's eyes. As a child she would watch her, and imitate her graceful movements as best as an 8-year-old could, holding her hand out to steady herself while walking downstairs, or slowly turning her head, then body, in the direction of whoever was speaking. She even remembered pretending to smoke. Nobody smoked cigarettes more beautifully than Aunt Kay.

"I would like to go for a visit," said Emerald, pulling out her ponytail holder and massaging her aching head. "But Dad, what if – what if Mother –" she said wildly, turning to him.

He was prepared with an answer. "I'll call you. If and when the time gets close, I'll get you back home. She's barely conscious now, and can't really enjoy your presence. And Sweetie, you're worn out. You've got to get away for a while. You know the doctor said it could be years."

He had already spoken with the Keckleys; they were delighted she was coming and had her room all ready. So Emerald packed two suitcases and a cardboard box, filled her tank with gas, and went.

From time to time, as the windshield wipers kept their relentless rhythm, Emerald's thoughts would be lulled to the years – now painfully gone – when Mother was herself. She thought of the last time they planted spring flowers together, the covert conversations, the fun little spats every so often . . . *swish-swish-swish* . . . of the shopping trips and the all-afternoon house cleaning sessions and the suppers they cooked.

She drove, re-living the conversation with Dad in her thoughts. She had felt so guilty; but he was right. She was exhausted and had to do something else for a while, a break from the round-the-clock cycle of shots, pills, and countless distasteful medical apparatuses. This wasn't turning her back on Mother; he was arranging excellent care for her, after all.

All these were very sensible reasonings, but when she thought of Mother's cool hand clasping hers – none of them could keep her heart from tingeing with remorse.

The swishing of the wipers lulled her back still further. Back to childhood visits to North Carolina. The memory of Kay's lilting, feminine voice had caressed her thoughts and found its way to Emerald's sore heart, giving it a sort of relief. She would be a friend, a lady to look up to, to enjoy something of the warmth of feminine influence once again – important to a girl of almost twenty-two.

She needed it badly just now.

Every mile from home released her a little more. Every mile separated her from – not from Mother, she was already a world away from her, even when close enough to look into her vacant eyes – but from the monster, the disease. The disease that had taken her beautiful mother away, and left an incoherent mess. She drove away from it.

Freedom and newness pulsed in her veins, the closer she got to Millcrest. At last the road carried her up the foothills, curving around and through the higher elevations; she entered the state, the valley, and the town itself. She hadn't been there since childhood, but her heart leapt to see familiar signs and landmarks as she coursed through it.

Coming into the vicinity of Ashmont she suddenly became nervous. She spotted the mailbox, the iron gates, the row of poplars leading to the massive stone mansion.

But her heart sank at the view. Was she sure she had the right place? It had to be.

However, this wasn't the "fairy tale house" that she remembered calling it as a child; it was an unsmiling, elderly matriarch of a structure, solemn and formal; the thunderstorm electrified it into blinding flashes, showing its age starkly, if briefly. It was all a mistake; she shouldn't have come! But there was nothing to do about it now. She found a place to park and walked, through the rain, around to the front of the house.

Why were all the windows black? It was late, too late to come as a visitor, she thought to herself – oh, why didn't she wait till tomorrow like Dad had wanted her to? Everyone must be in bed by now, and she'll wake them up by ringing that dreadful doorbell that sounded like a gong.

Two frightful stone gargoyles flanked the steps to the front door; she had forgotten about them. They stared senselessly into the whirling storm, caring nothing about the newcomer. She mounted the steps, slipping a little. Just then there was a noise, a movement – the double doors cracked open. One blonde head, then two, appeared; there was the flicker of a candle, a beckon of a waving hand. The next moment Emerald was received, dripping and shivering, into four arms and a blanket.

2

MEMBER OF THE FAMILY

With a little laugh, Aunt Kay removed Emerald's hat and shook it off. "What a drive you must have had!" said the lovely voice, wrapping the girl in warmth and welcome. "Let's get your shoes off. Here, put on my slippers." Kay was the same as ever. Her satin house dress brushed Emerald's cheek as she helped her off with her wet things. Hair, demeanor, stature – the very lipstick color was the same as Emerald remembered.

"Our electricity went out! We were afraid you wouldn't be able to see the house from the road," said Aunt Nora – a slightly shorter, slightly plumper version of her sister. "That driveway is so hard to find. It's like a thread."

"Thank you both so much for inviting me to stay here," she told them. "Since you take in boarders and are so near the college, it was lucky that you had an extra room available. Of course I'll pay. Dad and I both insist."

Both ladies gently squealed in protest, which made Emerald smile. "Of course you won't! You're *family*," gushed Kay. "I wouldn't dream of it. Would we, Mother Ann?"

"What's that?" croaked the pile of knitting. "Oh, she's here. I'd better hide this afghan —"

"No, not *her*. It's Emerald. Emerald, remember? She was about this high when we saw her last. She used to come with her parents during the summer."

"Oh yes! How are you dear? Here," she said, moving the knitting out of the way, "sit down next to me."

They sat by the fire. Emerald shivered and enjoyed the crackling heat and light, now serving a double purpose since the room would otherwise be pitch black.

Emerald clasped the old lady's hand in greeting. "Hello," she said. "Somebody told me I was named after you."

"That's right, you were!" she said in her quavery voice. "I'm so old I forgot that is my middle name! Ann Emerald. My father named me."

"Was it because your eyes were green?"

"Oh no! Mine are brown. But Father said that the first blades of green grass appeared the morning of my birth."

"Your mother always loved that name and said she would use it for her own little girl, one day," continued the old lady.

My mother always loved that name. *My mother.* The phrase echoed through her soul. She was handed a cup of something hot, and took it; bracing herself for the questions, the concerns, the inevitable queries that would come. They came.

"How is she doing, Emerald?" Nora asked in a softened voice.

Swallowing first, she fed them the rehearsed answer. "We – we had to put her into a home. It's a very good home; she's well cared for now." She thought of the empty places back home; the empty rocking chair where she used to sit; the empty kitchen, the empty dressing table.

Everyone was quiet, hearing only the lessening thunder. Most of the house was in shadow except when briefly charged with lightning, less intense now. During the pulses of light she glanced around, trying to recognize its features. A few things she remembered: that broad painting of two leopards; a red tartan pillow; the models of antique cars on an upper shelf.

She was startled to suddenly hear big stamping feet approaching the front door. A man came in, with a grunt and a groan, and hung up his wet overcoat. He had brought the traveler's suitcases in from her little car and set them down, along with a long wooden item he'd been carrying under one arm.

"Say, what is this thing?" he held it up for all to see.

"Oh, that's – that's my easel."

"Of course! I forgot, we have a bona fide *artiste* under our roof!" And the women cooed like doves at the admiration of this impressive talent. "Your father said something about your studying art at the college. It's been a long time since I've seen your work. Saxon, I can't believe you didn't recognize that valuable piece of equipment. She's going to think you know nothing at all."

"All I know is it's a delight to see you again, young lady; you wouldn't remember me, but I do you. You were about as big as my little finger, running up and down these stairs many years ago. I thought we had a mouse infestation, hearing those patters while working on the furnace once."

She smiled and greeted him warmly, shaking his hand. He was a bear of a man and would have intimidated her had this been a first meeting. "I remember you almost more than anybody! You used to let me play with the – what was it? Oh yes, that mechanical tape measure thing. Then I cut my finger on it and you bandaged it for me."

"And I've been bandaging wounds ever since. Oh, maybe not flesh wounds, but of other sorts – the emotional kind, let's say. With only ladies running this place, emotions can run pretty high. Somebody has to keep them in check."

"I'm sure we can take care of ourselves, sir," cried Kay, in the tone of mock offendedness. "We, emotional?! We are not babies in diapers. Mr. Saxon was hired by our parents," she said, turning to Emerald, "about thirty years ago as a handyman and gardener, after he hung around here so long they finally gave him something to do. So now, he's the only one who knows everything about Ashmont – well, almost everything – " (shooting him a look) "and he thinks he's in charge of everybody. I'll concede that you're no longer a servant," turning back to the gruff old man, who was half-smiling with a glittering eye, "and I'll even go so far to say you're my friend. But my father, you're not." And she sat down with a huff, as rebelliously as a precocious three-year-old.

The lights came back on, and the house made funny little noises adjusting back to the power now coursing through it.

They continued sitting in the den, the ladies chatting about some changes they had plans for at Ashmont, and Mr. Saxon protesting at almost everything they said, due to impracticability or cost; but Emerald detected that it was more banter than real opposition – that her aunts enjoyed having a barrier to overcome.

Inwardly, she was much at ease with them now, compared to the jitters she had first approaching the house. Only one thing caught her attention, to give her a feeling of discomfort. She had been very hungry upon arriving and had fully realized it once seated by the fire and detecting the scent of something freshly baked. Then Nora came in the room with a plateful of scones – exquisitely made, crunchy but with soft insides, and dripping with glaze. They passed them around.

"Oh how wonderful," she said between bites, "and I didn't have any dinner. Aunt Nora, you could make a million dollars, if these were on the market."

"No she wouldn't, because she wouldn't have the heart to charge anything for them," Mr. Saxon said.

Nora brought her the plate a second time – there was one left. "I feel bad taking the last one! I really shouldn't," said Emerald, though tempted. She reached for it slowly, feeling it was expected of her.

"Nora!" shot Kay. "Remember, those are *someone's* favorites. We do have more in the kitchen, don't we?"

"Oh no, I put them all on the plate, remember?"

"But you-know-who might be coming in tonight too. She said it would be sometime this week."

"But the poor child hasn't had any supper!"

"We should make her a sandwich. Nora, go make her a ham sandwich."

Mr. Saxon stood to his feet and intervened by bringing the plate back to Emerald with his own hand. "The young lady likes these very much, and she's already here," he said impressively. Emerald meekly took the last one but didn't enjoy an object of so much controversy. On the way back to the kitchen, Kay was whispering to Nora in words that sounded like scolding. Emerald was able to catch "just make some more in the morning, and don't forget." And, "No, I won't."

Who were they saving them for? Probably some important guest coming for the weekend, Emerald deduced. She guiltily swallowed the rest and finished her tea.

The tiger of a storm outside had subsided into a mere kitten, prancing off to play somewhere else, and Emerald sat staring at the fire quietly.   Mother Ann snored under her knitting and was awakened when her needle slipped out of her hand.

"Well, it's time we all turned in, isn't it? Emerald, come with me. I'll show you where we've got you. Saxon, you carry her things," said Kay, leading the way up the main stairs. The girl mounted the steps, gazing around with pleasure, remembering many of the family photos and framed embroidery on the walls – it was all coming back to her now. She even caught a glimpse of an old black-and-white picture with her parents, along with Kay, in it. All three, young and vibrant-looking, had their arms around each other, leaning against a black car. How pretty Mother was in it. But they were moving up the stairs quickly and she was so tired; she'd look at it more closely tomorrow.

"It's the sweetest room," Kay was telling her. "Your coming gave me the opportunity to fix it up like I've wanted to for years now. I'm afraid it's on the third story – and it's small – you know I had to keep my bigger rooms open for weekenders. But if I remember correctly, you never minded being up there."

"Oh! Not at all. I think I had more fun up there than anywhere in the house. I used to play with Nora's daughter, I believe? What was her name. . ."

Nora was at the point of answering her as they reached the landing leading up to the third floor, when they turned the corner and came face to face with a person wearing overalls, a crop of short, spiky hair, and long feather earrings almost touching her shoulders. Emerald almost gasped with the suddenness of seeing such an odd, hard-looking woman, especially here.

"Louise," said Kay with authority. "You were supposed to have helped us in the kitchen two hours ago."

"I been fixing the toilet you told me about," said the woman in her Yankee accent. "And it was a lot dirtier than you told me. Had to get it ready for visitors," she went on, turning her eyes on

Emerald.

Kay gave half a glance over her shoulder in Emerald's direction, then changed her tone of voice immediately. "That will do. I'm sure all is in order now. You know, Emerald," she said as they continued to the top, "we like to keep Ashmont in apple-pie order. It's kind of our reputation, our legacy. We are known far and wide, for our hospitality, cleanliness, and elegant atmosphere." Kay sounded like she was reading from a tourist brochure.

They had turned the corner and stopped in front of a door with a crystal doorknob. "Here it is!" she said, swinging it open.

3

LOUISE

When Emerald awoke the next morning in her new room, she became aware of a rumbling sound near her. It was the purring of a massive cat that had crept upon her bed and now lay alongside her.

"Well, hello there," she said to the gray mound of an animal, gazing at her with eyes the color of sea glass. "And what is your name?" He blinked and continue to purr, rolling over while she stroked him.

She looked around at her temporary home. It was a sweet place, like Kay had said – a little on the old-fashioned side, with its rose motif and vague scent of mothballs, but overall a cheery spot, especially with morning light piercing through the curtains and spilling onto the floor.

There were twin beds in satin, candy-colored pink, and matching pink rosebuds running over the wallpaper in a pattern. A dressing table sat in the corner. Between the beds was a tiny fireplace and a mantel above it. Saxon had lit it for her after bringing her luggage up last night; it had made the room a little smoky but otherwise gave great comfort to the weary traveler; and she had fallen asleep listening to the crackle of embers.

Her favorite thing about the room was that it had its very own share of a *turret*. It made it so castle-y. The two windows in the turret were a marvel. When she pulled back the sun-faded curtains she saw that the window frames and even the glass panes were curved to fit in the rounded wall.

The view from her third story room was spectacular! Ashmont's extensive, somewhat untidy grounds were spread out before her in deep green rolls, dotted with ancient trees and an occasional stone bench or birdbath. It must have been wonderfully cared for in past generations, when there were plenty of hungry villagers willing to be employed at the grand place. There was evidence of well-laid out paths and flower beds, now under-trodden and neglected.   There was one vegetable garden still in use – Mr. Saxon's territory – and a few potted plants around the terrace, but other than that, Ashmont was nearing a state of decay.   As for herself, she saw beauty in such a condition.   A crumbling wall was much more interesting to sketch, and the roses now growing wild were greater inspiration than orderly, well-disciplined ones.

But from up here at her third story window, her eyes could not dwell on any of Ashmont's imperfections long.   The region's mountains and valleys were in open view beyond.   At this early hour they were still shrouded in mist, like a lady's veil. For at least five minutes Emerald gazed out at them, scarcely breathing, transfixed. She was almost pained by the views, ravishing her very heart, of frosted hillside and meadows, swimming in morning mist, laid out like a feast for her consumption. A simmering cauldron of beauty.

Something caught her eye directly below. It was a blonde lady in a caftan walking around on the patio, watering plants: she couldn't tell if it was Kay or Nora.   The lady called to someone inside, and Mother Ann hobbled out, bending over whatever she was pointing at. It must be Kay; yes, that gesture looked like her.

She felt like a little girl around Kay. The same sensations arose from childhood: watching how pretty she looked, and longing to be at her side to absorb whatever she was thinking and feeling. Kay's motions had always drawn Emerald like a magnet.   There was something indescribable about her that Emerald wanted to capture. She found herself, again, wishing for time with her. She had felt guilty in coming to Ashmont, but now that she was here, as an adult, she would finally have it. She envisioned pouring her heart out to her in quiet conversations, and taking private walks with her; what a balm to her tired, aching soul it would be. The last time she and Mother had taken a walk was . . . well, she couldn't remember when it was.

She showered and dressed, then headed downstairs.   Upon

arriving last night she had felt a sudden dread, especially seeing the starkness of Ashmont in the storm; but being in the presence of long-lost family, precious family, filled Emerald with a faint but exciting nervousness, a thrill running through her soul, at being here again. She wondered at the resurrection of childhood memories – sounds, sensations – like hearing the forgotten yet familiar sound of an old clock somewhere in the house, striking the hour just now. They were popping up, one by one.

She remembered her way around, at least the main parts of the house. Overall, Ashmont's interior was not as spooky as it had seemed last night; but in the bright light of day she could see more wear and tear than she had noticed upon arriving. Stained wallpaper was peeling in the corners; doors creaked and the plumbing made funny sounds. She descended the impressive staircase down the middle of the mansion, her hand sliding along the slick banister. Let's see, where was that photo she wanted to take a closer look at? The black-and-white with her parents in it. Approaching the bottom she saw the same group—she thought it was the same group of photos that had caught her attention last night; but that one was missing! Instead, a pale rectangle on the wallpaper was all that was there. The naked space seemed to stare back at her quizzically. She wondered who had removed it, and why.

Sounds and smells came from the kitchen; as she came down the hallway she caught a glimpse of the dining room, and saw a few unknown people filling it, waiting for breakfast. The last thing she wanted was to meet a roomful of people just now – she wanted to slip outside, and alone. Then maybe later, if she could catch Kay alone, they could talk.

She passed unnoticed by the breakfasters and found a back door leading out to the lawn. She wanted to walk around the house and do a little exploring. Upon stepping out, her skin tingled with the sudden chilly pleasure of the open air.

Ashmont was nestled in the heart of the Smoky Mountains. Here was atmosphere and oxygen fresher, cleaner than back home in Kentucky, and she indulged herself in it, imbibing its vigor.

Striding through the wet grass, she wore a dark jacket and denim skirt; the only color was the limp red ribbon she had used to hastily pull her hair into a ponytail, which was somewhat askew. To an onlooker she might have looked like a forlorn laborer, a farm worker or – in days long ago – a milkmaid; but inside the subdued exterior beat an exhilarated heart, expanding with every swishing step, with every glance at distant mountain crests.

She wouldn't go far, since she would be expected at the breakfast table soon, just enough out into the lawn to gain a full view of the house. Wow, it was way bigger than she had remembered! How did they ever fill up such a house?? There were some low rambling wings that had been added after the main house was constructed, no doubt to house servants in its heyday of fame. Still, how ethereal it looked as it rose up before her, wrapped in its misty morning veil! It seemed the haunt of all her ghostly memories, and vaguely – of mysteries to be solved. She wondered what mysteries might be hidden there. What had happened in her aunts' lives the last fifteen years? Why had they kept so little in touch with her family? What type of people now resided there, and what hopes, joys, or heartaches would she brush with in the next few months? While wondering these things, she tripped on something.

It was a brick. She looked around, as people do after tripping, to see if anyone had been watching. Luckily she was the only backyard wanderer and had no fears of being laughed at. It was all coming back to her now: it was a portion of the old brick walkway that led around the rear of the house, in a herringbone pattern, among the clusters of crepe myrtles and rose bushes. She remembered once when she was little, she had fallen on them – perhaps some of these very bricks she was walking on now. Mother and Dad were gone to town, but Aunt Kay had rushed to her and picked her up, and carried her into the house. She had given her chocolate milk and let her lie on the couch the rest of the day, watching TV. Smiling at the memory, she wandered on . . . but gradually realized she couldn't remember exactly how to get back to the terrace.

She should have been paying attention! She was in a totally different section than she remembered, and couldn't even hear the voices of those on the terrace anymore. She kept walking along it until she found an entrance, but it was locked. With every few steps she found another wing of the building, each more unfamiliar than the one before, until she sighed with frustration. In her disorientation all she kept finding were walls and bushes. Now she thought of her pride in "remembering her way around the house" from years before; she humbly admitted she was totally lost.

She turned a corner and – smack! – ran into something metal. It was a tool bucket, hanging from the arm of Louise, the woman who had fixed the toilet. "Oh!" cried Emerald, with shock at the almost full-body collision. They now stood inches from each other; in such close proximity, that Emerald's first instinct was to apologize. She stepped back, noticing that Louise still wore the odd ensemble of last night – overalls and feather earrings.

"You kin to the owners?" asked Louise right away, not at all shaken by the surprise. Emerald, trembling, had to ask her to repeat herself.

"You kin to the owners?"

"Yes. Well, sort of," she said, backing away at a more comfortable distance.

"She your aunt?"

Again Emerald had trouble understanding Louise's clipped phrases, laden with an accent from New England or somewhere. Louise said it again.

"Not really. Kay and Nora are cousins of my father. But I've always called them my aunts, and considered them so."

Louise just stared at Emerald with a gaze that she didn't quite comprehend.

"I seem to have gotten lost. Could – could you show me the way back to the terrace?"

Louise, although not acknowledging this request, walked along, so Emerald joined her. She hoped to be within civilization soon.

"I been working for Miss Kay a few years," she volunteered.

"Oh?" replied Emerald pleasantly. "Working for the Keckley

family?"

"No. Not for the family. Just Miss Kay."

Emerald tried to follow whatever she meant by that. "She must need a lot of special attention," she answered, puzzled.

To this, Louise gave no response; she just stared. The feather earrings fluttered a little in the morning breeze. What she said next, in a lower voice, startled Emerald:

"She's off."

"What? What do you mean by that?"

"She's off, just off. She ain't like Nora or the others. Or anybody else. Are you off?"

Obviously this Louise was disturbed. Emerald, alarmed, walked faster, trying to disengage herself from her as gracefully as she could. "Certainly not," she answered. How else were you supposed to respond to such a question?

Emerald was glad to hear the voices of her aunts just ahead. She hurried and finally regained sight of the terrace. Unwilling to continue the strange conversation with Louise, she walked faster, with nothing but the sound of swishing grass between them, and the clanging of Louise's bucket.

There was Kay – the picture of serenity, with head leaning back, eyes closed, and pulling on a cigarette luxuriously. Emerald hungrily eyed the empty seat next to her. She walked even faster. At last she could gain the refuge of her presence, and chat with her.

But just as she walked up, Kay saw her and Louise (who walked just as fast as Emerald) and suddenly stood to her feet.

"There you are!" she called. "Are you out exploring this morning, and so early? Your boots are all wet. Let's go in and take them off," she said, holding the door open for her. "Come in to breakfast. I have somebody I want you to meet."

4

A SURPRISE

Every seat around the breakfast table was filled except one. Emerald prepared herself to meet the other inmates of Ashmont.

"This must be the new young lady," said a pleasant woman, tall, wearing an African turban and strands of beads. She patted the empty chair next to her.

"Emerald, meet Rita Canter, one of the professors at the college."

"Nice to meet you," she said, sitting down. Someone handed her some English muffins, and she busied herself with her plate for a few moments so she could be looked at by everyone present. Why did she still feel like a ten-year-old? Sipping her juice, she tried to take on a grown-up expression, by having a faraway look in her eye and nonchalantly passing the sausage. She nearly dropped it. Everyone glanced up at her for a few moments but, soon resuming eating, she felt at liberty to take a look around herself.

From what she could tell in the first few moments' casual observation, she already knew most of them. She was relieved to see only three unknown faces, and one of them was the friendly Rita beside her, who was handing her a section of the newspaper. A very good looking, white-haired gentleman sat at the head. He was alternately flirting with Kay and scribbling notes into a little journal. Then there was Mother Ann and a dog in her lap, then Mr. Saxon, the two aunts, and another man behind the sports section. She couldn't see enough to judge how old he was, but his hand, reaching out at intervals for another morsel of food, looked about thirty years old. The cuff of his blue shirt was a little frayed.

During the meal she was saved from conversation, since Kay and the older gentleman kept up their banter, with occasional laughing interjections from Nora. He turned to Emerald once or twice, asking about her college plans, and whether or not she was frightened of living in an old haunted house like Ashmont.

"Don't put odd ideas in her head, Lars," laughed Kay. "Anyway, she's no stranger here. Remember what I was telling you about her? She's family."

"Ah. So she probably knows that the warning about the house was a mere charade," he teased, winking across the table at her. "She knows what, or rather whom, to beware of around here." And he nodded once toward Kay. In return, she pinched him and got up to clear some dishes away.

"Have you gotten your classes all lined up yet?" Mr. Saxon asked her.

"No. I'm supposed to do that tomorrow."

"Ah, college. The best years of my life," sighed Kay.

"But my dear sister," Nora said, "you only went a year and a half. And it wasn't college. It was finishing school."

"Well, for all practical purposes, yes it was college. It prepared me for the life I was to lead here at our dear homestead. That's more than I can say for some institutions. So, I didn't go on to real college. No matter. It was the little graces of life, the proper way to conduct oneself, and adding to the joy of living that I learned, not numbers and facts."

"Well I'm glad of Ashmont's provision for you and yours, Ms. Kay," said Rita Canter. "One can experience the joy of living, but I'm afraid that won't guarantee you can make a living on joy. As I tell my students, seize the day, but make sure you have a plan for future days to be seized as well."

"That's what I'm doing," announced Nora mysteriously.

"What?" asked Rita with a laugh. "Are you seizing the day today?"

"No, the other thing you said. Making plans. . . making plans," she said in her sing-song voice that she used when especially happy. "I'm going on a trip."

"A trip? Where are you going, Aunt Nora?"

"I'm going on a cruise. A cruise to Rio dee Janeiro." She

pronounced it wrong, but nobody corrected her.

"Really! When?"

"Oh, one day."

"I'll tell you all when. The same day that I see Mr. Saxon give up his pipe, shave his beard, and remove those horrible nandinas," said Kay, nodding toward the window overlooking the flower beds. "And yes, I'll say they're all on the same day – because they're all equally impossible. That will be the day, dear sister, when I shall book your cruise."

"Oh, I have faith, I have faith, even if no one else does. Don't you, Mr. Saxon?"

"Let's just say, I have known Kay Keckley long enough to observe that she gets what she wants, even if it takes years. That woman has a will of iron once she gets something in view. That knowledge is the basis of my faith – in all that she said – except one." And he took out his pipe and patted it lovingly.

Emerald was surprised to learn that the white-haired man – whom Kay had never introduced, she only remembered Kay calling him Lars – was not a boarder at Ashmont. He was to leave right after his tomato juice, saying something about having to go back home to get ready for a game of golf. He was dressed in spotless white, and for a perverse moment of nervousness, Emerald imagined the ruby liquid spilling on it, ruining the perfection. She smothered a laugh by pretending to cough.

After he left the room, Mr. Saxon leaned toward Emerald and spoke low to her: "I do not trust men," he said, "with footwear such as his. Loafers – dress loafers – with no socks. He even has pennies in them." She had to cough again.

People were finishing up and moving on to their daily activities. Emerald looked out the window and saw that out on the lawn, Lars stopped to speak to the strange Louise. She was still walking around with her bucket, stooping now and then to pull a weed or pick up a piece of rubbish. He not only spoke to her: it was a conversation; and Emerald could see her short hair bobbing, nodding in answer to a question or something. What could they be discussing so earnestly, so privately-looking? He seemed to be instructing her about something, counting off his fingers as if he were giving her a list of things to remember. Then, with a quick glance back toward the house, he quickly walked off. Soon after, his expensive car was seen heading up to the main road.

"I'd love to see some of your artwork," said Rita, nudging Emerald, who was still lost in thought, wondering about the exchange between Lars and Louise.

"It's really not remarkable," she responded modestly. "I enjoy it though."

"Ah — art. I wish I could do that. One of the more refined studies. I take it, then —" (she said with a chuckle) "you wouldn't have any business classes this term. If so, you would've been in my department."

"Actually I took some accounting classes back home at our community college. I was helping Dad with his firm and he needed me to help him with the books for a while. But coming here, he told me — he insisted I pursue something totally different. I've always loved painting and he wanted me to get my mind off things." Her voice cracked and she was unable to explain about Mother's illness. Dr. Canter said nothing, but warmly patted her hand.

Emerald learned that the reason there were no more people present that morning was because it wasn't yet the weekend. It operated as a bed-and-breakfast as well as permanent boarding house; some guests, she believed, were expected to arrive later in the day. The nameless VIP mentioned last night — as Emerald had taken the last scone — was referred to again this morning. Kay and Nora both seemed in a flutter to finish the breakfast dishes and go to town for shopping, saying something about "her favorite soap, and some new towels;" and Emerald heard Nora ask Kay "how long she thought she would stay this time."

"Hopefully longer than last time," was the response.

And then, the ladies lowered their voices and spoke of something more private. Emerald couldn't help but lean in a little; she was curious to know what was so serious. She saw their work suspended, looking at each other, and Nora even wiped away some tears. Emerald caught Nora's last sentence – "Heartbreaking thing for her, so young."

With the ladies gone, and Mr. Saxon now roaming the lawn with a pair of hedge clippers, Emerald was fairly secure of an opportunity to explore the house a bit, and alone. She had said goodbye to Rita but didn't know where the man with the thirty-year-old hand went; she assumed he left. She started snooping.

Starting out at the main staircase, she suddenly remembered about the missing photo of her parents. She went back to the stairway wall and examined it. There was the pale rectangle where it had hung; and now, in place of the original photo, was an old, faded, cross-stitched robin and three eggs. How odd – why would someone want to take the photo down? It was the prettiest of the group, and Kay especially had looked ravishing in it; so young.

Oh, well. Walking the halls she knew, literally down memory lane, she peeked into various rooms and crannies at her leisure. Much of it she remembered – differently. What she had thought was a soaring ceiling and skylight was only ten feet high, with a tiny window. The "endless" roomy cupboards in one room, her favorite spot when playing hide and seek, was really just a cabinet with a few lower compartments; no way she could fit herself in one now. She smiled at the distortions and softenings that had come out of her own mind. But still, it was pleasant to look and remember. Opening a door and seeing an unknown hallway, she went further.

Many of the rooms were closed off, and she wondered what was in them. The handsome and furnished bedrooms she knew were in the main wing; those were reserved for paying guests. But this part of the house was dark and chilly. Door after door was either locked, or crammed full with stored boxes and old furniture. Neglect was the theme of this part of the house, apparently. It was a shame to see potentially handsome rooms cast off like orphans.

And then she found the library. From the moment she stepped inside, time flew twice as fast, because she was immediately lost in its ambience. A sleepy and musty room – some would describe it, and turn away uninterested; but her artist's eye was caught by the captivating design – a jewel of a space. It would have been gorgeous in its prime! It had wood paneling, a chandelier, and crown molding; but her favorite part was the gigantic fireplace: so big she could have stood inside it, almost without stooping.

Someone had visited here recently. There was a cleared-off spot on the dusty sofa, and the moment she saw the ashtray and wrinkled newspapers on the fireside table, she knew Mr. Saxon must have shared her appreciation for the spot.

She stayed so long that she got cold, but not yet finished browsing the bookshelves, she decided to go upstairs for a sweater and return. While in her room she saw the corner of her sketch pad under the bed and hastily grabbed it, along with a smock and box of charcoal pencils, then ran back downstairs.

Hearing Louise's bucket, she halted. It was too early in the day for another weird encounter with her! She turned and tiptoed back up to the second floor. Surely there was another route to the library. . . she stood and thought for a moment. She noiselessly did some looking around and checking of doors. Sure enough, she found another staircase hidden away behind a partition. She hoped it would lead her somehow back to the library wing. The secrecy of what she was doing added to the fun of exploring.

She couldn't help giggling to herself, out of glee or nervousness: she couldn't tell.

Wow, a claustrophobic person could never use these stairs, she thought, brushing both hands along the walls as she descended, and pulling a cobweb from her face. After a turn or two, she thought she had found her way again, but realized she was in a completely different hallway. She stopped when she heard a sound – just loud enough for her to perceive the presence of someone nearby. A small clicking, just ahead. It was in the next room on her left: the door stood open. She just knew it was Louise! But curiosity made her take one peek inside, to see what she was up to in there.

Carefully she peered around the door frame. It was not Louise, but Mother Ann.

The clicking was her dog Puddles' toenails on the floor. "Oh – hello," Emerald tried to say pleasantly. She noticed the old lady was holding something white, with a lid – a candy dish. "I was just about to replace these," she told her. "They're old – they're from last Easter. Don't you think they need to be thrown away?" Emerald stammered her agreement, wondering why Mother Ann seemed so dependent on her opinion of it. She took off the lid and showed the candy inside to Emerald. "See? They're pink; they must be from Easter. That's not good enough, is it?"

"Oh, I don't know, they look okay to me," she answered, taking one. "Yes, they're wrapped in pink paper, but they're not necessarily from Easter. Actually, they look pretty good." And she popped the piece of chocolate in her mouth.

Mother Ann looked confused, like she couldn't decide what to do. "But they're probably not good enough," she said in a low voice, as if someone would hear.

"Well, I like them. Can I keep them in my room?" Emerald suggested, hoping it would make her feel better. "Here, dump them in here," she said, opening her painting smock to show a roomy pocket. The old lady did so, and seemed satisfied. "I'll get the better candy out; you know, the more expensive ones." Emerald nodded in agreement, smiling at her. She hobbled away with the empty dish, with Puddles following at her heels.

With a few more turns, Emerald found the library again, this time noticing that the knobs to the great double doors were brass, and shaped like some fearful creatures' heads. She scrubbed them clean with the edge of her smock and saw that they matched the ugly stone dragons out front. She must draw them one day, if only to send to Dad, and see if he remembered such an atrocity. He would get a kick out of it.

Walking the whole perimeter of the room, she stopped at an ancient phonograph with a stack of vinyl records below it. Buddy Holly, Louis Armstrong, Brahms, the Bee Gees, Rosemary Clooney – she smiled at the relics and wished she could listen to them.

Would the machine work? It was dusty but she plugged it in, and after a popping sound, was surprised to hear the hum of the arm rising and moving. She chose an Eartha Kitt record and placed it on the turntable; it worked.

Settling down under the natural light pouring in the windows, her hands and eyes were busy for the rest of the day, and the only sound was crackling music, and the scratch of her pencil. First she drew the windows, extending way up and coming to a gothic point at the top. Next was a quick sketch of the dragon head doorknobs, and then came some flowers bobbing outside the windowsill. Working away, she felt like she was etching the images into her very soul, into some inner storehouse of her mind, and would thus be able to keep them forever.

A golden glow settled over the room, and ripening afternoon cast a spell of languor over her. Emerald yawned and surveyed the work she had done – as usual, was satisfied and not satisfied with it. She shivered and decided to take a break. There, that window seat looked cozy. She found a blanket and covered herself, curling up on the seat's cushion.

Leaning her head against the glass pane, she semi-consciously gazed at the waving branch of a mimosa. What music was playing now? The phonograph was finished – it had whirred to a stop after the last record was done. But she still heard something. A radio or TV must be on somewhere in the house. She yawned.

A single instrument, like a violin, was weaving its solitary notes, as delicately around her senses as a faint whiff of perfume. Not realizing it, her eyes closed as she wondered who enjoyed listening to classical music . . . it was probably Dr. Canter . . . it was so beautiful, haunting. . .

She slept. She dreamed of Mother, who had just come home from work and was bustling around her, tidying up the room – but quietly so that she wouldn't wake the sleeping one. Then Mother was standing over her; she could hear her very breath. It was so real. Emerald even lifted a hand up, in her sleep, reaching for her. She touched someone and it startled her awake. Not Mother, but a blonde girl, her own age, was standing over her, smiling.

"There you are, Cuz!" said the girl.

5

OUR LAMB IS BACK

shmont Hall had been built in the 1870's, by a very wealthy man from Austria. He had immigrated to America and met a noted beauty from Virginia, the daughter of a statesman, and she instantly fell in love with his expensive carriage and rolls of money he put on display for her. She was so single-minded in her admiration of his possessions, that his homely looks did not affect her at all.

Eager to secure her in marriage, he promised something she often talked about: a European-style castle. Naturally she was starry-eyed over such a proposal. He spent months searching for the perfect location, plan, and builders. A notch in the Appalachian Mountains was selected; it reminded him of the Motherland, and rejoiced that his bride would grow old with him enjoying mountain vistas that he had always known.

Then, just as the stone walls were going up, he got word that she had met someone else, and had obtained a similar promise of a mansion from him.

In the Austrian's eyes, it was now a race. No expense was spared, and his plan doubled, tripled what it originally was; every luxury was installed, every ornament possible was added. The motif he had instilled throughout the home was the head of a lion, his love's favorite animal. He selected the best metalworkers he could find, and orders were placed for lions of all sorts: doorknobs, light fixtures, stained glass, and statues. Wherever he could place a lion, he did so, in her honor.

The other man built his mansion, too. But living in New York, he had much easier access to marble slabs and copper pipes; and his fine house was finished faster. So she married him instead.

The ugly Austrian had just received word of the marriage when the final touches were being put on. Now, with no lady for it, he became alternately enraged and dejected.

The lions had just been installed when he had gotten the word of her decision. Livid, he walked through the house, ripping out the doorknobs, smashing the windows with every image of it, then gave orders that they all should be replaced with the head of a dragon – as snarling and evil-looking as possible, to match his state of mind.

To accomplish this extraordinary request, not often heard of in the Appalachians, iron workers with artistic skill were recruited. One was selected and he produced perfect specimens of the frightful heads. It was the ugliest of the ugly: sort of a cross between a dragon, and troll, and a catfish. The workman brought his smith equipment to the worksite and stayed there until he had completed the order; or rather longer, since his friendly daughter was with him, and had helped the Austrian overcome his heartache much sooner than he had intended.

Within a few short weeks, the two were fully in love, and bound by promise to each other. It would have been a very poetic story had she been beautiful – and visually impaired (so as not to clearly see his ugly face), or both. However not only was she not blind, but she was just as homely as he was. But great love was born between them, and he christened the mansion Ashmont at that point – "out of the ashes of my life, has risen a mountain of secure love."

The young married couple was very wealthy, and now had a very spacious home, but – as sometimes happens – no children to fill it. But they had many friends and hosted frequent visitors. Parties of all sorts were held. The castle was a startling, imposing feature in the mountainside, among the humble cabins and shacks; but it gave great distinction that drew many tourists, and eventually – some enterprising young men who decided to build a sawmill nearby. Oak and cedar were plentiful on the hillsides and made much money for them; thus the town of Millcrest was born, along with a few family legacies. Millcrest grew; the people got rich; and Ashmont Hall was its jewel.

When the Austrian and his wife died, however, the house fell into neglect. It had been bequeathed to relatives of the wife, but the only ones still living had moved away and showed no interest in feeding, by that point, a white elephant. It was then acquired by the town of Millcrest and refurbished; a caretaker was hired for it. At last, after about forty years of faithful stewardship, this caretaker was given full ownership of it – mansion, grounds, stables, and all. He and his wife, and their little grandson, whom they were raising, inherited it in full. Their name was Keckley.

For the next few days, Emerald forgot about the heartache back home.

Sybilla was here. She was the daughter of Nora, but much more resembled her aunt Kay, in her countenance and demeanor. She had Kay's aura of cool, calculating charm, winsomely drawing people to her by her careful, alternating distance and intimacy with those around her. It was a gift shared only by these two; Emerald could never imitate it.

The joy of the household at her arrival revealed that she was the "important guest" long anticipated: she hadn't been there in years. From the moment Sybilla's high-heeled boots came tapping up the Ashmont front steps, and her silver fox was hung back in its former place in the foyer closet, the aunts had come alive. They fawned over her, cooked for her, and asked her opinion on this or that new alteration in the household. Even Mother Ann's watery old eyes would light up, looking at her great-grandchild; she presented her with the afghan she had made.

"Mother Ann, your fingers are as nimble as ever. How exquisite. I love you."

The ladies all sat in the den, the most common family chatting spot. Mr. Saxon was dozing in the recliner in the corner.

"Darling," said Nora, "your aunt Kay and I worked so hard on your room. How do you like it? You always coveted that set of French windows that overlooks the courtyard."

Sybilla dropped her pretty eyelashes in humility, thanking them for going to so much trouble just for her. "Y'all didn't need to work so hard on it, just for me. You've done a ton of work! I didn't recognize it." And after the all-around hugs of appreciation, she added in a small voice – "It's too bad that, well. . ." She looked as if she couldn't decide whether or not to say something. "Oh, never mind."

"What? What is it, my precious? Is the adjoining bath alright with you? Oh, I knew we should have gone with peach tile, instead of the turquoise."

"No, it's not that, the bathroom is *divine*, like the rest of it. It's just that – since you mentioned it – the courtyard –" As she said the word, she slightly leaned over to peer over at Mr. Saxon, reclining with his pipe, his slippers just barely hanging on to his elevated feet.

"Don't say it, I know," said Kay, with a roll of her eyes. "He's slipping. He's getting on up in years now, you know. The courtyard is atrocious – all overgrown, and the patio is cracked and full of weeds. But don't you worry. We'll work on that next."

To their surprise, or not, they found that Mr. Saxon had heard every word. He lowered his pipe a moment to say – "I'm not going to kill myself over a fifty-foot square of weeds and broken bricks, that nobody ever goes into. Your aunt keeps me busy with the visible part of the Ashmont, until I'm worn out. I don't see why we have to worry about the invisible part. The wall around it blocks the view."

"But our lamb is back, and she sees it. It's plainly in sight from her window," returned Kay. "Anyway, once we get it back in order, we can start having backyard parties again. And dances. At least monthly dances." The sight of Kay's sparkling eyes filled Emerald with warmth, and she was thankful to be a witness of these exciting changes to come.

The two girls had fun together. The first day of her arrival, when Sybilla had found Emerald asleep on the window seat, she took her around the house, just as she had done years before, showing her all the favorite kid haunts (except without leading her by the hand), Emerald felt claimed by her cousin: she liked the feeling. She was wanted by another, for companionship – not for daily care or medical needs. She realized this with a stab of guilt, and at moments was tempted to forsake her budding life at Ashmont and pack up and go right back home, to Mother's side.

But all Dad's letters said the same thing: he was making sure she got the best care, and his one comfort was knowing she, Emerald, was with friends – more than friends. Yes, she thought, folding and placing the graph paper (Dad wrote everything on his engineer's pad) into her dresser drawer – he wanted her there. And it was good for her, to be with those not merely friends, but blood relatives. Each day fermented in her a sense of belonging to them.

6

MYSTERIOUS MUSIC

The Keckley ladies had reverted to the family surname some decades after their marriages, however demoralizing this fact was to the men they had married, to preserve the link and legacy to Ashmont Hall. Even Sybilla went from being a Leonard to a Keckley as a high schooler. She had found the name helped her in her acting hobby at the local theaters and beyond.

The young actress enjoyed some years climbing the ranks of performing, starting off as a pot of geraniums, and from there progressing to a variety of characters such as newspaper boys or singing cats; blind demoiselles, and tragic queens. Her genuine talent was helped along by her natural self-confidence and her butter-blonde hair, which was a magnet for admiration on the stage and everywhere else.

Now in her mid-twenties, she had added to her personal repertoire the element of worldly sophistication. She had been traveling overseas. Upon graduating from Millcrest High, the urge was strong to test the waters beyond the sphere of where she'd grown up. Having enjoyed the spotlight and being brought up as the darling of Ashmont, she realized it might be only a taste of what was to be enjoyed by a having a larger number of admirers.

Indeed, armed with such latent self-confidence as she embarked upon the world, she could not fail. It had started when she had accepted an internship at an acting company in New England. She was perhaps humbled by having to work hard, really hard, for the roles that she had been used to claiming as a right; and very often had to settle for the lowly inconsequential ones. Even then, just knowing that a larger number of eyes was upon her, whetted her appetite for more.

From Boston to New York, New York to London she had gone, on a trail of semi-success with a company that filled the smaller theaters, mostly. But to perform as a "passerby wearing yellow hat" in London, sounded more exciting than as Queen Mary in only in Millcrest, and her aunts lauded her to all their friends as if she had won a Tony every year.

A little dazzled by this fashionable cousin, Emerald soon became Sybilla's accessory in daily life at Ashmont. It was still two weeks until classes started, and she hadn't found a job yet; so she did pretty much whatever Syb led her to do. Dodging chores, making fun of the guests, spending lazy hours in the mansion's hideaway nooks, or lounging on the terrace, gossiping – she had never laughed so hard, never felt so detached from sorrow.

One day they were wandering among on the grounds and came to a wooden slab that someone had built between two trees, creating a bench. Sybilla took a seat there and propped up one foot. "I used to be able to stretch out on this all the way, when I was little," she commented.

Emerald sat on the ground and said, "They say the Austrian built this bench for his wife ages ago, and somehow it hasn't fallen. It's protected by the position of the trees against the elements, or something like that." Emerald had learned a little history of the place, and asked Sybilla more questions about it. But Syb didn't share her fascination, having lived there her whole life; so her answers were disappointingly scant.

"Syb! There it is again!"

"What?" she answered, now with both feet on the bench, and her arms wrapped around her knees.

"That sound. Listen."

It was what she had first heard weeks ago – the song of a single instrument played by someone hereabouts. Was it from the village? It sounded much nearer. The notes were clear, and executed beautifully, but mournful somehow.

"Have you ever heard it before?" asked Emerald.

"Yes, I think so," said Syb. Her mischievous nature was stilled and serious for the moment. "I have. I remember now. But I don't know where it's coming from."

"Do you think it's a recording? Is someone listening to a radio?"

"No – it's not coming from the house. Outdoors, somewhere."

Emerald doubted that her aunts played any sort of instrument; she wondered, though, if it could be Rita Canter. Wasn't she carrying a horn case one day? Or was that someone else?

There was silence for a few minutes, as each girl speculated the likely source of the music. But a *pow*, and a clanking of metal, rudely interrupted any sentimentality for the time being. A whizzing motor started and Syb expressed frustration.

"Oh good grief," she moaned. "He's at it again. Mom and Kay hate it when he's so noisy while guests are here."

"What? Who?"

"Danny Gross," sneered Syb. "Is what I call him. 'Grosch' actually. He works in that garage. Keeps the cars up and stuff like that. Fixes things."

"I've seen him but haven't really talked to him. He only comes inside to eat."

"He's got another job in town, but yeah, he lives in the carriage house. That building over there, where those sounds are coming from. He's probably working on one of the cars. It was made into a garage years ago, and they kept the rooms on top the way they were. The grooms lived in it, you know, the men who took care of the horses. Danny gets it for free. Because," she said, her eyes beginning to glitter, like they always did when she was about to divulge something, "when our dear Aunt Kay wants to really make a splash, she has him get out the black Cadillac, polish it up, and drive her places. To keep up the image of the family, the grand Keckley reputation. You should see – " and Emerald had to wait a minute or two, for her to stop laughing again – ". . . you should see the getup she makes him wear to chauffeur her around, to parties and things like that. A black uniform and shined-up boots, and a hysterical cap! I nearly died when he drove us to the governor's ball one Christmas. We had to get out acting like that was an everyday thing, and call him by his last name. Oh lord, I couldn't keep a straight face. But afterward, he was mad I guess, and nearly got us killed by speeding around the mountains back home."

"I haven't even talked to him since I've been here. He must keep to himself a lot."

Syb finished her indulgence of ridicule, wiping tears from her eyes, and sighed with satisfaction. She then sat up straight, as if seized with a great idea. "Hey," she said, flicking Emerald's shoulder, "Let's go hire him."

"What?"

"Let's hire him – that's what Kay always says. Let's get him to take us somewhere. Anywhere. It's his job, after all." And with her leading the way in this scheme, Emerald had no choice but to follow, feeling uncomfortable; especially when Syb named off seven or eight places they "needed" to go to Danny's irritated ears, when they found him in the garage. He stared at them both, incredulously, but turned back to work on the pieces of greasy metal (whatever they were) at his workbench.

Syb had a way of staring at people when she didn't get her way, that could have driven a hole through steel, so Emerald thought. She shifted uncomfortably while Syb stood her ground, tapping her fingers, and insisted he drop everything and take them.

"Really, Syb, we can go in my car," she stammered, attempting to defuse the simmering volatility before her. Danny kept right on working, while Syb, pristine in her perfect outfit, stood at his elbow threatening him.

"Syb, don't worry about it –"

But her cousin held out, and Danny finally straightened up and dropped the car hood shut with a bang that made both girls jump. He briefly wiped his hands off, looking from Syb's triumphant face to Emerald's sheepish one.

"Fine," he grunted. "Let's go." He took a seat, grime-covered and all, in Kay's champagne Lincoln, leaving the girls to open their own doors.

He drove them into town. Syb had been chattering about a new restaurant she wanted to see, and a shopping center that was being built, and several other places – all very far apart from one another – that she required Danny take them to.

"Hey! You missed that turn. I said take us to Bridgestone!" piped up Sybilla.

And after a few minutes of Danny's silence, and Syb's repeated directions, it dawned on the girls that he had zero intention of obeying any of the orders, or regarding any of the pokes of Syb's finger into his shoulder.

On they rode, straight toward downtown Millcrest. Syb was angry but whispered to Emerald that they would jump out at the first opportunity, then send for someone to pick them up. They stopped at a red light and Emerald waited for her cue, but Syb shook her head and motioned something unintelligible. They stopped at another red light, then another. As for Emerald, she was secretly enjoying this, as she had not seen the pretty town in daylight since she had arrived; so she took this opportunity to observe the various shops and eateries as they rolled by.

At last they approached the city's center, surrounded by tall corner buildings and shoppers and suited businessmen walking briskly past. Syb motioned for Emerald to get ready to get out. Danny, who was perfectly aware of their plan, moved over to an inside lane, making it more difficult for their escape. Furthermore, to their horror, he locked all the doors, forcibly rolled down all windows, and proceeded to play the most obnoxious music he could find, at the highest level of volume.

The girls shrieked with mortification, hiding themselves as low down in the seat as they could, and Sybilla screamed threats of dire circumstances toward Danny. Such commotion only added to the attention they attracted, as well as to the driver's amusement. "That's the thing about these new cars! These automatic controls sure come in handy!" shouted their greasy chauffeur, not at all concerned with the curious glances of people around them.

Sybilla managed to unlock her door and hop out, disappearing through the traffic and to a cafe nearby. She waved at Emerald to join her, but just as she figured out how to open her door, the light changed green and Danny stepped on the gas. The last sight she saw of her cousin was of her being joined by a good-looking guy; then they went into the cafe together.

Oh well!

Emerald, now stranded alone in the backseat all the way home, felt more like a kid being driven to the dentist than as any employer of a family chauffeur. She looked at Danny's profile under his ball cap and tried to figure out if he was mad or not. His blackened hands rested easily on the wheel as he drove, and he seemed to be leisurely taking in the late summer day with enjoyment; but otherwise he was expressionless.

"I didn't have anything to do with that, I hope you know," said Emerald.

"Sure, sure," he answered, with a touch of sarcasm. His voice was not fierce, though.

"I didn't! Why would I want you to drive us around? I have a perfectly good car."

"A car, yes; 'perfectly good' – I doubt it," he answered. "It's at least twelve years old, right? Got a lot of miles on it, even for that. I can tell by the sound of it, it needs new brake pads asap. Also, your oil was low the other day, dangerously low. You didn't thank me for changing it for you."

"Change the oil? I had no idea. Dad usually takes care of that. Well – thanks, then."

She went on, feeling a need to explain more to him. "Back home I never did drive it that much, only to school, and to band camp in the summer. But Dad used it for work trips sometimes."

Danny was quiet, but seemed to be considering what she had said. However he didn't voice his thoughts, he just continued to make his way back home without any more conversation between them.

At dinner that night, Sybilla, to Emerald's surprise, said not a word about their escapades with Danny at the wheel. All the threats so generously lashed against him had evaporated somehow, and Syb ate, drank, and talked as gleefully as her first night home had been. But during dessert she turned a saucy look upon Emerald and asked her, pointedly, if she had had a pleasant companion this afternoon? Had she enjoyed her time with a certain young man about the town?

Instantly the attention of the aunts was on her, with inquisitive smiles and looks. Emerald was red-faced and glared at her cousin, shocked. Syb was taking the last bite of her crème brûlée and did not notice her. But she said to the curious ladies, "I got Danny to take us to town today, and told him to let us out downtown. I tried to get Emerald to go with me so I could show her some of the fun spots on Main Street. Thought it would be a good opportunity for her to do some job-hunting. But apparently she was having so much fun that she decided to let him drive her around without me. I saw them laughing as they drove off."

Emerald heard this highly embellished tale with astonishment, and could not even refute anything since Syb had slipped out and the aunts were now in spirited conversation with their guests about how romantic a place Ashmont was. There had been so many matches made here, down through the decades.

The one thing Emerald was grateful for was that Danny was not present. Someone said something about his being at work at his other job, whatever it was.

7

DISCOVERIES

T here was absolutely nothing wrong with Emerald Johnsey's appearance. She stood at a nice height, with a ladylike figure and toned slender limbs; and having somewhat flyaway hair, it was thick and dark, and gave significance to her presence. It looked quite nice when it was under control. As for her face, when you looked beyond her dominant glasses, you saw eyes, nose, mouth all well-formed and in harmonious proportion to each other. She usually had a pensive look that indicated deep thought, whether that was the case or not. Often she was processing her environment and looking with artists' eyes at what other people would call drab or dirty, and seeing something very different. When not lost in thought, she smiled at people, finding interests easily. Her personality fell somewhere between shyness and friendliness, that was becoming for a young girl.

There was nothing wrong with her appearance, as said before — except that it wasn't pretty.

She paid little attention to her apparel, and none at all to makeup or hairstyle. All her efforts toward refinement of beauty were poured out by her hands, upon the pictures she painted. Also, the hobby marked her with a perpetual occurrence: dried bits of paint on her hands. This trademark was noticed by her aunts, who held their glasses up to examine why her fingers would be so dirty, but then giggled at and patted with their own smooth hands, in a loving, indulgent manner that warmed their niece's heart. Nevertheless, she took care to scrub them before appearing at table again.

Art was her great escape, her passion. Nothing thrilled her more than ripping the plastic cover off a brand-new canvas board and setting in on its easel, then ceremoniously setting out her brushes and opening the tubes of paint. The smell, the colors, the image that was bursting from her very heart, that she would try to project upon that canvas – it all was intoxicating to her.

And here she was in this ancient mansion, with inspiration in every room. From the architecture, to the dusty chandeliers, to the irregular window panes, Ashmont gave her fresh scope that she happily indulged in those first few weeks. After she learned the usual haunts of the tenants and what times to avoid them, she would steal away in the rooms alone and let her eye rove over every detail, every odd shadow that fell across the floor; even the fine cracks and chips in the woodwork had charms for her. Perfections and imperfections, she found, and loved each one.

Or if the weather was nice and she preferred organic subjects, she would get up early and walk the grounds, delighting in the mellowing colors of late summer, taking quick sketches of an ancient tree or a dilapidated fence. Frequently, as she sat and gazed out at the valley – then back at the regal house – she shivered pleasantly with the realization that she had a part in owning such a house. It belonged in her family. The same life that flowed through it pulsed in her own veins, by birth.

But she saw that, after a few instances of being seen alone, her aunts thought this odd behavior. "Is Emerald alright? What has she been doing outside all this time?" Or, "Is she still in that damp little sitting room? What on earth is she doing in there?" was heard by her, in a low voice once or twice outside the door. They couldn't imagine why anyone would want to sit in an empty, quiet room, with no television or other means of entertainment. The Keckley ladies would no more do such a thing than voluntarily sign up for karate lessons.

Emerald knew that Sybilla was, in one sense, the centerpiece of their world. They delighted in her presence and in granting her every desire; but she looked upon this without jealousy, since she had been so far away, for so long. It was understandable. But in her heart, Emerald still entertained gaining a footing with Aunt Kay, the mother figure she still idolized. She would watch her, she would sit near her, she gained comfort just being in the same room with her.

She looked for quiet moments with Kay apart from everyone, but had not been able to find any. If only she could have a few minutes here and there to herself, and sit under her sympathetic gaze and listening ear! It would be Emerald's meat and milk in her times of loneliness.

The days went on, and Emerald began to spend less time alone, and more time mingling with the others. She began to mesh with them. Her routines and conversations became fitted to theirs, and they accepted her propensity for solitary roaming. She enjoyed the laughing hours with Sybilla – as unpredictable, as selfish as she inevitably was – but she really had fun. There was only one person in the house that put Emerald on edge, as soon as she walked into the room. Louise.

She always seemed to be in surprising places, and at odd times of the day. Walking the halls in the middle of the night. Standing around a corner silently, as if listening for something. Cleaning a random shelf up on the third floor, when the dust in the main wing bore testament of neglect there, where it was more visible to paying guests. More than once Emerald had found her standing unnaturally close to herself, especially when in conversation with one of her aunts. Kay would fix her eyes on Louise in a way in which Emerald wondered how she could bear it – Kay could have a paralyzing stare – but Louise remained totally unabashed, doing her little unnecessary tidying up, or whatever flimsy pretense she had at the moment for hovering near them.

How did she get established here, wondered Emerald more and more. Yes, Ashmont was huge and they needed hired help, but was this the best they could do? True, Louise was only a maid, but she was constant visible presence to those visiting the mansion, usually genteel people with money and refinement. Her manner was abrupt, her appearance awkward, and her skills not up to the boasted standards that Kay was always referring to.

As soon as Emerald heard Louise shuffling into a room, her stomach tightened. It was impossible to relax around her. It wasn't so bad when others were present; then, it was only the discomfort of having someone so ill-suited to the family in their midst. As a hired employee, her presence should have barely been perceptible. As it was, however, she often butted in, if not verbally, physically; imposing her awkward self right between two people who were having a conversation; or clattered around doing her work, with no eye for how things ought to be arranged. More than once Emerald saw Kay come right behind Louise, softening the military-like severity she had left behind.

Louise's interpretation of housework was not what it ought to have been. Garbage emptied and the room cleared of unnecessary embellishments, like flowers, was mostly what it entailed. Chairs and ottomans would be arranged at right angles, giving the appearance of neatness; but dust bunnies aplenty would peek out from beneath them, and Emerald often found herself nudging them back into their lairs. On tabletops, signs of a rag hastily swiped showed by what it left behind. And apparently, Louise considered the sickeningly sweet air freshener she frequently used, to fill in any inadequacies in her work. This aroma, like a wall, was walked into by Emerald for only a couple of times before she recognized it as Louise's signature scent.

But there was a deeper irritation. Louise seemed to latch herself to Kay whenever she had conversations with others – especially Emerald.

She thought about this as she lay down in bed one night, listening to the mountain wind outside. Time and again, Emerald had tried to draw nearer to Kay. Opportunities seemed to be dangled before her – just like the empty chair on the terrace that day – and then be suddenly snatched away again. The phone would ring, or someone would walk in; often, Louise would abruptly remind Kay of a task to be done, and bustle her away.

Did Louise even have access to Kay's personal space? wondered Emerald.

Kay's suite was directly under Emerald's room. She had not seen it yet, but imagined it as elegant and feminine as Kay herself. A canopy bed, dreamy waves of curtains, French doors opening to a private bath . . . these images filled Emerald's mind whenever she thought of it.

But she would hear disturbing sounds from downstairs. Muffled talking, deep into the night. Sometimes quick footsteps, such as someone in a hurry. Tonight as she lay in bed, she heard something again: a lady's voice – Kay's voice. It was upset. Sobbing. Emerald stared at the cracks on her ceiling, afraid of what she was hearing. Then there was the sound of the voice rising, in yells and even shrieks. Then it would die away again.

Back and forth the pattern continued, for an hour. Emerald would drift off to sleep and then wake again. Just as she was on the verge of a deep sleep, thinking she was dreaming the sounds, she heard something that jerked her upright in bed. This was no dream. It was a tremendous crash of breaking glass.

8

PUZZLES

Emerald mentioned the crashing sound at the breakfast table the next morning.

"I'm sure it was Tiger John. He knocked over something or other," answered Nora. Kay was busy and didn't hear her, apparently. Lars was probably stopping by again today, the way Kay's eyes were sparkling and she swirled around, straightening up the room.

"But lately he's been sleeping in my room," continued Emerald. "Although I can't remember if he was with me last night or not . . . anyway, I've never seen him reckless. Mischievous, maybe – but not breaking things."

"That cat," said Mr. Saxon, "sleeps twenty-two hours a day. And for the two hours he's awake, he exhibits a most disproportionate amount of energy from the lethargy of the preceding ones. So yes, I'd say he was capable of breaking a glass, running savagely wild, and terrorizing a village, all at three in the morning."

"He messed up my puzzle the other day," joined in Nora, with a little pouty lip. "At least two-thirds of my Paris landscape had to be re-done. Scrambled it all up, when Puddles came running in, and startling him. But I won't scold him, poor baby," with a glance at the elderly dog in Mother Ann's lap.

"Just how old is he now?" mumbled Sybilla, grouchy as usual in the mornings. "I expected him to pop off years ago."

"I'll help you with your puzzle, Aunt Nora, if you want," Emerald volunteered. She was waiting for a call from Dad about some recent tests Mother had had done; it made her nervous, and she wanted to be doing something.

Later they sat at a vast desk, sorting through puzzle pieces, with the only sounds being snores from Puddles and her elderly mistress, whose head was tipping forward in slumber. She wore a flowered hat with a veil, and Emerald saw that her hands were gloved, folded upon Puddles' back.

"Does she have a party to go to today?" whispered Emerald to her aunt. "She's all dressed up."

"Oh no, dear, no parties for her, at her age. Ninety-one, you know. It's just that sometimes she has the idea that she needs to dress up; that her everyday clothes aren't good enough."

Not good enough. Emerald remembered the day that Mother Ann insisted the candy wasn't "good enough." She mentioned it, and Nora explained it with pity in her voice.

"Ah, the effects of being married to my grandfather," she said, nodding. "He was almost obsessed with getting Ashmont on the map again – really restoring it to the glamour of its first days. And he did, too, to a large extent. But poor Mother Ann, from Appalachian people, you know, had a time trying to live up to his standards; she hardly knew what it was to live with indoor plumbing, until she married him. And now, in her old age, she seems to hear his reprimands again. Where she would have worn simple cotton dresses, he had her in velvet gowns. And her poor little wild flowers from the mountainside, in cracked mugs that she thought were so picturesque, were thrown out by his own hands, and replaced with expensive florist shop ones."

Emerald thought of this suppressed quality of simplicity in Mother Ann's life, and felt the affinity in herself. She, like the old lady, often valued the natural and pretty over costly, man-made embellishments. She dwelled on the satisfaction of this family likeness for a few moments, while her fingers sifted through the puzzle pieces, grouping all the blues together.

Aunt Nora's chief occupations were cooking, hostessing, supervising Mr. Saxon in the household repairs, and working puzzles. She had boxes and boxes of them, stacked on the shelves of the family den, and she loved to receive a glossy new one for her birthday or Christmas. The more pieces, the more tedious, confusing, and complicated – the better. It kept her head and hands busy on many long afternoons, especially after a disagreement with Kay; and it soothed her when she fretted about their finances.

She was about halfway through with her present one, a picture of the Eiffel Tower.

"Can you help me find some of these missing sections?" she asked Emerald. "I'm trying to find this man's foot."

"Paris looks like an amazing city," said the girl. "Have you been there?"

"Oh no. Have you?"

"No, never. But Dad has. He's talking of us going there on a vacation soon."

"They say it's like New Orleans; I have been there. And oh, one year we went down to Miami. It was just heavenly, all that bright blue water. As a matter of fact, I have a picture album here in this drawer."

"Did you and Aunt Kay both go?"

"Yes, she likes to travel. Well, mostly she likes shopping in new places. She enjoys re-doing the guest rooms, you know," then – "she spends a little too much if you ask me."

"One day maybe you can go on that cruise you said you wanted to. Where, Brazil? Is that right?"

"Oh, I am going, whether she takes me or not. I don't know when, or how; and she insists that we will never set foot on a ship. She gets sick. But ever since I worked a puzzle about Rio, I simply knew I had to go one day."

"Well, maybe with what Ashmont brings in, you know, from renting rooms, you could save up for it one day."

Nora answered with a sort of sideways nod of the head, and a little sound that could have been yes, could have been no. Emerald was intrigued, but asked no more questions. Instead she opened the photo album.

"Did you say this is – Florida?" Emerald saw nothing but pictures of tulip fields, with a row of Holland windmills.

Nora adjusted her glasses and peered at them. "Oh yes," she said confidently.

Emerald was confused. Then she looked closer and noticed

hairline squiggly cracks in the photos – running through the colorful rows of flowers. They were pictures of a puzzle that Nora worked on while in Florida.

"Fifteen hundred pieces," sighed Nora happily. "That's why I took several shots of it. I was trying to get one without the glare of the overhead light."

Emerald stifled the outright laugh and forced herself to keep it to a smile.

Flipping through the pages, she saw scenes of three other puzzles Nora had completed – a candy shop, a field of moose, and the planet Jupiter. Not a shot was taken of Florida; unless you counted the edge of some palm trees on a balcony, accidentally showing up in the background.

"And there's nothing more aggravating than one missing piece. Luckily all the ones I found in the condo were complete. But I'm afraid this Eiffel Tower will have a small chunk out of it. I just can't find that part," she said, pointing to empty space.

"That would drive me crazy," said Emerald. "But here's the foot."

They worked in silence awhile, then Nora sighed. "I need a piece of tape, dear. Would you reach in that drawer and find it?"

Reaching all the way to the back, she found a roll of tape knocking against a velvet box. She pulled both out. "What's this, Aunt?" she said, opening it.

Nora adjusted her glasses and peered inside. "Oh! I can't believe it! I've been looking for that for the longest!" She cracked the case open and tilted her head with admiration. Emerald breathed a gasp of surprise and peered closely at what was inside: a ring with a crimson gem, delicately surrounded by tiny clear stones, and mounted in silver.

Nora took the ring from the casing and slipped it on her finger; it glittered under the desk lamp. "Look at it – watch those facets. Have you ever seen a deeper, clearer red in your life?"

"It is breathtaking!" said Emerald. In spite of Nora's weathered manicure and calluses, her hand looked queenly wearing it. "Where did you get such a piece? It looks like an antique."

"Oh yes, it's an heirloom, and one of a kind, for sure. It's been in the family for many decades." Then, lowering her voice – "I had to hide it, you know."

"Oh really?" asked Emerald, matching her tone to Nora's whisper. She tried not to look too curious about this revelation. "Why is that?"

"Oh my, it's worth so much, of course!"

"But what about a bank? Or a safe? Surely you could keep a safe here at Ashmont."

"Lars – he is a financial person, you know, who deals in investments and things – does not advise we move it from the premises. And as to a safe, yes we have a large roomy one in the kitchen, and another small one or two upstairs. But" (whispering again) "she knows all the combinations, has all the keys around here, you know."

Instantly Emerald knew she was referring to Louise! The Keckleys employed her, but did not even trust her!

They stared at the ring in silence. Mother Ann and the dog snored on, and Emerald's heart beat quicker. Apparently this ring was an important antique, proven with documents – from where? She asked Nora.

"This one came from Spain. From one of their queens, you know."

Breathlessly Emerald looked at her aunt. "You mean to tell me it's from a historical collection? From Spanish royalty?" Nora was already nodding in agreement, proud of the piece. "Oh yes, I have the document to prove it, my dear." They looked at one another in solemn awe. Emerald was further stunned by what was said next.

"I have many more like it. Not only from Spain, but from all over Europe, my dear. France, England, Malaysia . . . "

"What? Where are the rest of them?"

"Oh, over the years we've had to hide them," she said, dropping her voice. "All over the house. In the backs of drawers like these; behind books on the bookshelves; in the sugar jar; places like that."

"But who are you hiding them *from?*" Emerald whispered, bravely trying to get a confirmation of the truth.

But before Nora could answer, a slight wave of a plant, in the corner, caught Emerald's eye.   Part of a hand could be seen, reaching out to steady the movement.   Whoever it was had been hiding there, listening!

9

AN EARLY CALL

YOUR MOM IS DOING WELL. I GAVE HER THE SKETCH YOU DID, OF THE FIREPLACE YOU TOLD US ABOUT, AND IT HANGS RIGHT WHERE SHE CAN SEE IT WITHOUT HAVING TO STRAIN. SHE SMILES WHEN SHE LOOKS AT IT. THE DOCTOR IS OPTIMISTIC ABOUT THE NEW MEDICINE THAT HAS JUST BEEN APPROVED. BUT THE BEST TREATMENT IS YOUR CHARCOAL DRAGONS AND POPPIES, IN MY OPINION.

Dad hardly ever sent text messages, but his letters were arriving every few days, as promised. Her heart ached to think of the small comfort he got in making the situation sound better than what it was. The wording was sternly positive. She folded the graph paper and noticed the little cartoon animals he had included on the other side. Emerald had sat for hours, as a little girl, imitating his animals, the fat little pig and smiling cow, laboring over his examples until she perfected them. Those simple, funny doodlings were what had first piqued her interest in art.

Dad was attentive in minutiae of farm life but sadly absent-minded in boring, humdrum details, such as money to live upon. He had forgotten to send her any. She looked in the envelope to be sure: no check. Mother had always taken care of the bills – and it wasn't hard, since Dad made a very sufficient living as a mechanical engineer. In her decline, Emerald took over, just in time too, writing the checks to pay bills and getting them off before too many late fees had been applied. Dad hardly knew where the checkbook was, and was content with the handful of pocket change for his daily cup of coffee, and a sandwich from a machine.

And so: she needed a job. She couldn't bear to ask him for money right now. Anyway, Millcrest was full of interesting places, like the shops and cafes she had poked around into after registering for college classes. A florist or a dress shop would be nice; or maybe the year-round Christmas store she had gotten a glimpse of. She would go tomorrow, and check a few places out.

Another motive was – she must admit it to herself – to get away from this house sometimes. Louise was becoming more than her nerves could bear. Why oh why did they tolerate her odious presence? Sneaking around, eavesdropping, meddling where she had no business. Rearranging some things, hiding others, twisting things around to suit her strange habits, it seemed. And on top of all that, barely even fulfilling her paid duties of keeping the rooms clean.

But of course, now, Emerald knew what Louise was really up to. She was looking for the hidden pieces of jewelry! She had probably already found some and sold them . . . how many left could there be? Even with Aunt Nora being so secretive about them, ubiquitous Louise surely had stumbled upon some in her housework. And if not, Emerald had no doubt that her far-reaching ears had picked up on their existence, just by paying greedy attention.

One morning, Emerald (who liked Ashmont best early in the day, before it was on its best behavior for paying guests) went into the kitchen, confident of solitude and fresh coffee; formulating plans for her next round of job hunting. She had applied at several places that week but had had no luck. But today Syb promised to take her to a place or two, downtown, and she felt that with her assistance, today would be the day to land something.

Going to the cabinet for a mug, she jumped when the phone rang; she almost dropped the cup. So early! Who could be calling? she thought. Glancing at the clock, she saw that it was barely 6:00 am. She quickly answered it between rings.

The voice on the other end was that of a man. Emerald knew that voice to be Lars, Kay's beau and business associate. She was just about to tell him that Aunt Kay wasn't up yet, when he surprised her by asking for Louise McSee. "She's expecting my call," he told her.

"Hold on a moment," said Emerald, laying the phone down and wondering where Louise would be found that early. She was about to go in quest for her, but the instant she turned she found Louise standing right behind her – nearly smacking right into her for the second time since they met. Louise certainly had a talent for moving from place to place in total silence. Without a word, she picked up the receiver and moved into a corner of the room, as if to guard the privacy of her conversation.

Emerald resumed her spot at the kitchen table and had no intention of leaving. She was too interested in hearing what type of talk those two would have, even if she could only hear one side of it. She nonchalantly turned the pages of a gardening magazine while really straining to hear what Louise was saying to Lars. So far, just several yes's and no's. Next Emerald took up the newspaper and began working the crossword puzzle. Now her ears began to pick up on a phrase or two: "No sir, not yesterday," and "Yes sir, I'll let you know if that happens."

Emerald itched to hear more! She moved to the window, pretending to check the weather. Louise glanced at her over her shoulder, feather earrings swinging, and lowered her voice into the phone. She mumbled something Emerald couldn't catch.

Just then the back door opened and in walked Danny. He scraped his boots on the mat and glanced up at Emerald. He didn't greet her, but proceeded to the pantry and noisily started looking for some breakfast.

Louise, in a serious voice, was telling something to Lars – something about "going over the edge" and "not this time." But the more intriguing it got, the more sounds issued from the pantry; and Emerald vented her irritation by glaring at Danny when he came out holding an armful of cereal boxes. Next came the clinking of dishes, which he was now making by finding a bowl and spoon, and she sighed in frustration. Louise moved further away, continuing her confiding talk into the telephone.

Danny joined Emerald at the table, pushing back his chair with a scraping sound. *Does underline everything require so much noise?* She demanded mentally. He set several almost-empty boxes down, and began pouring the remnants of cereal into one big bowl, combining them all. "Pantry needs to be cleaned out," he commented, shaking and tapping each box until it was empty. Giving up on hearing Louise, Emerald turned a disgusted eye on his creation: chocolate pebbles and blueberry squares, colored puffs and shredded wheat, all blended together. He topped it with milk and began to devour it as if he were starving. Watching him, she couldn't resist one comment: "That's just nasty." He just looked at her, and seemed to enjoy it more because she said that.

She took her cup to the sink and washed it, drowning out Danny's crunching sounds. In the meantime Louise was still talking on the phone, or rather listening, with the appearance of receiving some type of instructions. At last she hung up, but without Emerald finding anything out, except that Louise was more suspicious – of something – than ever.

Frustrated, Emerald went outside to walk it off, and enjoy the morning freshness. She meandered a little ways beyond the patio when Danny walked out as well, joining her.

They didn't say anything at first. But a movement in the edge of the woods caught Emerald's eye, and she cried out softly. "Oh! Look at that."

"We see them around here all the time," he answered, unimpressed. "Beavers are destructive though. They tore up the little bridge over that stream."

"But – look. That's not a beaver."

"Yes it is."

"No it's not."

"Yes it is!"

"No it's not! See how small it is? It's a woodchuck. Or a groundhog; same thing."

Danny kept asserting it was a beaver, and Emerald became frustrated at not being able to reason with him. He eventually assented, though, saying maybe he was mistaken. She had the pleasure of knowing she could wear him down; but secretly she thought he must be terribly stubborn. The brown animal waddled along the grass, and was followed by two more. "Oh how cute!" she said.

"Wish I had my twenty-two with me," said Danny coolly.

"What! Why?" she said, turning to him.

He didn't answer, only held up an imaginary firearm and squinted one eye, then firing, complete with sound effects.

"But why would you want to kill them? They're not doing anything!"

"Like I said, they messed up the bridge. Or at least, they probably dig holes or something."

Emerald was disgusted and moved away. What had appeared to be a pleasant walk on the grounds was now turning her stomach. She left him without a word, and sought out the path to the ravine that she'd found when she'd first arrived at Ashmont.

The cool pine air and fast walking were therapy for her, flushing away the irritation and filling her with more pleasant feelings. Just as she caught a glimpse of the foggy valley beyond, her heart leapt with the beauty of it and she stopped and actually twirled. Nobody would notice her way out here, so she didn't care. In spite of a few grating personalities here at Ashmont, there was much, much to enjoy. Dad was right, she needed to come here for a while. Looking back at the mansion – which was becoming less formidable to her – she admired it from her heart. Suddenly she realized how lucky she was to have family here, at this unusual place; she began to feel it belonged to her, too.

Then she heard it again. The music. The same clear tones she'd heard when falling asleep on the window seat, the day that Syb had come home. Where was it coming from? Her own thoughts? Was her imagination stronger than she realized? No, the sound was real; and the notes began spinning themselves delicately on the air just as before, hypnotizing her. Maybe it was coming from the valley? Someone down below was playing a fiddle, perhaps; some eccentric old man sitting on his front porch, not dreaming that the morning breezes carried the sound to the great castle on the hill.

Then it stopped, and she sighed, feeling suddenly lonely. Just as she came up over a little knoll and gained sight of the terrace, she involuntarily flinched: there was Kay, just like on that first morning, seated alone and resting her head on the back of the chair. An empty chair sat next to her, and Emerald aimed for it, glancing around jealously. Kay looked up just as she reached it, and greeted her in a sleepy voice.

"Ah, what are you doing out so early, sweet Emerald? I remember your mother doing the same thing."

The mention of her mother, and the closeness to Kay all alone, triggered something inside the girl. She was unable to answer. But welling up in her were all the fears and longings of past months, and she finally had the opportunity to confide in her.

Before she could say a word, the sliding door opened, and Louise came bustling out with her gardening tools, noisily getting to work just a few feet from the ladies. Then Nora brought out breakfast things to spread on a patio table, with two guests following her, accepting her apologies for oversleeping.

Her quiet moment, alone with her beloved Aunt Kay, was now filled with people and noise, and the precious opportunity evaporated like a vapor. Emerald vacated her seat for them, blinking back tears, and fled upstairs to her own room.

10

CHURCH AND A GIRL

On Sunday mornings, Aunt Nora went to church. Emerald had been at Ashmont three weeks before she realized this, and the next day being Sunday, she offered to go with her.

Nora seemed appreciative of the company. They got into the Lincoln that the sisters shared and buckled their seatbelts, and in the next quarter of an hour Emerald experienced a fear so approaching terror that she was the one to insist upon driving after that. Nora's driving skills could be described as subtracting thirty years' experience, and adding the same amount of human aging, the result being that Emerald wondered how her aunt could be still alive!

It occurred to her, between wide-eyed gasps that first morning, to wonder why Danny hadn't been driving Nora. "This is the way I always take," she had said, hugging a curve and straying slightly into oncoming traffic, "it's a little faster. And the scenery is so nice." The scenery was soon to be adorned with mangled metal, Emerald thought, gripping the door. Kay surely knew the driving habits of her own sister; she should see to it that Danny was behind the wheel whenever she wanted to go out!

They at last reached the safety of the parking lot, and got settled into the formal sanctuary. Then Emerald discovered why Danny's services were not used.

He was there at the church, right up in front, suited and tied and with no appearance of grease on his hands. The familiarity of his head and glasses first caught her eye, or she would have not recognized him so readily. He was glancing around the room and saw her too. The unsmiling, discriminating stare in her direction, across the rows of velvet pews, was exactly the same as she had encountered at home.

Opening the church bulletin, she saw the printed name of *Daniel Grosch, Director of Music*. What a surprise! So *this* was his other job. She had thought he must be working at some factory or maybe an auto parts store.

She observed him now, scurrying around under the long silver tubes of the pipe organ. He was holding a conductor's wand and preparing to launch the little orchestra into an instrumental hymn. Sleeves rolled up, tie askew, he decisively – almost fiercely – waved and poked and signaled the music into existence, creating a rather stormy introduction to the Presbyterian service. As for Emerald, she had great fun watching him. The performers labored under his direction, visibly tired when they were finished.

Next, Danny straightened his tie and mounted the platform, announcing to the congregation a hymn number. Everything he did was done severely. She had to cough in order to avert outright laughter. Once or twice she was afraid he noticed her, and she looked away to hide her smile.

"Did you notice Danny there?" asked Nora, as they were getting in the car later. Emerald was preparing herself for a repeat of the alarming journey back home and didn't hear what she said at first.

"I said, did you see Danny? He directs the music. That's a nice little job for him, don't you think?"

"Yes ma'am," she answered, making sure her seatbelt was fastened securely.

"When he first moved in, I'll never forget, he was the most exasperating thing."

"Really?" said Emerald, not really listening; she was trying to determine whether she should lock her car door or not. If it were locked, the paramedics might have difficulty prying her out.

"Kay had hired him to drive us around sometimes. And then, what with Saxon getting older and everything, he started helping mow the grass, or washing the cars, you know, that we realized how much we needed him. So between the two men, they fixed up the carriage house into a little apartment, and he moved right in. I'll never forget, I went out and bought him some food and supplies for his little place, while he was off visiting his brother. I had such fun getting all the things he didn't have! Or that were so pitiful he couldn't have used them. New pillowcases, towels, dishes. He didn't even have a fork and knife. He was gone for two weeks, so I worked hard, and wanted to surprise him."

"Oh?" said Emerald, trying to be interested, but actually watching how fast the street signs were whizzing by.

"Well, I just knew he would be delighted with it. A real home for him, fixed up so nice – I was excited as could be. It was just as if I were taking care of my own son. I couldn't wait to see his reaction. But after a whole week he still hadn't said a word about it; just as silent as stone, like he always is. And I finally went out there to see him. Do you know what I found?"

"No, what?"

"I knocked on the door but no one answered, so, since the lights and radio were on, I went right in. All the food I had bought and prepared for him were still in the fridge, and even the bowl of fruit on the table – I had arranged it so pretty – were all untouched. But on the counter was a can of cinnamon rolls, open, with the dough inside – raw – with teeth marks in them. Teeth marks! That young man doesn't even know how to turn on an oven. And I went down into the garage to find him, and do you know what was sitting all around that nasty old worktable? The good dishes I had gotten him, nice porcelain bowls with a sort of geometric pattern, you know, that men like – and they were filled with greasy nuts and bolts and all kinds of garbage!"

Emerald was amused in spite of her bouts of occasional terror. "Why didn't he eat the food you stocked for him?"

Nora was animated in her answer, in a way that delighted her niece; with a little squeal of wonder. "You won't believe it. He said he saw all that nice stuff in the kitchen and assumed it was for some guests coming in that weekend; he was prepared to vacate it for them. As if I would make my crab salad for someone, and then let it sit a week in a fridge. Really!" She said with a huff. "And I asked him what in the world he was doing with those good dishes in the garage, and he said something about not being able to find any cans or buckets, but that he was planning on rinsing them out before the weekend guests needed them." Here Nora shot a look of incredulity, as if Danny, and probably all men, were completely off their rocker.

"Although," said Nora as an aside, "I was the one who threw away all his old plastic buckets and things sitting around the garage, so no wonder he couldn't find any; I thought it was just junk — but still" (louder) "I tell you, he's just as backwards as he can be, sometimes. Of course I understand, from his raising, that his people were no gentry; sort of backwoods folks. I hope," she continued, now turning into the long Ashmont driveway, "That his wife will improve him."

"Oh, I didn't know he had a girlfriend. When are they getting married?"

"They're not even engaged yet, but they will be soon if all goes right. I asked him last week when he was buying her a ring; but he acted like they weren't ready for that yet."

Emerald was intrigued with the thought of Danny having an almost-fiancée. She surmised what type of person she was likely to be.

"Didn't you see her this morning? She passed us as soon as we sat down. Red-haired girl. She was wearing an ecru dress, sort of like yours, but in ecru," Nora told her.

But Emerald couldn't remember anyone of that description; probably because she had had to keep her eyes down, off of Danny, so he wouldn't see her amusement. She had a new respect for him now, though.

So, he was a church music director, and had a red-haired girlfriend in an ecru dress. Very interesting! She was glad to know he wasn't completely the gruff hermit he portrayed to people.

To be honest, she was relieved. She was afraid of someone trying to fix her up with him. More than once, her aunts had hinted at being on the lookout for a romance for her, and she was afraid Danny's close proximity would make them appear to others as a natural pairing. It only took a few encounters with him to solidify the feeling in Emerald that there was no attraction of that sort whatsoever between them.

Emerald's imagination took fire once she realized Kay would love to host a wedding at Ashmont! Perhaps Danny and his bride could be persuaded in that direction. Emerald foresaw the mansion coming to life with this prospect, possibly as early as Christmas or even fall. How happy this would make Kay!

11

SECRET PASSAGE

As long as Kay Keckley had lived at Ashmont, which was practically her whole life, she had been conscious of its prestige. The name had been circulated among the upper classes for decades, sometimes the 'in' place to be, and sometimes waning in popularity, but usually fully restored to its reputation after a very successful party, a wedding, or a visit from a celebrity.

Kay never mentioned that the house was not really built by her ancestors. The fact was, that it had passed into her family's hands because no one else wanted it, decades ago, and it was finally given to the man who took nominal care of it; much like Mr. Saxon.

But that was long ago, too long for anybody to remember details like that. What was really important was that the name of Keckley was now irreversibly associated with the prestige of Ashmont Hall. The underside of this fact was that Ashmont had long been established as a somewhat creepy place. It all began with the family cat (an ancestor of Tiger John). He unfortunately had a bad habit of walking on the piano keys at odd times, such as the middle of the night, terrorizing any visitors who happened to be there. From that grew all sorts of wild stories of ghosts, demons, and the like, tormenting every soul within its walls. Also, a rumor had circulated that Ashmont was built on top of a cemetery, and nobody knew if it was true or not. At any rate, people were becoming afraid to visit it. The dragon heads certainly didn't help.

The Keckley grandson of the early 1900s – Kay and Nora's grandfather – grew up known as the boy from the haunted house. Local boys perpetuated every flight of fancy in how haunted it was, and, being too scared to actually pick fights, instead threw things at him. When he grew up he married a lovely Appalachian girl named Ann, and they produced a son who had as much fervor as his father could have in lifting Ashmont's curse and establishing it in respectability. Also, in making lots of money.

With the son's help, that's what happened. Ashmont had fertile acreage and they used it well. Through the planting of orchards and raising of tobacco, they made enough money to send the two little granddaughters to the finest boarding schools, away from the negative rumors. The girls boasted of having their very own castle back home, and had photographs to prove it; winning the admiration of many schoolmates and respect of their teachers. The Keckley plan worked very well and the granddaughters came home elegant, graceful, and having a zest for the finer things of life.

They had made many friends at school and were just as eager to invite them to Ashmont as the friends were to see this interesting place. Great parties were held, even rivaling those given by the original owner. As the youngsters became women, Mr. Keckley wanted to improve their standing – and Ashmont's – in society even more, especially since politicians and wealthy businessmen were among his acquaintance. He wanted to send them to finishing school.

The girls were overjoyed at this prospect. Their tastes had improved just as much as their father's. It was decided that only one would go, right now, to a very exclusive school in Switzerland; she would return home and the other could go. Kay was the most eager to go first. Nora was disappointed – she was older, by a year – but she acquiesced, because she was used to it; Kay had a stronger will than hers, as everyone at Ashmont well knew. But when Kay returned after less than two years, Nora's desire to go had vanished. She had met a young man and wanted to marry him. It was all the better for their father; the family funds were considerably less than before, and anyway – he reasoned – perhaps Kay could just teach everything she had learned to her sister, and save that tuition.

Now, in her *(ahem)* early middle age, Kay had hundreds of friends, and they were always coming to see her. They seemed to come out of the woodwork. A senator and his wife; a set of siblings from out of town; old friends from school; sorority sisters; and businesspeople from places near and far. Observing Kay interacting with people like this was a treat for Emerald. Her flair for entertainment was a constant source of wonder. The prettiest, most luscious-looking foods were prepared, often by Kay's own hands (to Emerald's surprise). Homemade cakes with pale chocolate or butter-colored frosting, adorned with sprigs of lavender; bowls of fruit with sauce; shrimp and grits; skewered kabobs; the list went on and on. She seemed to know how to do everything.

She would have friends over, or, more often than not – Emerald suspected – they got themselves invited over, then carefully select what type of party it would be: tea in the afternoon, or a casual supper; she even had a group of friends come for berry-picking, and procured for each one a straw hat and basket for the occasion. Mostly it was an intimate meal on the terrace. Linens, china, wine were all selected with impeccable taste, but to all this was added the quality that so few possessed: the wisdom to not make everything perfect. She would stand back to look at her festive tableau – and then change something. Some little thing was left purposely askew; or something was removed; or a chair was taken away and hidden, so that they had to use an overturned planter as a seat, and therefore have something to laugh about. Once, Emerald even saw her set up a whole scenario based on the lie that "our dolt of a maid has gone and scratched all the flatware by putting them in the dishwasher," and an "impromptu" picnic was in order, complete with checkered cloth and finger foods. As soon as they were out of sight, happily tramping out on the lawn, Emerald opened the kitchen drawers to see every piece of silver perfect, in its place. She knew that Nora was the one to take care of the good dishes, not Louise.

Watching her aunt at work with all her society friends made her hunger for interaction with her all the more. Whenever she herself was not needed in the conversation, she could fully be absorbed in the workings of her aunt – every gesture and smile, compliment and tactful joke. It was all done with exquisite talent somehow. She wondered how she learned it. She made people feel she was doing them a great favor by visiting her, doing things for her.

Fall classes began. Within a few days Emerald was fully installed as a student at the college. She gained her footing, mingling with the other fresh-faced newcomers, finding her way around the campus, and discovering the best places for studying or sketching.

When she knew people well enough to talk to them, she was somewhat surprised at their reaction to knowing she lived at Ashmont. Often she was met with a variety of curious glances and questions. Some people only knew it as the castle on the outskirts of town – not even realizing a family lived there. Others, especially professors who had lived in Millcrest awhile, said very little. She was proud to be the (almost) niece of Kay Keckley and willingly dropped this piece of information in conversations about it. This was usually met with silence, or a polite "oh."

At Ashmont itself, she was falling into rhythm with its ways very nicely. Autumn was a popular time in the mountains, and there was a steady stream of weekenders that provided her with a reason to escape somewhere within. The Keckleys busily entertained their guests, and Emerald found a childlike glee in seeking out hiding places without being noticed.

Dr. Canter had told her about a rumor that there was a secret downstairs room, the only cellar space beneath the house. "There used to be some stairs leading down to it, but I have no idea where they are. It's possible that the entrance to the stairwell was walled over. In the olden days they stored canned food and winter vegetables down there," she told her. "But the children of the house had the most fun with it, using it as a secret dungeon for their escapades. I've heard Kay and Nora talk about it before." Apparently it had fallen into disuse and was boarded up.

Emerald's ears were alive to hear of this secret part of the house; and yes, she vaguely remembered playing in a dank room with old furniture, stacks of newspapers, and household debris, all drenched in the musty smell of a basement. No one but children

and servants who would go down there . . . what better place for .
. .

The jewels.

Dr. Canter saw her eagerness and told her, "I believe you are the only one who truly appreciates this house! Much more than even the Keckleys, in my opinion. Oh, they put on a show for guests, but when no one is around, they always find things to groan and complain about. It's nice to see you relish it, as it deserves."

Emerald pretended to adjust her interest to only natural curiosity. "It's too bad they sealed it off," she said. "Unless there's a staircase around here I haven't noticed yet."

"You should ask Louise McSee. If anyone knows every square inch of the place, she does. Even Mr. Saxon admits losing track of which hallway leads where, and even forgetting some rooms altogether."

"But Louise hasn't been employed by the Keckleys for very long, has she?" quizzed Emerald. "I can't imagine her having such a thorough knowledge of any part of it that she doesn't clean regularly."

"Louise knows just about everything about Ashmont, and about the Keckleys, for that matter," said Dr. Canter, with a reticent look. These words left Emerald with a chill.

12

THE NOTE

E‌merald took it upon herself to find the forgotten cellar. She went up and down the slim stairwell that she had found that first day, feeling along the walls and pressing in to see if any gave way. No luck, though.

Where could the door be? She examined all the corners of the library, the den, even the dining room, but all was sound and immovable.

The kitchen, she thought suddenly, of course. There had to be a way downstairs to where canned goods used to be kept.

But even when she could snoop alone, which wasn't often, she found no evidence of anything. Not even a trapdoor in the floor, like she knew some old houses had.

If it's sealed on the inside, maybe at least there is a basement window to be found, she thought, walking around the outside of the mansion.

When roaming around she would take her sketchpad with her as an alibi. "I love to keep finding new spots to sit and draw," she would say, when found in an odd spot.

And she wasn't lying. Her fruitless search for a cellar window had made her stop and rest awhile on the tree bench. She was frustrated. It was impossible to find a way to the cellar since evidence of it had been so thoroughly glossed over, no telling how long ago.

After a while she heard the lone violin. The notes drew her spirit up, up among the leaves and limbs, out into the pure mountain air, above the flying fowl and the mountain peaks. Taking her sketch pad she poured her irritation out onto it, depicting the musical waves physically catching her up, and making her airborne.

She was working so intently that she didn't realize Sybilla was standing by her. Emerald flushed and felt vaguely guilty. She always felt this way when someone stood over her drawing, observing it.

"Hmm. That's pretty good." Syb tilted her head and looked at the sketch pad. "What is it?

"Oh," said Emerald, folding it up to put away, "just the way I feel when I hear that violin. I wish I knew who was playing it; some farmer I guess."

Syb hesitated, which added to the pain of Emerald's being discovered. "Oh. I've never known anyone who drew – *feelings*."

"It's interesting, trying to capture it, in my opinion."

"Well, hey. Speaking of interesting. Let's go to your room and look at what you brought to wear. You know, something – a little bit more grown-up." Emerald caught Syb's eye just as it looked away from her brown clogs.

"Grown-up?" laughed Emerald. "Why? Most people around here know I'm not a kid."

"Well, I have a little project in mind, but it's my secret. Just to help you come out of your shell; realize your full potential. I do know a few young men in this town, you realize that, right?" Syb had her by the arm and was leading her down the hall. "Of course, I wouldn't want to make your boyfriend back home mad."

"Boyfriend!" snorted Emerald. "You wouldn't have to worry about that, since I don't have one."

Syb looked like she had expected her to say exactly that. "Well, one day that might change. You never know."

Emerald had had very little experience with beaus in her twenty-two years. From an early age she enjoyed boys' company and had a best friend or two who happened to be boys; but as she got into her teens, and found herself to be the object of a crush, the realization of that had made her extremely shy. In class one day she had even received a juvenile love note from him: "Do you love me?" with two little squares drawn beside the "yes" and "no" responses. She had been so petrified by receiving such a note, and added to that, the pressure of knowing he was three seats away, and was waiting for its return, the experience was unbearably awkward for her. In cowardly fashion she had drawn a third box of her own at the bottom, and the answer "I don't know" written in a shaky hand. Then she checked the box and sent it back.

In high school, she fell in love several times, with much older boys, or movie stars; all equally unattainable to a ninth-grader. When she reached sixteen she had the misfortune of a next door neighbor who attached himself to her in friendship, being seen with her everywhere, thereby making the world think they were "going together." She liked him as a friend but never seemed to be able to distance herself from him. It would have been a profitable situation had this boy been a handsome, muscular athlete. However, he was so skinny that he looked terminally ill, and anyway he himself was in love with someone else. His constant attachment to Emerald, even out of insecurity, kept her inoculated from obtaining any real boyfriends all the way through high school.

"Do you have somebody particular in mind?" Emerald asked her cousin, who was now rustling through her closet and surveying her wardrobe.

"Maybe. Yeah, I'm thinking of somebody. He would be just right for you. Hey! Why don't you ever wear this?" Syb had been skipping past almost every article of clothing until a silky gray dress caught her eye. She pulled it out and held it up to herself in the mirror. "Oh! How I wish I could wear this color. It just never has looked good on me. It's just right for you though. Why don't you put it on?"

Emerald laughed outright. "Are you kidding? I only brought that because it's been in my closet for years, and it would be decent enough to wear to a dressy occasion. Dad had said something about the famous Ashmont parties, and I just wanted to be prepared, sort of. It's my 'emergency' fancy dress." She eyed the sleeveless garment with suspicion, doubting her appearance in the silver fabric. She couldn't even remember where she had gotten it; oh yes – the senior banquet from high school days. A friend had given it to her at the last minute, and she was to have worn it that very week; but fortunately she had gotten a virus and couldn't go.

Syb was still admiring it and holding it up to her cousin with a critical eye. "This is very basic. It needs just the right accessories. You know, strands of beads around your neck, and heels – really high heels. You would be gorgeous." Emerald smirked to herself and let Syb run off with her flight of fancy. But the idea was planted; what if she was right? She began to become interested in spite of her doubts; and thoughts of the 'mystery guy' gave her mind a reluctant little spark. Who knows?

"Come with me," said Syb. "I know where just the right jewelry is. Mother has some old pieces in a room down the hall. Actually, everywhere. She loves jewels, fake or real. I believe they're hidden everywhere in this house."

Unsuspected by Syb, Emerald's heart raced with this opportunity, falling right into her open hands! This was just what she was waiting for! If they could but find some of the good pieces, maybe she would suggest they keep it in a secure place, safe from Louise's roving eye.

Five minutes later the girls were delving into dusty boxes, happily in search of treasures; Syb looking for baubles for fashion, and Emerald on the hunt for the genuinely valuable. But she was intrigued, in spite of herself, by some old knick-knacks and photos stashed haphazardly in an old trunk.

"There's probably some stuff that Aunt Kay doesn't want us looking around in," commented Sybilla. "She's always had secrets from people. How she stays mysterious, she says. That's the reason she won't let anybody in her room."

"Really? Not your mom? Not even Louise, to clean?"

"No one. Mom told me to stay away from her room a long time ago. It's like Kay's private world, I guess."

"Entertaining people all the time must be stressful."

"I guess so. She's real sensitive about her personal space."

"There it is!" said Emerald, snatching a framed photo stuck down into the side of the trunk. "The picture that used to hang by the stairs. It went missing and I didn't know why. See? It's my Mother and Dad, with Aunt Kay. Look, how pretty. It must have been taken thirty years ago."

Sybilla looked at it for a minute, then shrugged. "Weird stuff goes on around here sometimes," she replied.

"What kind of stuff?" Emerald asked, trying not to sound too intrigued.

"Oh, I don't know. Things being moved around a lot. Something will be there for months, and then suddenly it's gone. Like furniture and stuff. Nobody will know anything about it. Sometimes arguing."

"Arguing?"

"Kay gets – upset sometimes."

"Sybilla, I want to ask you a question."

"Yeah?"

"What about that Louise person? How long has she been here?"

Syb dusted off her jeans and put the lid back on a box she'd been rifling through. "Louise? Oh, maybe five or six years."

"Does anybody know where she came from? She sounds like a New Yorker, or somewhere like that."

"Mr. Franklin just brought her over one day, and said she was our new employee. As far as I know she just cleans and does odd jobs. But I've found Kay really tearing her apart a time or two. Kay seems to keep a close eye on her; wants to know where she is every moment of the day."

"Mr. Franklin – Kay's boyfriend, right?"

"Ha! She wishes! I'm sure she'd love to get her claws into him, as rich as he is. He's the curator of Ashmont, or something like that. Come on, let's get out of this creepy room and go downstairs. I know a few other places we can check tomorrow. I have to be at play practice in an hour."

Syb was already walking out the door. "Be right there," called Emerald, wanting to look around by herself for a while. A piece of paper caught her eye: it was sticking out from the box Sybilla had opened. It was on pale blue stationery, and folded several times, into a tiny triangle; Emerald remembered folding notes like that as a young girl. But when she carefully spread it out and examined it, she sank back down on the floor, absorbed. For some reason, the writing looked so familiar. It was addressed to Kay:

"Dear Kay, dear 'cousin' – We got back home too late last night for me to call you. And since I had to be at Nan's all day today, I thought I'd scribble this note out and just mail it to you. I wanted to use my new stationery anyway. Father wouldn't have liked the phone bill if I'd called you, too, of course. And I knew you & I couldn't shorten our conversation enough for his taste, or his checkbook. This trip to see you was the most fun I've had in my whole life, especially because of a certain someone who shall be nameless. Mum's the word there. But be sure not to give away our secret (the other one). Ashmont's a wonderful place for secrets, that's for sure. I left you two things to remember me: one in the clock, and the other in the books. By the way you are a genius. The way you sealed off the pages and cut the holes out in the middle, then covered them up perfectly. Nobody will ever find our stuff inside those dusty old books, that nobody looks at. Our <u>magic</u> is safe. Remember, top shelf – Q through R – Encyclopedia Britannica. Burn this when you read it. Nora hinted that she knew where one of them was, so look out. As for the first secret, the most important one: when you two were walking on the bridge last week, before he left – did I tell you how good you looked together? Your blonde hair and his – "

Here the first page ended, and Emerald sat upright. She knew why this looked so familiar. It was the handwriting of her own mother!

She eagerly shuffled through the stack. She had forgotten all about jewelry, and only thought of finding the second page to this note.   But looking through piles, in drawers, under books — nowhere was the continuation to be found. Since the stationery was colored she thought it would be easy to spot among the ordinary white paper. The room was getting dark, but she wanted to keep looking; however, hearing sounds coming from downstairs, she knew dinner would be served soon.

She sighed and gave up – until another day.

13

FLIRTING

S ybilla and Emerald sat at a tiny round table and picked up menus. A striped awning shielded them from the noonday sun. *The Peppermint Pony* was swirled in painted letters on the window facing Ashmont's main street, and a window box filled with dusty miller made a silver fringe at the street level. College students milled in and around the little shop, either ordering lunch or browsing the artwork and books on display. One empty corner held a small stage and a microphone.

"Somebody will probably sing today. They have open entertainment on Fridays," said Syb. "Which means it will be horrid."

This was the same place Syb had escaped to on the day Emerald was trapped in the car with Danny. She had been wanting to get a better look at it.

The girls placed orders for salads and Emerald admired the ease of how Syb interacted with the handsome waiter. She looked pristine in her chic, neutral outfit, with the only color being the flirty red of her lips and nails. Emerald slid her clogs out of sight under the table; then looked at some of the artwork nearby.

"Did I tell you I'm going to be in a new play? Opening night will be held in Finley's theater. Say, why don't you see if they need artists for the backdrops and things? You could so do that."

Emerald appreciated the thought and agreed to think about it. "I don't know. I've never done anything like that before. I'm used to just painting for myself, really. Just small pieces for my family and whoever else cares."

"You should *so* bring some of your pictures here, Em. You can submit them for display, or even sell them if you want. Yours are way better than these, anyway." Emerald didn't remember that

Syb had seen any of her finished pieces, so she wondered why she said that. In spite of that thought, she couldn't deny a thrill from the suggestion!

The cute waiter brought their order, and then, to Emerald's surprise, twirled a chair around, straddled it, and made himself at home with them. He leaned forward and gazed at Syb with unmasked admiration. She did not even so much as smile in response, but scolded him. "Get back to work, you idiot. You'll get fired if they see you."

"Well it would be worth it, to spend the rest of the day with you." Emerald watched their interaction, fascinated.

"You'd best shut up and do as I tell you. You're ignoring paying customers, you know." Syb acted cold, but her eyes twinkled. Just then the manager appeared, and the waiter jumped to his feet. He leaned over to whisper something to Syb and give her a playful pinch.

"Who is that?" Asked Emerald after he'd walked off.

"His name is Julian. Do you like his accent? He's from New Zealand. He's been in a couple of plays with me. He's a cutie, isn't he?" Emerald studied this confident behavior of hers: praising him behind his back, but chilly and aloof when he joined them again.

"Julian, you haven't even asked me about my friend here," said Syb, and Em felt her cheeks warm as he turned his blue eyes on her. "Actually she's my cousin. Emerald Johnsey. She's an artist. Tell her she needs to bring her work here. I see the perfect spot, right over the coffee bar."

"Ho! Yes! Emily, eh?" And her embarrassment increased under the correction of her name, and how unusual it was, and questions about how she got it. She was used to explaining it, but not to blue-eyed guys who had a slight dimple in their chin, and an adorable cow lick that made their hair look boyishly out of order!

Julian had to leave them once again to meet the demands of others.

"He's a sweetie. Not a very good actor, but nobody minds.

"Syb! Look!" A Now Hiring sign was taped under the cash register. Syb's eyes widened. "Of course! How perfect for you!

"I'll go ask for an application," said Em, beginning to stand.

"Uh, no. No. I have a better plan. I know how things work here. I will call them myself. They won't know your name in a stack of applications; it will get over-looked. Let me talk to them."

"Oh would you? That would be great!"

They ate while listening to a few people perform. When a lady was singing a throaty ballad, Syb seemed drawn in and affected. It took a while for her to speak again. Emerald wondered what, or who, was on her mind; so much so that she broached the subject with a baited line.

"You and Julian would make a good-looking couple, Syb."

The blonde rolled her eyes in response. "Not my type," she snorted under her breath. "What do you think about him though?" She asked slyly.

"Me!" Em was abashed at the thought.

"I should fix you two up sometime." She went on. "You could wear that silver dress." Em knew she was teasing now, or if not, the idea was still a thing beyond the realm of reality. But the mention of the dress reminded her of the hunt for jewelry, and her discovery of her mother's old note.

"Sybilla, you know what I found yesterday? When we were looking for jewelry?"

"Hmm," she half-replied, sipping her frappe.

"A letter, an old letter written by my mom to Kay. Decades ago, when they were teenagers. I had no idea they knew each other back then! They sounded like best friends."

"Yeah, I heard Kay and Mom talking about that before. But they acted like it was a big secret."

"You heard them talking –? When was this?"

"Oh, a long time ago. Maybe a month."

"A month! But I've been here two months already. Why would they be secretive about it? It seems they would want to tell me." Did they want to spare her pain from hearing her talked about? Mother wasn't that bad, or was she –?

She went on: "Syb, I only found the first page of that letter, and I'm dying to read the rest. Do you know where I could find it?"

But Em couldn't get any more answers from her. The freeform performances continued, and once again, Syb had fallen silent over a sentimental song. The warbler was no great talent, but it was a love song, and she even saw her cousin dabbing her eyes.

"Is everything okay?" she asked after several minutes of silence.

"That song reminded me of someone I used to know. Someone special. His name was Frederick. He was along with my acting company in Vienna, then in Budapest, then Rome. We performed six nights a week, and he would take me out on the seventh. He would buy calla lilies and French chocolates for me. So you see, Julian and his types can flirt and flitter all they want, but I'm afraid my heart is in Europe right now." Her voice had trailed off, and her gaze was fixed on something unseen.

Emerald couldn't speak after such solemnity, and felt a deeper respect for her cousin. She wondered what had happened to the young man? She realized Syb was speaking again, as if within her own soul.

"The isle of Capri . . . a lovely place for a honeymoon."

Someone was now stammering poetry from the corner microphone, and Em tried to turn her attention to him, but she was stunned by her cousin's revelation.

She was in love with someone, and had to leave him behind!

Or had something happened to him?

Perhaps they'd fallen in love and wished to marry. Maybe his family objected to his marrying an American, so they wanted to elope. They had plotted when and where, and even knew they wanted to honeymoon on the Isle of Capri.

Emerald burned with curiosity to know what fatal event had aborted such dearly made plans. Had they broken up? Had he . . . *died?*

She couldn't say a word until the amateur poet was done, and even then it seemed too delicate a subject to bring up again. But Em couldn't bear it much longer.

"Syb, tell me. What happened to him?" Her cousin was just rousing from her reverie, and looked at Emerald as if she needed clarification.

"What happened to your fiancé?" repeated Em. "You were saying that you two had planned a honeymoon. In Italy."

"Planned it? We've already been on it!"

"What!" Em tried to adjust her thoughts to what Syb had just said.

"Yes, we had our honeymoon there."

"You're – you're *married?*"

"I was. The divorce was final last June."

14

EMERALD MAKES A CHANGE

Two or three times, the cute waiter Julian came to Ashmont to hang around. Sybilla was her full self when he was nearby. Any moping or depressed spirits flew away as soon as his sports car was heard on the gravel. By the time he walked in with a wink, and sat down with his signature posture – one leg hanging over the chair's arm – Syb looked refreshed as the morning sunrise.

Emerald continued to marvel at her manner of holding him aloof while still teasing him and keeping him on her line. Back and forth they would banter, fun flashing from their eyes, with Emerald usually the silent third, trying to keep her mind on her drawing.

As fascinated as Emerald was, after a while she found it hard to endure so much obtuse teasing over flimsy topics, so she would slip away to let them enjoy it alone. She would much prefer the grounded feeling of a straightforward conversation, were it about nothing more than today's weather.

But she couldn't help but wonder if he sought more than just banter from a pretty blonde. Because – she reluctantly noticed, with a thrill – he never left Ashmont without seeking Emerald out, wherever she was, and talking to her. At first she thought it was only to further tease Syb, in giving her an obstacle of sorts to overcome. But Julian would hang around longer and longer until Emerald got rid of him, half flattered, half alarmed. The longer he stayed, the more piercing glances she had to dodge from her cousin; and she would rather do without that.

One day, after Julian had just left, and needing to process her feelings about him, Emerald was in a mood to wander the halls again. She had sat through tea-time, the antique custom of

Ashmont that was scrupulously upheld by the ladies – as indeed it was one of the delights of visiting guests. When she was home in the late afternoons, she participated, enjoying the ceremony of it. The guests present absorbed all of her aunts' attention, and when she saw she had little share, as usual, she really didn't want to stay. She had slipped away as soon as the dishes were removed and the crumbs were wiped away.

Her room was being cleaned (supposedly) by Louise at the moment, and Mr. Saxon was heading toward his library with a fellow smoker or two. A thorough rain was soaking the grounds. Still craving solitude, Emerald was forced to search for it in some new, unexplored area of the house.

She pushed open the heavy door of a room she'd barely seen. A poof of dust greeted her as she walked in.

Finding a lamp that worked, she looked around and reveled in the ghostly findings. Fine old furniture, a marble fireplace, rugs and spittoons seemed to blink sleepily in the sudden light. A marvelous place for moping, if you didn't mind the veil of darkness and dust. Brushing off a couple of pillows, she nestled into a chaise and thought.

In the last twenty-four hours, and just when she had begun to feel comfortable in her new train of life, Emerald's world had shifted yet again. With an effort she brought recent developments to the surface of her mind and began to sort them out.

Sybilla seemed on another plane now, and Emerald grappled to find her footing in this changed relationship. Where she had been awed by the flirtations with men – so vividly on display when they lunched at The Peppermint Pony – she now recognized evidence of the pain her cousin must be in. Julian was so appealing and warm that he could elevate any female depression, just being around him. At the time, Emerald had had a hard time stomaching all the little touches and glances Syb had showered on him. But when she thought of her damaged state of mind, she recognized it as only a surface manifestation: to cover the ache beneath.

She had been a man's wife and returned home a wounded lamb. Where better could she go to heal those inner scars than among those who adored her so? Who could blame her for nestling into the healing love of her mother and aunt? Their very hearts bled for her. How much more of a claim she had on their affection, than some vague relation who had not grown up within these walls and among such devotion and care? Perhaps Sybilla had been rather spoon-fed upon the nectar of overactive tenderness, as a youngster; but that was all in the past, and it was but natural that she would seek healing within the same nest that had nursed every other pain she had suffered.

And yet Emerald's longing to be under Kay's wing was stronger than ever. With a feeling alarmingly raw (she wouldn't call it jealousy), she would watch her cousin in private talks with Kay, or walking the grounds together, or emerging from one another's rooms. Daily Aunt Nora cooked her favorite food, and almost as often, Kay brought her some trinket, scarf, or novelty she had picked up in town.

A bond impenetrable seemed to exist between Kay and Sybilla. Emerald thought she was imagining it, at first, but when she considered how alike they were, she recognized an affinity that even Nora couldn't enter into. Nora often needed Kay, and Emerald certainly wanted her, but they each had to be content with a few moments here and there. To Syb's lot fell the greatest portion.

There was always time enough for Sybilla, when it came to Kay's schedule. Heaven and earth were moved to preserve those moments of affection and confidence, for her; but Emerald's efforts at nearness to Kay were thwarted, again and again . . . never by Kay herself, oh no. She had made it clear from the very beginning that, being the gracious hostess she was, her ears and arms were always open to Emerald. It's just that every moment was so unlucky as to call her away to an urgent need of one of the guests, usually. *Usually.*

Emerald had never been so provoked to anger when, just yesterday, during the beginning of a tête-à-tête with Kay, Danny burst into the dining room demanding Emerald help him with something. Kay remembered she was to assist Nora in the kitchen, and rushed off. Emerald turned to the interloper with sparks in her eyes.

"What instrument do you play?" he had said, not noticing her irritation.

"What??"

"You said once that you were in the band. I need you for the concert next month. Tell me what you play."

"I didn't even bring my oboe with me! It's at home in Kentucky!"

"Oboe. Good. Yes, I can use you. There's one you can borrow. Wednesday night at seven, in the church basement. I'll get you your music."

And he had turned from her without the slightest expression of thanks.

She sat in the dark room thinking of that scene and became frustrated all over again. To vent her feelings, she glared at the heavy drapes covering the windows. Ugh! How ugly they were! Faded and dusty, and the color of a tired maroon that had been out of style for decades. She pulled at them and wondered what they covered up. They resisted the motion as much as an old dowager would an impertinent child, tugging at her skirts.

She took hold of one of the heavy panels of fabric and swung it back to see what was behind it. Tall, perfect window panes, letting in precious rays of light now that the rain had passed. Each one was beveled to reflect little rainbows on the edges. Who in the world would cover them? Such windows should be showcased to every visitor.

She worked for several minutes, hoisting the panels open as far as she could, then stood back to view the effect. By now, splendid afternoon sun came pouring in through the gaps, igniting the tomb-like room with a blaze.

Ah, she could finally look around and appreciate it, now that it was awash in life-giving light. Wood paneling, beautifully crafted, soared up to the coffered ceiling. Thick, gilded frames held paintings of the seaside. A grandfather clock, lifeless and mute, anchored the west wall. A fireplace took up a huge part of one wall; like the one in Saxon's library, it was so big she could almost stand inside it without stooping. It was marble, delicately veined, and creamy white.

Walking back to the bay windows, she recognized this room now. It was visible in the front of the house, but was always so dark that it never attracted the eye. But if you stood on the front lawn you could see it was the centerpiece of this entire wing! The windows went all the way up and were set inside a huge turret – much larger than her tiny one upstairs, that she took so much pride in.

Why didn't they make Louise pay more attention in here? This room could be the crowning glory of the mansion. The furniture was sadly old-fashioned, but it could be replaced. The more she surveyed the architecture, the more in awe she was.

She fetched a stepladder, and a half hour later the maroon drapes were down. She had been able to reach each drapery panel, dismantling them and casting them to the ground with disgust, one by one. The windows were now fully disrobed and displayed in all their glory. "Oh!" She breathed, in ecstasy of admiration. The whole room was transformed. It was grand as a cathedral, compared to the dungeon it was before. A tarnished plaque, which she had not yet noticed, hung over the door; she went to read it. The Vienna Room, it announced in embossed type.

The Vienna Room. Yes, that is quite a name for this remarkable place. It deserved its own name.

Then she thought of Kay. What would she say? Emerald's heart beat faster when she thought of her reaction. What an improvement this was. She visualized the room cleaned and with new furniture, and Kay and Nora leading guests in, serving tea, and – yes – relating how they had not thought much of this room until their niece Emerald came. She did this; she showed them the worth of such a room, and oh, how glad they were to have her artist's eyes recognize such an asset. "Our niece Emerald, she took down the drapes," rang in her thoughts while she gathered the fabric from the floor. And Kay's approving eyes would turn from the windows, to her, with pleasure.

She couldn't wait to show it to them. But glancing at her watch she saw it was time to leave for her evening class now. Where was everybody? She walked through the house and was surprised to find an empty kitchen. Not a soul was there, not even the ubiquitous Louise. Oh well, she would show them later. Returning to the Vienna Room, she took the pile of dusty cloth and crammed it into a closet nobody used; they wouldn't be needing them anymore. Then grabbing her books and purse, she left for the college.

It was past ten o'clock when she came back home and pulled her little car down the driveway and parked it in the carriage house. Her heart thudded palpably when she looked up and saw several lighted windows, though none shone in the Vienna Room – apparently no one had seen the windows uncovered yet. She ran inside.

Apparently everyone was in bed. She was disappointed that no one was up to share her victorious discovery and congratulate her. Oh well, that could wait till tomorrow morning. The delay couldn't remove the satisfaction of her labor, and she could surprise them with it at breakfast, when Kay was at her brightest and cheeriest.

She yawned and looked forward to soon being in bed herself, but before she mounted the staircase she glanced down the hall toward the east wing and couldn't resist. She would take one quick look at it, just a peek, for her own gratification.

Quietly she found the right door and turned the knob. It swung open with a creak. All was dark. That's funny, she thought, since the moon was nearly full tonight. Switching on a lamp, she stared at the wall of windows – and was mystified.

The heavy, deadly, maroon drapes were *hung back up*.

15

LOUISE'S WARNING

Maybe I just dreamed it, was her first thought the next morning. As soon as she went downstairs, and was sure of not being noticed, she went to that part of the house and cracked open the door of the Vienna Room. Instantly, the sick feeling from last night returned, because there they were: the dusty old drapes hung back on their rods again. And they had the addition of new wrinkles from where Emerald had wadded them up and stuffed them into the closet.

Who in the world did this?

She knew, of course.

At breakfast she did not expect the situation to be mentioned, and it wasn't. Her eyes followed Louise and her absurd, swinging feather earrings as she slung the dishes, staring at her sloppy movements until her head began to ache. The woman had no conscience. She did not even meet Emerald's eye. Who did she think she was, intercepting Emerald's actions in such a way — a blood relative of this fine old family, whom she was dependent on for employment!

Her poor aunts! They were completely deluded, she was sure. Just now, Kay was listening to some guests recount their flat tire the day before, and how the wife had sprained her wrist trying to help her husband change it. She was sympathetic, offering to ice the wound, and naming the best doctor in town whom she insisted on them visiting that very day. An elegant, refined woman like her — all tenderness — could not conceive of the treachery going on in her own home! She had probably hired Louise out of that same pity that was written on her face just now.

The question was, should Emerald confront Louise directly, or enlighten her aunts first? She debated upon the most effective method of ridding them of her.

Later, when Emerald knew Louise to be in the laundry room, she took it upon herself to at least question her.

There she stood, knee deep in the never-ending linens and towels, yet not paying the slightest attention to them. Instead she was looking deep into a brown paper bag, her face almost immersed in it, searching for something. Emerald moved closer.

There was a clinking of what sounded like small glass bottles, and a rattling sound, and a shuffling of papers, all coming from the bag. What did Louise have in there? What was she looking for so feverishly?

Emerald watched as Louise gave up and rolled the top of the bag down, then stuffed it behind some dirty clothes in the corner. Her face was still red from bending and searching. Emerald chose this moment to speak.

"Louise. Do you know anything about some drapes that were removed from one of the rooms?"

But she had started the washer and dryer; they drowned out Emerald's question.

Louder, she repeated herself, stepping closer.

This time, she was heard, and Louise met her eye. Emerald had expected a guilty look and an apology, but she got neither.

"I figured it was you who took 'em down. Ever-body else knows best not to meddle."

Emerald was taken aback at this accusatory tone. "Meddle?! How was that meddling? Did you see how much improved the room looked? It's not like I damaged anything, or made any kind of permanent change." Emerald was seething. Her aunts did not even have a chance to see the drapes down!

Her anger gave her courage to reprimand Louise directly. "When I inform Aunt Kay of this, she will not be pleased. I was only thinking of the best for the Keckleys, and for this house. That room could be used by guests. As a matter of fact, the rest of the house could use improving too! There is grime on the baseboards, and dust in the corners, that you overlook – "

Louise looked right back at Emerald and said, "Miss Johnsey, don't do it. Don't tell her. *I'm warning you!"*

Emerald was shaking. She turned from the room, nauseous from this exchange, and from the smell of the dirty laundry. She almost ran out to the back lawn; then going to the tree bench, she sat on it, holding her knees to her chest, and fumed, horrified by the wicked control of this woman, this servant, living at Ashmont.

She wished she was the type of person to deal with problems head-on. It was a miracle she confronted Louise the little bit that she did. She wished someone would come along who had the stamina to see it all the way through, to get all the cards on the table for all parties to see, and to effectually solve the problem. Coming face-to-face with such horror made her able to do nothing but flee it.

But she had to continue to live in it, to tolerate it, knowing Louise was nothing but a drain in the ship, a gauged-out place where all the goodness of the house was fast leaking out. And no one knew about it but her.

She thought of Lars Franklin. He had to be privy to the workings of the house, and, like Emerald, seemed to be the only one who suspected Louise of anything devious. He was often talking with her in a quiet manner and she seemed much more responsive to his commands than Nora's or even Kay's.

She began to watch for him purposely, and to look for opportunities to speak with him. Surely he had the power to see to her dismissal! And to get the proper employees to replace her.

Tonight was the first practice for Danny's concert. Emerald was late. She found a side door and slipped inside, wondering if she was in the vicinity of the church basement. The hall was dark and she looked left and right while walking, until she ran smack into the illustrious director himself. He immediately pulled her arm to follow him through a doorway. In one hand he held a black folder, filled with music.

"You're just in time, the rest of them have only warmed up," he announced. He grabbed a case off a shelf, explaining this was the extra oboe they had; and it hadn't been opened in several years, but she was to use it. He handled the pieces and began to put the horn together (incorrectly); she took over and adjusted it the way she wanted it, looking at it doubtfully. Not even enough time to soak her reed before she must play with people she'd never met.

Emerald stepped into the practice room and all eyes turned to her. Putting her music on her stand, she felt her face grow hot, and wondered how awkward would it be just to be suddenly sick, and leave? But knowing she wasn't a good actress, she stayed.

To make it worse, Danny commanded her to sight-read and play the first few measures of a song he placed before her, entirely alone! There was a moment of tormented silence before he motioned for the first beat to commence. Then, of course, having not warmed up at all, her notes came limping and squeaking out. After this charming introduction, he violently cut it off, and gave her time to go over some scales first. She timidly did so, thankful that the other players took this time to shuffle through their music, and converse in quiet voices.

After a second and third run-through, she had improved so much as to at least blend in with the others and not mar the song with too many of her own wrong notes. Most of these other players were, she deduced, students at Finley, and much better and more devoted than she could be. Tonight was the first time she'd played in three years.

As they were walking outside, after he had given her many instructions about practicing runs and breath control, he asked her a question on a topic that had been on her mind incessantly.

"Did I see you taking down some curtains last night? I saw lights coming from some windows that were usually covered. Were you up on a ladder? You should've asked Saxon to help."

"Yes! Did you see me? Danny, it was awful, I spent all that time taking them down, and you should see how gorgeous those windows were – the whole room was – without the darkness of those drapes. And you know what? I went to class and when I got home, they were back up again! Louise McSee did it, she told me so. There is something wrong with her!"

He listened, or seemed to be listening, although not making eye contact. The parking lot was dark and a lone streetlight wanly lit their path to their cars.

"And this morning when I called her out, she threatened me! She literally ordered me to tell no one, and threatened me with – I don't know what, but something – if I told my aunts."

All Emerald's gestures and emphasized words did little to awaken his alarm, as he was coolly examining his keys and scraping something off one of them. "Well?" she asked. "Why would she do that? What do you think about her?"

He shrugged. "Once, she was snooping around in my garage, cleaning or something. She poured bleach on some of my gaskets and ruined them."

"But I mean, about her personality. The way she listens in on everyone. The way she takes over when she has no business to."

"I guess I haven't noticed anything about that. But I still think you should get Saxon to help you next time you're climbing ladders. Or me, I'll help you do it."

"Danny, I haven't told anybody this, but I think Louise might be – might be stealing. Not money, but – I think she is looking for something much more important. Aunt Nora told me that the family owns dozens of invaluable jewels, collected since her grandfather ran the place. She said they've had to hide them. I think Louise knows that, and – she's looking for them herself. Any day now, if she disappears, I'm sure that's what happened."

This disclosure made the moment a solemn one. The only sounds were a few frogs and some distant traffic. Danny now looked up and met her gaze.

"Oh no," he said.

Finally, she had gotten his attention. She felt she had an ally at last!

But what he said next made the illusion pop like a bubble.

"I can't believe it. Didn't you get your horn? I told you, you need to practice at least a half hour every day. There's no other way we'll be ready for the concert, unless everyone practices."

16

FIRST GLIMPSE

She must tell her aunts about Louise, *today*.

Like a puzzle in her mind she mapped out her day: what times her classes were, and which tasks had to be done, and exactly how much time would be taken up in between times, like driving. Kay would be home all day; she had heard her mention it. When home, she was in her own suite during the times between lunch and mid-afternoon. Meal planning was done by Nora, and when that was ready, someone was sent to town for necessities; sometimes Saxon, sometimes Kay herself, rarely Louise. Kay just went yesterday, so she was sure to be home for a couple of hours, unless Emerald miscalculated.

Ashmont was so large that it was easy to avoid people if you wanted to – except twice a day, at the carefully-adhered-to, set-in-stone times for the morning meal and afternoon tea. As an inn, this schedule was vital, and it was the one unifying routine that held the household together. A somewhat late supper was usually offered but was often not attended by the guests.

That meant that Kay would be available, alone in her room, around two o'clock. With a flutter of spirits Emerald raced home after biology, and parked in Danny's garage. He was there. She had to field a few questions about how her practicing was going, which seemed absurd coming from a disheveled person in tattered, oil-stained clothes, holding a wrench.

When free from him, she flew to the house and headed for the main stairs. Before she got past the foyer, however, she heard the alarming sounds of raised voices nearby.

It was Saxon and Nora, embroiled in an argument. He was actually standing on a table, half his body inside a wall duct, trying to coax Tiger John out. He had fallen through one of the upstairs vents and into the wall. This had happened before, and each time he had had to be retrieved before doing any damage to the wiring.

Muffled sounds of questionable character issued from the wall, from both Saxon and the cat. Grunting and mewing ensued from within, while Nora was poised perfectly on the floor, surveying the scene, and fancying she was helping. She was the picture of serenity, except for the worrisome look on her face which was something of a trademark for her.

Apparently she was using this cat extraction as a way to capture her audience (Saxon) and torment him with questions about some project.

"But we *need* that courtyard, Saxon. Kay's been calling for its repair for years. It would just be replacing a few bricks and pulling some weeds. I'll help you."

"You'll stay a hundred feet away from it, if it's ever to be touched."

"She has it all envisioned. A nice smooth patio, so no one trips while dancing, you know, and with the pergola covered in vines, and a fire pit or two, and string lights. And the music to be piped in, of course, unless we can hire Danny and his people to come play something. This renovation won't cost much! Less than a thousand dollars, if that!"

"Ten times that! I well know the tangents of expense applied to projects around here. I cannot so much as change a light bulb, without having to do it three times over to suit yours and your sister's taste."

"Oh you exaggerate as usual! We will all chip in on the courtyard, me and Sybilla, and Louise and Danny too – just show us what to do, and we could have it done in a weekend, I dare say. Even Mother Ann could scrub the old flower urns. She loves to be outside. You know she takes Puddles out there several times a day, to do his business."

Puddles came up just then, toenails clicking on the hardwood, and sniffed around Saxon's bag of tools. He lifted a leg toward it.

"Ma'am, I have many years' experience in propping up this old homestead and dressing it in its Sunday best. I know that I will not and cannot succeed in ever fulfilling the desires of yourself and especially those of your sister. The illustrious image in her mind is miles beyond what this place could ever hope to attain. Wallpaper and furniture and now, dancing patios. It goes on forever. You will have to replace me, before long, you just remember that!"

Sybilla brushed by at this moment, kicking Puddles aside, and hurrying toward the door on her way out. Emerald, who had not seen her cousin for a few days, took a moment to grab her and ask about another matter that had been weighing on her mind.

"Syb! What did they say when you called?"

"Hmm dear? What are you talking about," she replied, re-rolling her cuffs on her tailored blouse.

"The Peppermint Pony. You said you would call them about that job opening for me."

"Oh! Yes! I did."

"You called? Great!"

"No, I mean, um, I told you I would call them. I promise to do it *asap*. It's my director's fault, he keeps changing my lines. My head is all mixed up. But I'll let you know. I promise." And she rushed out the door.

Emerald was aggravated. She needed a job! Well, forget Sybilla, she would go herself. First thing tomorrow she would go apply. It was exactly the type of place she would love to work at; and so close to the college, too.

The argument between Saxon and Nora was not at all resolved, as usual, and they continued sparring in their habitual way that Emerald had a hunch they rather enjoyed. It spent some of their nervous energy.

She went up the stairs to the next landing; all seemed quiet in Kay's hallway.

Now was the time.

She skimmed up the staircase and went directly to Kay's suite. Her heart beat faster and her throat went dry. In spite of what Syb had said, that Louise was not allowed in there, Emerald knew she had entrance: she had seen her with her own eyes, unlocking the door with her own key. What if Louise caught her now? Would she scold her away? Would she threaten her again, and report her to her superiors?

But Emerald reached the door with no sign of the strange woman, so she lifted her hand to the doorknob and tried it gingerly. She was startled by a cough from within the room – Kay's cough. This unexpected noise froze her, and before she could react, the door opened and there stood her aunt.

Emerald felt as if she had to explain her presence as fast as possible.

"Oh, Aunt Kay, I – I thought you might be out shopping, I didn't know – I just thought I would check to see – "

But her anxiety evaporated at Kay's gentle reception of her. Other than looking a little disheveled, and trying to straighten her appearance by patting her hair and tightening her house dress, she acted as if it were the most natural thing to find people staked out at her bedroom door.

The bedroom itself was barely visible. All was dark within, but the open door allowed a shaft of light to illumine a little of it. Kay still stood in the doorway, but from what Emerald could glimpse beyond her – she could not have believed her eyes!

17

KAY'S BOUDOIR

No satin bedding, or elegant furniture; no French doors opening to a sleek bath; no expanse of soft carpet that Emerald pictured Kay walking back and forth on, plotting her parties. Instead was all . . . a mess!

Clothing, papers, dishes, seemed to be strewn about, on the table and unmade bed; the bed itself indeed had a canopy, but looked more like a garage-sale relic than an antique from Ashmont's early days.

Emerald was thoroughly stunned. She could not speak. Her own embarrassment made her back up into the hallway, but her aunt drew her back in. After a few moments she averted her eyes, aware that Kay must be ashamed of the chaos. However, she didn't seem at all fazed, and in fact invited the girl right in.

"Come in, dear, have a seat there," she said, not apologizing for the box of shoes and dirty glass that she had to move in order to sit. Kay switched on a lamp, and Emerald saw that the floor-to ceiling windows were blocked by drapery – much like the Vienna Room – shrouding its contents from the world. On a sunny day like today. The sad little lamp looked overstrained in its attempt to brighten such a space.

"I was just about to go over these bills and things," said Kay. Emerald had not noticed until now that she held a stack of envelopes and papers. Still clutching them, she waved toward the desk just behind her niece. "Did you ever see such a mess?" she asked with a groan. "I'm such a ninny about things like this. Look, a bill for the new refrigerator. I thought we had signed up for monthly payments. But here, it says we owe the whole amount." She waved the paper in front of Emerald.

She took the paper and studied it for a moment. "No, Aunt Kay, it's not a bill – it's a quarterly statement. See? You did pay the last payment – here, it says it was received. The balance isn't due until February though."

"Really?" she cried, putting on her glasses and taking it back. "Well! You're so smart. I didn't know that's what it meant." And she hugged Emerald in appreciation. In turn, Emerald tried not to acknowledge that her aunt evidently had not bathed in a couple of days. There was also a vague medicinal odor; but maybe she just imagined that.

Kay walked about the room, her housedress trailing and showing off her pretty bare feet. "Nora knows even less about numbers and stuff than I do," she fretted. "And . . . some months. . . I just don't know what we're going to do. This business fluctuates so much, you know. And I know we spend a few dollars on our parties and events, but the reputation of Ashmont must be upheld," looking at Emerald earnestly as if trying to convince her. She nodded in agreement, trying not to look alarmed that a stack of papers was sliding off the desk and spilling it onto the floor. Kay just ignored it. "Our interaction with society," she continued, lighting a cigarette, "is just a sacrifice we must make."

"Aunt, I insist, I need to pay for my roo –" but before she could get all the words out she was quickly hushed. "I would be absolutely offended if you or your father tried to pay us! After all – you're family! Do not mention this again." Her voice was firm and impressive.

Emerald glanced around at the squalor and had an urge to help in some way. "What if – well, you know I used to help Dad with his books at the office for a while. You know, paid the bills and wrote payroll checks, stuff like that. Could I help you, um, organize it to make it easier? You won't let me pay; I want to do something."

Kay looked reluctant at first, shaking her head at the innumerable pieces of paper blended with bits of trash and cigarette butts. "Oh, I couldn't let you," she began, although seeming to weaken her resolve to receive help.

"Please," added her niece.

"Well. . . are you sure you have time?"

"I have mostly morning classes, and you know I haven't found a job yet. I could work on it an hour a day or so."

Kay inhaled her cigarette, then scratched her eyebrow with her pinky fingernail. "Promise me," she said, "you will stop if it gets overwhelming. I don't want to take away from your artwork, that's important. You must continue with your passion, your lovely paintings. I still think you ought to try to sell them."

Emerald started work that very day, while Kay took a rather long shower. She began by picking through the tipsy pile on top of Kay's desk. Wafts of dust arose, making her sneeze. She began to sift through the scraps of papers and envelopes. Most of these were fairly recent, but here and there she was astonished at finding papers from eight, ten years ago! Looking in envelopes, some of them still sealed, she found bill, bill, monthly statement, and occasionally – a check. How on earth did Ashmont operate in this state?

Was there any framework of financial stability at all? And, to add to her concern, she saw that there were many more stacks, and boxes filled with papers, stashed underneath the desk and behind the furniture.

The dank atmosphere and overwhelming clutter gave her a headache, and she sat in silence for a minute. Kay finally emerged from her dressing room, fully dressed and accessorized. She wore a trim yellow pantsuit and a scarf at her neck; as fresh as a spring morning. Emerald almost laughed outright, in amused awe, at the contrast of the woman and her bedroom.

"Are you able to make any sense of that mess?" asked her aunt, strangely cheerfully.

Emerald pulled out a document or two and began asking about them, but her aunt could offer little knowledge. While Kay was putting on earrings and shoes, Emerald grasped the opportunity to mention the reason she came here in the first place.

She spoke of her surprise in finding the Vienna Room, and examining the furniture, and being dismayed that such a room should be buried in obscurity; being careful to appeal to her by praising it and pointing out its potential. Then the curtains, and how lovely those beveled windows would look in the sun. Then, their removal. But before she could get to the next part, her words seemed to choke in her throat. A combination of her latest accusing encounter with Louise, which was still fresh, and the headache brought on by the surrounding clutter, made her cry.

Kay rushed to her. "My darling! What could be the matter? I believe this work will be too overcoming for you!"

"No – no . . . that's not it . . . it's . . ."

Kay cradled Emerald's head in her arms; she laid her cheek against her sweet-smelling skin.

"What is it? Tell me."

"When I – when I returned home from class and looked in the Vienna Room – the curtains – they were hung back up!" Emerald wept more openly now with her aunt's gentle touch. Kay cooed her concern.

"Oh! After all your hard work uncovering them, too!"

"But Aunt Kay, I need to tell you something – I think I know who did it!"

"Who did what, lamb?"

"Who hung the drapes back up. I am sure it was – it was – Louise McSee. She admitted it to me. She even threatened me, if I should let you know about it. And I've seen her do strange things. She seems to be – nosy – about you, about this family. I haven't been able to tell you yet, until now." Emerald's eyes shone with tears and with this pent-up revelation.

"I know, dear."

"You know?"

"Yes, I know it was Louise. In fact – I saw her do it."

"You saw her!" gasped Emerald. "But Aunt, why didn't you stop her? Why do you let her meddle in such a way? If you could have seen the room, how it looked transformed – "

"Hush now. You're right. I probably should have stopped her. But Lars made me promise to just report things like that to him, and not take these matters into my own hands. He says it's too stressful for me."

"Mr. Franklin! I thought he knew about her! I have seen him

question her before."

"Yes, dear. He is curator of Ashmont – was made so many years ago, by our parents. I advise you to do as he has told me, and simply take note of episodes such as this and let him know about them in privacy. Don't you worry, I will tell him about it. I'm seeing him this very afternoon."

"But why is she allowed to stay here?" Emerald almost cried out. "Why is she paid to do such indifferent work, and spy on others in the process?" She could have added her suspicions of theft, but did not hazard such thoughts – yet.

"Shh. Stop crying now. I know it's a frustration. I assure you, I want her gone as much as you could. I keep telling Lars this. He says he will replace her in the near future. Just keep notice of her doings, and we will pass them on to him. He may not realize how dire the situation has become." She squeezed her shoulders and turned her face up, wiping tears away. "Now you know why I do not allow Louise in here. You and I are the only ones who know the truth about her."

18

REHEARSAL

Emerald's mind was immeasurably comforted. At long last, she finally knew that she and Kay were now on the same page about Louise. She could encounter the crude woman with breezy unconcern now, only throwing a glance of contempt in her direction if the other's gaze was fixed on her in scrutiny.

Every day until now had been steeped in uneasiness about Louise. Now relieved of being the sole bearer of such a burden, she began to love being a part of Finley College. Her drives to the school were delightful. With her music turned up she zipped through the streets, relishing the reddening foliage and saturated autumn sunshine in these precious few weeks before winter. And when she walked on campus to the various unique buildings, she felt her eyes opening to so much she had already missed! She met other students with a smile, she felt fresh joy in her pursuits; signified in the reckless swirls of autumn leaves she tramped through, as she went from class to class.

Her success at school was all the more satisfying knowing it brought joy to her parents back home. Then, she got reports of Mother doing better than expected with her new medicine. Dad would call almost every night, and sometimes Mother herself. She said she loved the newest sketch Emerald had sent her and kept it by her bedside.

It was a copy of the removed picture of the three young people – Mother, Dad, and Kay – leaning up against the old roadster in the black-and-white photo. Ever since Emerald had found it in a cardboard box that day she and Syb were looking around, she had kept it in her room among her own things. If no one appreciated it enough to display it, she did, although still puzzled as to why it was taken down in the first place. This instance, among the many other things that had bothered her, were chalked up to Louise's presence; she was still there, but any day now she would be removed and Emerald could fully relax again.

Emerald wasn't only cheered by crisp weather, good grades, and news from home; she had another bolster to her spirits that added a spark to her eye. Julian had been coming to see her.

The first couple of times, he had given Sybilla a ride home and just hung around for a while. Then the next time he showed up alone. Again and again it had happened, and when he was told Syb was at play practice, or shopping, or getting a massage, he most resolutely made a point not to rush off.

If Emerald was in the den, he settled into the big leather sofa and watched TV with her. If she was outside drawing, he chewed grass and threw acorns, making her giggle with funny stories. He even came up to her room and helped her with homework, or said he was helping, by making fun of American idioms and telling her what schools taught back home in New Zealand.

He had a deep voice that made her smile shyly. And his accent was enchanting to her ear. A few times she couldn't understand certain words, and he seemed to enjoy stopping to reiterate them, or explain their meaning back in his homeland.

He was hilarious! As an observer of the typical customs of genteel Southern hospitality, he saw and noted the ironies of it that made Emerald laugh. She watched him engage Ashmont's visitors, claiming to be either the gardener or cook or long-lost son to the Keckley family, whatever his current mood had an inclination for. He liked to put Nora especially to the test, utterly confusing her with made-up requests from their guests, or running to embrace her when she entered the room. Emerald would come to her poor aunt's rescue and Julian would receive scoldings in her sweet voice, which only seemed to fuel him for future mischief.

He was a friend, only a friend, she was sure; but just a friend was exactly what she needed right now. The dynamics with her cousin had changed since the revelation of her recent divorce. In Emerald's immediate sphere, there simply were no other equals for her to connect with.

With Julian, she was never hearing lectures about how she should be practicing music. There were no suspicious stares in silence, as she was always on the watch for, from Louise. No rushing off to more important things such as her aunts were called upon to do.

He offered her the undervalued – yet vital to a young person – qualities of relaxation, fun, and laughter. She looked forward to his showing up at Ashmont (he never called ahead) more and more. A few times, Syb came home to find him there, and she always shot a fast glance at Emerald that made her blush. This was nothing but two friends hanging out together, but even if it were something more, why would Sybilla seem so sensitive to it? Unless she really did have feelings for him, herself?

Emerald even enjoyed practicing in Danny's orchestra. That is, she would have enjoyed it, if she could forget how uncomfortably needy he was of her (dubious) skills. She soon found out that he very much depended on her for the winter concert, and did not allow her a single absence from these all-important rehearsals. She didn't mind playing, and acknowledged the therapeutic effect of musical oneness with the ensemble of mostly college students; but could never rise above the level of mediocrity and achieve the superiority Danny wanted her to have.

She wished she could play splendidly. She imagined herself lifting the audience to lofty heights with swelling arias and rapid runs; with Danny directing her, prompting her and glowing over her brilliant strains. Of course the pressure of this had the opposite effect on her actual performance and she usually tooted along more like a schoolgirl.

For a while, indeed, Emerald was on the verge of quitting altogether, in spite of the impending performance around which Danny seemed to revolve. She mentally arranged the wording of how she was going to get herself out of playing anymore. At first she thought she would resign in an angry huff, after he had criticized her too much; sometimes a polite but icy statement of finality; sometimes a note left for him after rehearsal was over; and the other option was just to stop showing up. But something always seemed to happen to keep her coming back. Either he would thank her for being there, and talk about how desperately he needed her to carry the melody, or he would simply assign her an important piece of homework and require her to play it next time. The third but most rare occurrence was that she actually received a word of praise from him. This last method was by far the most effective to work on her, but the most unlikely.

She soon found out she was not alone in her feelings. One night when the trumpets were in surgery under Danny's scalpel, she heard voices of the brass section directly behind her. She heard a low groan, and then "Come on already! It's eight fifteen. I still have most of my term paper to write!"

Emerald turned in her seat just enough to see the euphonium behind her. He continued to hiss, "Every single Wednesday night we sit here and waste time because he has to play tutor to each instrument."

The tuba player joined in. He was a huge, burly young man with thick hair, and exactly fitted the dimensions of his instrument. "Are you going to play in the concert? Grosch is stressing out bad about it."

"If I can keep my grade point average up; meaning, if I get my term paper turned in. I don't think the excuse will fly – 'but I can play the intro to the Sonoforio perfectly'."

"Well, I'm not," said the tuba. "He'll have to do without me or find somebody else. I just started law school and I'm having to commute. No time for concerts for me. I like playing okay, but I'm looking forward to getting out from under – " and he left the sentence unfinished, with just a nod toward their director.

"Did you see the way he yelled at the pianist over losing her place at the key change? She was almost in tears."

"And he's always losing his place! For one thing he hardly follows the score. And when he writes changes on our music, I can't make heads or tails of it."

Here Emerald felt a twinge of defensiveness, since she herself had noticed this and had a hunch that he had trouble with his glasses. He probably needed new ones and couldn't afford them. The euphonium and tuba kept up their commiserating, venting their frustration against Danny, until Emerald began to actually feel sorry for him. He was totally unaware of the whispered mutiny simmering among the brass. She looked at his face – so earnest – intent on forming the music, brows knit together; and then a look of satisfaction when the chords came together perfectly. In that moment she felt she understood him for the first time; she sensed a particle of affinity – the appreciation of the beauty attained, the same beauty she strived for in the earnest work of her hands.

Suddenly Danny took his baton and cracked it on one of the music stands – their least favorite demonstration of authority.

"Emerald Johnsey! You were supposed to have come in at measure 24. Did you not hear me say for the woodwinds to join this time?"

19

WADING THROUGH

Now the possessor of a key to her aunt's suite, Emerald would slip into the dark room, usually while Kay was entertaining visitors downstairs, and tackle the clutter a few minutes each day.

All was chaos here and she didn't really know where to begin, but just picked a dusty stack of papers and started working through it. In spite of this being very depressing work, surrounded by neglect, grime, and confusion, she felt a sense of purpose and usefulness. She was doing something to repay her room and board; but mostly she was glad to be of such help to Kay. She obviously needed it!

She learned to approach the mess like she did her paintings: step by step, she would find pleasure in wading through the barrage of images that flooded her creative mind, plucking one from the whirlwind and focusing on it, and setting about bringing it under control, putting it to order in a meaningful way, tangibly, so that it could be viewed and evaluated. It was a transforming of vague, fleeting imagery to solid and unchanging reality.

In this way she was able to gradually make sense of what she was finding. Little by little, she formed a truer, though increasingly frightful, picture of the financial state of the home. Kay's spending habits seemed to be running rampant and unchecked! What was worse was that as Emerald dug deeper in her bedroom, she found bags of merchandise still with tags: bought and then squirreled away, never to see the light of day. Purses, scarves, soap, bottles of shampoo, and the like, still in their fancy store bags and hidden under mounds of clutter!

Aunt Kay had a problem! This was appalling. Merchandise in perfect condition – sometimes bought in doubles or even triples – still in boxes and bags. Receipts inside were dated as far back as several years! This whole set of rooms seemed to be swimming in layers of items, clutter, and catastrophe. Items of zero value – like an empty tissue box, a sock with holes in it, or still-full ashtrays from who knows how long ago – were blended with brand new sweaters and watches and other expensive items. Nothing could be thrown away without carefully examining every inch; Emerald had even found cash mixed in with pockets of wadded-up trash!

What would Mother and Dad say about this situation? But of course Emerald would betray Kay's secret to no one. She was entrusted with access here, one of the few people – perhaps only person – of this house to be allowed in. In fact, the first few times she entered, she was filled with joy of the exclusive importance of it. It was only after she began to uncover the reality of the problem, that alarm started to take over her feelings.

And she was angry. Emerald had thought Louise was to blame just for neglecting her employer's room, but now she was convinced she was the very source of it!

Because there was no way her aunt would live this way if such an interloper weren't constantly present at Ashmont! No wonder Kay would retreat here so often, locking herself in for hours. Of course she wouldn't let the woman clean in here. It was the only place where she could get away from her ever-watching eyes. Emerald thought of the times she herself flew upstairs to her room to escape Louise.

She thought of the times Kay's face revealed some personal worries, some inner vexation that she had wondered about. It was only natural that it was the only place she could let go of the incessant cares of running the mansion. Poor Kay was totally overwhelmed and it was manifested in the worsening mess in here. She was hiding this dreadful knowledge from the rest of the world; and she, her niece, was one of the few admitted to the sight of it.

This room used to be the sanctuary Kay deserved, Emerald was sure about that. The bones of the room were of elegant design and décor, as shown by the now-stained wallpaper and graceful furniture, currently loaded with junk. It had been a true lady's boudoir, pristine and elegant, until Louise came on the scene.

Emerald figured out that old letters and receipts were dated from about the time of Louise's arrival five or six years ago. Lars had been the one to hire her; Kay couldn't do anything about it. She was afraid to disappoint him by complaining, so she did her best to live with his choice, coping with the stress by any means that came naturally to her.

Kay had turned to *shopping*. How exhilarated she always looked, coming in bearing packages of newly bought treasures: Emerald had noticed this from the very beginning of her visit. More and more purchases gradually led to utter denial of her habits. She had become ashamed to let anyone know.

She remembered the day Syb had said no one is ever allowed here. In this state, it was the only part of the house that was off-limits to anyone except whom Kay really trusted from her heart. Then, that meant that Emerald was one of those special few. And what if she hadn't come here to college? Who else would be in a position to intervene and rescue? Her sense of purpose was doubled in importance now.

Emerald had by no means forgotten the stowed-away jewels that Nora had told her of. She kept an eye out for anything that could look important, to her untrained eye at least. So far, it was mostly clothing and paper, gobs of paper. All these receipts and documents she was finding certainly gave her a good look into Kay's private life! Trips to Knoxville, Asheville, and Charlotte at exclusive inns; rentals of the finest cars; visits to wine cellars for bottles that cost in the hundreds. She thought about what Syb had told her about Lars Franklin and how wealthy he was. Was lonely Kay using material means to make him woo her? It seemed that way. How much was he interested in her, if at all — beyond the small flirtations Emerald had witnessed? And did he have any inkling about her personal flaws?

One day, a couple of weeks after beginning the unearthing process in Kay's suite, Emerald came downstairs with wide eyes and a fast-beating heart. Not so much because Julian was waiting for her and wanted to take her for a drive; but because of something she held tightly in the palm of her hand.

"I'll be back in a minute," she told him, dusting off her clothes like she always had to do after working on Kay's stuff. "Let me grab my purse and jacket." When up in her room, she put the item in her table-side drawer. As flattered as she was to be going out with Julian, she couldn't wait to get back home to examine it closer.

20

A NEW JOB

"Take this mail to Danny, please, dear," said Nora, with her untied apron hanging from her neck, and handing her niece a handful of envelopes. "If I don't get this cobbler made tonight, all our home-grown pears will be for naught." Emerald wanted a chance to talk to him anyway. He had not been satisfied with her performance of a few certain measures that she had struggled with, and she was going to try to convince him with a simplified version she came up with herself.

He was heaping some stray branches onto a cleared-out spot and trying to start a fire. After arranging them and putting some more dead wood on it, a blaze took hold. She had given him his mail, and he flipped through it and tossed most of it into the flames, making it flare up. The crackle and smoke made her shiver, thrilling her with the bite of cool air that was settling in for the afternoon.

Next, he took out some cloths and started wiping down Kay's car.

She sat on an overturned bucket and watched. "Is that part of your job?" she asked idly.

He never answered any question right away, but waited until he was fully ready. "You could say I'm the Keckley chauffeur. When they want me to be."

"So I've heard. How long have you been doing it?"

Again, a pause while he finished wiping the fender, then the headlights, with meticulous care.

"Few years now." This time he had a question for her. "So you're a niece of the family, huh."

"Actually, my dad is Kay and Nora's cousin. Second or third, something like that. I've always called them my aunts. Say, Danny – do you hear music around here sometimes?"

"Music?"

"Somebody playing an instrument, somewhere here on the grounds. Surely you have; being outside a lot, and all."

He stopped to look for something on the work bench without answering. Finally he said, "Animal sounds come up from the valley quite a bit. Maybe that's what you heard."

They were silent a few minutes, while she listened for it again. When she heard a distant bird she said, "There it is," but as soon as she said it, realized it wasn't. It was a blue warbler, Mother's favorite bird. The thought made her speak of her. Danny listened while she told him about the illness, and that death was possibly looming; and that Dad wanted her to come to Ashmont for a few months because she'd been worn out caring for her. She sat on the bucket and rambled on, about Mother and what she looked like before the diagnosis, and what she looked like now; where she had grown up and gone to school; how she had enjoyed coming to Ashmont as a child, haunted memories and all; and before she knew it, she was confiding to him her discovery of Kay's atrocious hoard and how alarmed she was about it. Danny said nothing at all, just letting her go on; he kept wiping and scrubbing. Occasionally he would glance up at her, indicating he was still listening, and she appreciated the token of politeness. Usually when talking to the Keckleys, they would hear her words but their gaze would be elsewhere, and she didn't know if they were listening or not.

She fell silent, mesmerized by the crackling flames. She had forgotten what she wanted to talk to him about; her thoughts were on the item she had found in Kay's room yesterday. It was something that gave her new insight into her family, and that pecked at her with unanswered questions, too.

Danny stood straight up from his stooped position and thanked her for bringing his mail. Then he surprised her by saying, "Go upstairs," and nodding his head toward the steps leading up to his living quarters.

"What?"

"Go upstairs. There's something for you up there. Door's open. Look above the desk."

What could be upstairs, in Danny's apartment, that was meant for her? She went up and looked for it. Taking a look around the room, she noted a sort of masculine untidiness, from dirty jacket on the chair to the uncovered food left on the counter. *It's pristine compared to Kay's room,* she thought with a smirk. She spotted a desk, somewhat coated with dust and miscellany, and poked around a little, but not seeing anything that looked like it would remotely belong to her. During this search she saw how the bricks in the wall behind it were formed, and that there was one brick protruding forward a little bit, making a tiny shelf. On this brick were Danny's glasses, propping up an envelope with *Emerald* written on it, floridly. She picked it up and opened it.

> Em – I'm sorry I had to leave this with the Composer. You had already left when I found out, and he was the first one I saw, going out the door – and my phone is dead, as usual. I'm in the wildest hurry. But I'm about to bust, with the news I have for you. I got you a job today. A JOB!! See how good I am to you? And they need you right away. Just call this number: ----. You can thank me later. Love ME

And beside the *ME*, Syb had drawn a little winking face.

The Pony had hired her! She came through on her promise, and Emerald felt a little guilty about doubting her before. Wasn't it Sybilla's idea in the first place, that day they had lunched there and she first mentioned it to Julian? It would not have occurred to Emerald to apply, much less bring her art.

She went quickly to her room, grabbing her purse and keys. Then she remembered what her family had told her so emphatically. "You must take some of your paintings!" and "Oh, yes, when you apply for the Pony, do take some! Yours are far better than the ones they have!" came flooding back to her mind. Well, she wouldn't actually show them to the management today, but she might as well have a few in her car, just in case. She selected four or five and took them with her.

Driving down the ribbon-like road, her hands trembled on the wheel. Why was she nervous? Well, maybe not nervous, but excited. This was the first time she had really looked forward to something solidly good, waiting for her. The job itself — and the person she would be working with — filled her with pleasant anticipation. She blushed when she thought of Julian's smile, his nearness as they would be working under the same roof. *Just a friend, remember,* she scolded herself.

When she parked and got out, she suddenly remembered that Syb had said to call the phone number. She had forgotten, in her hurry. Oh well, she was here now, and was encouraged by the sight of the shop being almost empty. She could bring her paintings in and speak with the manager without being the center of attention.

Glancing around for Julian, she was a little relieved not to see him. Not today, on her first day, when she would be learning the ropes and probably bumbling about. But where was anybody? She looked behind the counter, then peeked into an office — all empty. The only person she could find was a customer, an old man reading a paper at one of the tables.

Finally a back door opened and somebody came inside with a huge garbage can on wheels. "Excuse me," she asked the boy, "Is the manager here?" But he was wearing headphones, listening to music, and didn't hear her. She was about to signal to him when someone tapped her on the shoulder. It was the old man who had been reading his paper.

"Ma'am, you dropped this," he said, handing her something. It was Sybilla's note.

"Thank you," she said. Opening it again, she re-read it and decided to get out her cell phone to call the number. After tapping the numbers, she expected to hear a phone ring in the Pony somewhere; but none was heard.

The line crackled so she stepped outside to get a better signal. At last someone answered on the other line, mumbling. "What?" she asked into the phone, feeling that this must be a wrong number. A female voice answered her, and she still was unable to make out the words. "I'm sorry," said Emerald, "I'm trying to reach someone about a job opening. I must have the wrong --"

"Oh, that's us!" exclaimed the voice on the other line. "Are you the one we've been expecting? Emily? Yes, dear, we need you right away. You're coming, right?"

Emerald was confused. So the job was not at the Pony after all. But -- what type of place was it? Even after getting directions and hanging up, she still didn't know the name of it.

She drove there, seeing that apparently this establishment in question was not in the pretty, quaint center of town, but flung out to the nondescript streets – among mostly industrial-looking, drab buildings. Her sense of excitement had fallen significantly since the exciting moment of receiving Syb's note.

She found the place. "A black door with a faded green awning," as had been described to her, appeared as she turned a corner where she was supposed to. Squinting up in the sunlight, she found the words painted on brick: MILITARY SURPLUS STORE. What? What did that even *mean?*

She was obviously not equipped to be employed in such a place, whatever it was. Her artistic brain knew nothing of the military, or the array of paraphernalia displayed in the window. What on earth did they sell? She visualized machine guns, helmets, and camouflage. She hesitated, then entered the store, to find the owner and explain she could not take this job. A jaunty bell above her head announced her entrance.

21

ODD COUPLE

Not a soul was in sight, so she walked around as if browsing. Among the mysterious packages and accessories were very few items she recognized. A glass case filled with pocketknives, which folded into themselves and held every tool imaginable. A wall full of ropes and chains and fasteners. Camping supplies. Gardening supplies. Strange-looking weaponry of some sort. And clothing: flannel shirts, denim jeans, and khaki galore.

The wooden floor creaked as she stepped from one aisle to the next. Was there even anyone here? There was no sign of life here whatsoever!

She no sooner had that thought when sudden noise coming from the back room made her jump. A rhythmic, steady cadence, soft at first, then a bit louder. What could it be? She listened closer.

Walking toward the sound, very slowly, her eye followed the rows of merchandise to a doorway. Coming out of the doorway was a pair of boots, exactly like the ones on the nearby shelf. These boots were . . . *dancing.*

Shuffle, step, ball and chain, shuffle, step, ball and chain, shuffle, shuffle, shuffle. The boots moved steadily out of the doorway, into the open store, among the shelves, creaking the planks of the wood floor just as her own feet did.

From where Emerald was, she had to move over to see who was the wearer of the dancing boots. She saw him.

Not only did his footwear match the store's goods, the rest of his clothing did, too: tan cover-alls with silver buttons, and a camouflage cap. It was as if a store mannequin had been dressed, and had come to life; but this mannequin wore a very human beard and untidy shock of white hair. His lips moved with the words of an inaudible song, and his feet went right on, keeping time perfectly.

Smiling at this spectacle, she kept out of sight for a little longer. As it turned out, this was not a solo performance. His wife joined him a few moments afterward. Her plump little form came twirling out the same doorway, skirt afloat, and soft-shoed right up to him. He took her hands into his own. Their feet fell in time together – stepping in the same directions, back and forth in their music-less dance; then he whirled her several times until Emerald became alarmed that the sweet old lady would stumble! But stumble she did not, although her face was pink and she huffed a little. They apparently had completed their finale.

Emerald could not resist: she applauded them.

They looked up and saw her. Instead of being shocked or embarrassed, they answered her applause with one more twirl, dip, and bow, looking as if they were glad to have an audience for a change.

"Hello! Hello! Can I interest you in a gunny sack? Waterproof pup tent? A folding shovel?" said the gentleman, waddling toward her.

"No sir, actually I'm here about the – "

"How about our newest model of hiking boots? You look like a, let's see, size 7?"

"Yes, that's right, but no, I don't need any."

"But you see we have an assortment of colors here, and several feminine ones."

"Sir, I need to tell you, I'm here about the job. Someone else spoke on my behalf, but the truth is – I really cannot – "

But the little woman was already coming toward her with open arms, as if greeting a long-lost granddaughter. Emerald saw that her waddle was exactly like her husband's.

"Oh! Gordon! She's here!" she gushed. "We've been praying for you!"

"Ma'am, thank you, but – really – there's just no way I can take this job," she was telling them. "My cousin spoke too soon. She didn't know about my schedule conflict, and it's a little too far for me to drive, and . . ." They stared at her rather mournfully, wondering how she could abandon them as soon as she appeared in answer to their call.

Just then, the front door burst open and admitted a string of several farmers. The little bell superfluously sounded over and over. The owners hurried away to attend their various needs; Emerald could have escaped then, and was tempted to, but was accosted by a man asking where the new corduroy jackets were. "They've been promising me they were coming in for two weeks now," he groused.

"Yes, I think I saw some boxes of jackets like that right over there. The owners know all about it. If you'll go ask Mr. – "

"Would you check and see if they ordered my size? Forty-two large? I've got to get to my field and the nights are getting too cold. Tonight's gon' be an all-nighter again. Expectin' a calvin; ol' Bella always gives birth at night."

And so Emerald was swept into immediate demands of the little shop, not knowing the first thing about the products or procedures, but out of necessity to the nice couple, who really were swamped – she couldn't imagine them handling this tumult by themselves. More men came and went. She meant to stay fifteen minutes; she stayed two hours. As the crowd thinned out, she looked at her watch and realized how late it was.

"Well, I don't know how we could have handled that without you!" said the wife. "But," she said with a lengthening face, "I understand if you don't want this job. It's not very exciting for a young college person."

"Oh it's not that, I'm not looking for excitement. I mean, it would be a very good job, here helping you two, but I'm afraid my schedule won't allow it. I have classes every day."

"Oh, what a shame!" she said, turning to her husband. "And right here at inventory time – "

"Blanche," said the man, "we'll have to close the shop tomorrow afternoon and just finish it. Surely we can get it done in an afternoon, if we just close up. But we will lose that income," he fretted. "We sure did need someone by tomorrow at the very latest."

Now Emerald was wavering. Just two or three hours. She could come between classes, just for tomorrow. But being a regular employee was impossible, though. She told them this.

"Could you, sweetie? Just help us out once more? It would help so much. We simply cannot afford to lose customers . . ."

"Yes, I believe I can come at two o'clock. See you then." She was glad to help them out just this once, since they hadn't found another employee yet.

Emerald was irritated at Sybilla. What did she mean by not mentioning the type of place she had "found her a job" at? Well, she did say in her note she had been in a hurry, so she probably forgot. But still! Military Surplus Store! Obviously she was trying to keep her from Julian and wanted her installed as far away from him as could be.

22

THE SECOND PAGE

The next day at two, and the following day at ten, and Saturday at seven. "Just once more" turned into three more times that week.

Their names were Gordon and Blanche Sylvester. Emerald had only known them a few days but was sad to leave them – especially since they hadn't gotten through a fraction of the inventory yet! To be truthful they worked slowly, being apt to stop all work in favor of a spontaneous dance.

She found out they were avid members of the Appalachian Barners, a dance community meeting twice weekly for lovers of square dance. Hence the hasty closing up on Tuesdays and Fridays so they could make it to the hall in time. They even made an appearance in their official attire one evening, to Emerald's delight: Blanche looked like a doll in her bright colors and frills, her bigger-than-life skirt, and tiny patent leather shoes. Gordon's white hair was slicked down, and his beard was neatly combed; he wore a shoestring tie and tucked-in shirt. Emerald could hardly keep from smiling as they gave her last minute instructions on closing up.

"Now, don't worry about taking those boxes out back, Gordon will do that in the morning. Just count the money from the register and put it in the bank bag. Oh, where's my hair ribbon? It's fallen off – oh, there it is, among the hand grenades. My goodness."

"Blanche, don't just pile them back up all willy-nilly," said Gordon. "Have some finesse."

"My dear girl," said Blanche, when Emerald reached forth to help her, "what are these marks on your hands? Is it a rash?"

She laughed. "No, just paint I forget to scrape off. It's my hobby."

"Well we must get you to re-do some of these old countertops and cabinets. They're antiques, you know, that we inherited with the store."

"Actually – "

"It's getting dark so early now, Gordon, I worry about her going home. How far away do you live, dear? At the college dorms, is that right?"

"No ma'am, I live a little out of town. I live at Ashmont with my family."

"You live where?"

"Ashmont Hall. With the Keckleys. They're my family."

The couple was uncharacteristically quiet as they glanced at one another. "Oh yes. We know the place. And we know someone else who lives there," said Gordon slowly.

"Really? Dr. Canter, or Danny Grosch, maybe?"

"It's a woman who has been living there a number of years now, isn't that right, Blanche? Her name is Louise."

"Yes, Louise. She used to come in our store quite a bit." Blanche looked flustered as she gathered her things. Then, giving several more directives about being extremely careful on the curvy mountain roads in the dark, she placed the store keys in Emerald's hand. They were nearly on their way, when she stopped them.

"Just to remind you both, I really appreciate the chance to work here, but I cannot after this weekend. I have an important class right during your busiest time. You probably need to find someone else as soon as you can."

"Oh, that's right," said Blanche sadly. "Thank you so much for your help this week. I hate to lose you. But I do understand. Just put the keys in the mail slot before you leave tonight. And, if you know any other sweet girls like yourself, send them our way. But I'm sure no one will have been so good for us as you, my dear."

"I'll spread the word that you're hiring," she said promisingly. The couple, looking as if – in spite of their white hair – they could have been going trick-or-treating, hurried away.

Now Emerald wished her job was permanent; not only to work for them, but for the sake of obtaining information. They knew Louise! That must have been why the couple looked at one another so mysteriously just now. They looked like they were conscious of something important, and probably unfavorable.

She thought more about it on the way home. She tried to figure a way to remain with them, but could only come up with a couple of hours here and there, and they needed to be able to depend on someone. She smiled at their foibles, self-destructive as they were, as far as store-keeping went. Blanche would give Emerald precise directions on what to do, and then would fret so much about it that she ended up doing it herself. Gordon would chat with his gentlemen friends, talking them into buying some needed item, then just as successfully talk them out of it again! Even recommending another store with a lower price.

And of course, the dancing. This delightful interruption occurred almost hourly. Spontaneity would strike and take over, and the couple never seemed to worry about it impeding their business whatsoever. Their real business was twirling and stepping and heartily enjoying the music they alone seemed to hear.

Emerald suddenly remembered the way Blanche had said it: "we know a woman who has been living there a number of years." Not employed there. How odd . . .

She found Sybilla lying on the sofa, reading something. Emerald's irritation with her had not evaporated, no matter how often she had tried to make excuses for her, concerning the confusion of not telling her where she had "gotten her a job." She felt there was a kernel of jealousy regarding Julian, in spite of Syb telling her she could never be interested in him.

"Back from work already? I'm so glad it worked out. I told the Sylvesters you were perfect for their store," said the blonde, kicking off her shoes and appearing ready for a chat. But now Em was familiar with her moods, and when she saw her eyes twinkling, and her posture of attention, it usually meant mockery of someone. Emerald didn't feel like making fun of anybody.

"So, what do you think of them?" began her cousin, suppressing a smile.

"Syb, you should have asked me before taking that liberty – of promising them I'd work there! You know how crazy my schedule is right now. I can't take the job."

"Mom said you've been working all week!"

"Right, just to get them through a few days. But I've been late to class because of it. You should have told me, asked me ahead of time. You had said you'd get me a job at the Pony, anyway."

Syb looked up. "Well, I tried. They said they couldn't hire anybody without an application. You should have at least filled one out."

"But you told me not to! Remember?"

"Everybody knows you're supposed to turn in a resume, or at least fill out an application. If you want to work at such a popular place, anyway. But I know that's not the *real* reason you wanted to work there."

Emerald was numbed by this sting: so petty and childish! She stood to her feet to leave the room, secretly wishing she could think of something clever to retort. But just then, the sight of paper – light blue, folded – that Syb was fingering, stopped Emerald in her tracks. She stared at it, disbelieving her eyes. It was her mother's note!

"Hey, where did you get that?" Emerald walked over to take it from Syb. She saw that it was both pages: the first one she had found in the box of old photos, and the other she had found in Kay's room just the other day. Both were written on the same pale blue stationery, with a teenage girl's bubble handwriting, but had been folded back the wrong way. The creases were off.

"It was just lying here, I just picked it up before you walked in! Defensive much? It's not even yours."

"Yes it is! I had this in my night table drawer! That's where you must have gotten it!"

"Are you kidding me? Why would I go through your stuff in your room? Anyway, you were wrong. It was here under this pillow!"

Emerald narrowed her eyes trying to understand this. Was Syb lying? She looked very earnest, and very mad, now. She must be telling the truth, because her (rare) moments of perfect innocence were defended so fiercely whenever questioned. She left the room in a pouty flourish.

The job argument, and the mean-spirited allusion to Julian, were forgotten in this much more important matter. Someone had certainly gotten the precious paper from her room.

She paced the den in contemplation. But then, suddenly hearing a rustle just outside the doorway, she braced herself for the sight of Louise. She realized she was trembling with anxiety and distress. Planting her words firmly on her tongue, she stepped out to confront her.

23

SCANDAL

But no overalls, no feather earrings or spiked hair met her confrontation: only Mother Ann and Puddles in her arms. Emerald wasn't sure if the sigh she breathed was that of frustration or relief.

The old lady settled into her chair and began working on her current afghan, a bright confection of yellow and pink. Puddles snorted and then yawned. Emerald sat on the couch Syb had been on, still holding the precious papers in her hand.

"Mother Ann, have you ever noticed —" began Emerald. But her companion could not hear her. Instead of raising her voice, she moved a bit closer.

"I said, have you ever noticed any strange behavior from anyone living here?"

"Oh dear, yes, of course. My family has always been strange."

"But I'm talking about particular instances. Have you noticed anything amiss — anything that seemed underhanded? Such as — thievery."

Mother Ann gazed with her watery eyes, requiring the last word to be repeated, and halted her work. "Thievery! I thought we had solved that problem! Puddles!" she scolded, looking down at the dog, "have you been taking the neighbor's garden hose again?"

Emerald, clearing the dog of any crimes of the sort, relinquished getting any insights from the elderly lady and sat back down to think. Mother Ann resumed her work, and Puddles his nap, in the quietness of the room for a while longer.

Emerald thought she heard sounds of arguing upstairs. She listened.

Yes, raised voices, and sounds of abrupt motions were heard, and her alarm increased. Mother Ann knitted, oblivious. Was

Sybilla complaining to the aunts about Emerald's accusation of her? Her face grew warm at the thought, knowing how they defended their lamb against any distress. She began to mentally prepare for a showdown.

But no, it wasn't Syb's high-pitched peals, or Kay's soothing tones to calm her down. The voices, at least one voice, was totally unfamiliar. Someone was almost shouting. It was – it was one of the guests.

Mother Ann heard none of this. Emerald peeked outside the room and saw figures on a landing up the stairs. She was torn for a second, but decided to dart out into the hallway to listen better. There was a corner nook she could stand in without attracting notice.

She was able to decipher "how could you ever allow her" and "the most disgusting" and, as she leaned out a little more – "in all my years of staying in inns, all over this nation, I have never encountered something as vile as this!" in an irate manner. Kay's responses were now heard, in a calmer tone, but firm and polite. Still, Emerald detected a note of panic in it.

"I assure you that –" was all Emerald could catch from her aunt's lips. Footsteps were now coming down the staircase, so she hid further into the corner. Ow! Something hard pressed against her back! It was a door handle. Apparently this was a closet she had never noticed. Quick as lightning, she got inside it and watched through the crack in the door.

Nervousness tingled through her, a mixture of alarm and glee, like the feeling of escape when a classmate is being punished. What on earth could have happened? She thought, trembling with excitement and curiosity.

Through the opening she saw Kay, as regal as ever even in crisis, standing with a little fat woman and her husband. Nora hovered around them, wringing her hands. Louise was a little further away, making her appearance as the culprit.

Promises of a full refund were given for the couple's two-night stay, but this overture was not even acknowledged. The lady wagged a finger first at Kay, then Louise, while the husband looked on, patiently holding all the luggage.

"How could anyone make a mistake such as that?" she shrieked. "What kind of employee is she? Has she been properly trained? You will receive a list," then turning to her husband – "Ralph, remind me to send them a list, detailing every single fault of your employee, and I'll send one to the town council, too. They ought to know what goes on in this establishment. First, the dirty ashtray in our room. We do not even smoke. Then, the way the bed was made. Why, it wasn't really made at all, this morning. I pulled back the cover to see our top sheet shoved down to the foot of the bed. But all this," she paused to breathe deeply, and steady herself, "all this does not compare to the atrocity I discovered just an hour ago. My toothbrush was missing. Missing, and replaced with another. And do you know what this other toothbrush had written on the side? Do you??" They all already knew, but Emerald was glad she was about to hear it herself.

"The toothbrush that was placed in my holder was labeled, plainly: *TOILETS ONLY!*"

Her voice was now escalating to a pitch higher than had yet been used. "And I didn't notice it until I'd already brushed my teeth!!" she shrieked. Emerald held her hand to her mouth.

And with that, they stormed out the front door; rather, they would have stormed out had her husband not dropped a hatbox and a pillow on the way out. Nora, eager to perform for them the only service she could, rushed to pick the items up and help them down the steps. The stone dragons stared at the decamping couple in dismay.

A laugh was hovering in Emerald's throat and she had to fight to keep it back. Horrible! How could Louise have made a mistake like that? She watched Kay say some low words to Louise, with an expression of severity on her face. She went on lecturing her for several minutes. Not a word was audible, though. Emerald wondered how Louise was taking this scolding; her face was not visible to her.

This was it: Louise was a goner. How would Kay dismiss her? With kind words and a month's salary? Or with a swift fall of the axe, and no fond goodbye, no letter of recommendation, no well-wishes for the future. Whatever the business associated with Ashmont, Kay seemed to take each case on with an equal amount of cool decision. She could handle anything.

Emerald still hid in the closet, watching for an opportunity to slip out. Thinking Kay and the others would gravitate to the kitchen, she waited for them to leave, but through the sliver of crack she saw Kay turn on her heel and walk directly toward her hiding place! What would she say when Kay flung the door open and saw her there, standing in the dark? While she tried to think of an excuse — she got lost, she was sick, was confused, etc. — her alarm subsided when she saw her aunt stop at a shelf right next to the closet door, and get something off it. She still had no idea Emerald was mere inches away from her.

"Nora, here are those stamps. Let's get busy on the thank-you notes," she said briskly, with no reference whatsoever to the catastrophe. "Have you started the peas for dinner yet?" and her voice trailed off as the two walked off toward the kitchen. Louise had returned upstairs, no doubt to pack her bags. Emerald smiled to herself and realized how many hours of worry she had wasted, for nothing. Louise would be gone by morning.

Safe to make noise now, she stepped out. But she soon found she had not been alone in witnessing the recent scene.

Rita Canter had just entered the foyer, glasses in hand, staring at the ladies as they walked off.

"Oh! Dr. Canter! Did you hear what happened?" whispered Emerald.

The woman stared quizzically at her as she repeated the scandalous mistake, but Emerald's mixture of fright and hilarity caused somewhat of a jumble of words that she couldn't follow. No, apparently she did not know what had happened. Emerald was suddenly aware of how ridiculous it looked for her to babble such a crazy story to the professor, and that after emerging from inside a closet!

Oh no! Kay was coming back for more stamps. Having no time to slip upstairs, and awkwardly standing in the foyer corner, she retreated once again to her closet and closed the door. Hopefully Dr. Canter did not notice, as she was now beginning to talk with Kay about a completely different topic.

The buzz of their words was heard awhile longer and Emerald began to feel the need for air. She adjusted her body to make the most of the enclosed space. But she lost her balance slightly and reached out to steady herself by grabbing a vacuum cleaner.

Her hand missed it entirely and she fell against a wall. The wall moved! Her heart took a little drop when the firm wood swung away from her. Oh, where was her cell phone when she needed it? Here, thankfully; it was in her jacket pocket. She turned on the screen, and shone the light of it at her feet.

It wasn't a wall at all, she found, but a narrow door, inside the closet, well hidden behind cleaning supplies and a shelf of extra blankets.

What a weird, wonderful house this was! Shining the light further, she saw that the inner door opened to a stairway that spiraled down. It was impossible to see where they led unless you descended them all the way. She shivered, and went.

24

AN ACCIDENTAL FIND

F eeling her way down the musty flight of steps, running her hand across a wall that felt as cool as stone, she circled her way to the bottom. She was surprised to see a dim light; there apparently was a window down here. She was right. It was very small and covered in cobwebs, but after a wipe-down she saw that the patio floor of the courtyard was on the other side. So that's why she hadn't seen it, the times she had explored outside. The window was almost completely obscured from view.

She found herself standing in a strangely shaped room, with many angled walls, like a hexagon. It was still too dark to see everything, so she used her phone light and shone it all about. Shelves covered every wall and ancient books nestled in them. It was like a mini library. "Book room" would be more accurate, since the volumes here were apparently the castoffs of its great cousin upstairs – the real library, formal and complete; no gilded edges or leather bound copies here, just cracked and faded old volumes that were one step away from the trash bin. Emerald randomly pulled a copy down and opened it, breathing its fragrance. This one was poetry.

There was a matronly stove in the middle of the room; she almost opened it until the thought of insects and mice struck her. One day, when she had time, and courage, she'd clean it out and try to light a fire.

She coughed from the damp, sweet basement odor, and wondered if she could get the window open for some air. It wouldn't open, but she did find – to her surprise – a door leading outside. It took a little trouble to unlock, but finally the latch turned and she was able to crack the door ajar. A set of narrow steps led up to the courtyard itself. She went up and stood, getting her bearings.

She remembered how Nora had pestered Saxon to renovate this courtyard. Kay, also, had referenced it often to her guests: "Back when I was a debutante, we would often *soiree* in the courtyard. It was just the right size to hold ten or twelve couples." Emerald herself recalled scenes from childhood of watching the dances that had taken place here, gazing at the twirling couples from any secret spot a little girl could find without being scolded away.

But this was beyond the old man's strength and ability, Emerald was sure! You couldn't even walk on the crumbled stones without imbalance. Decrepit urns were overturned, disintegrated by years of rain and wind, and strange weeds grew up through every crack and crevice. This spot would need professional help to be anything but the graveyard of former gaiety that Kay kept parading before them, still young and fresh in *her* memory.

After a while she retraced her steps back through the underground room, then up the steps to the foyer closet, still marveling at the ingenuity of this house. She planned on using the room as her new retreat, whenever she could slip through the closet without being noticed. Her new escape from Syb, Danny, and especially, Louise.

Not that she would have to worry about her much longer. The toothbrush crime was beyond anything Ashmont could tolerate and still keep what reputation it had. No more Louise lurking in hallways to stare holes in Emerald or question her oddly. No more pilfering among her personal things. She and her oddities would be purged from Ashmont, at long last, and replaced with a proper staff to handle things correctly. Kay's nerves would settle from the change; there would be no more need for overblown shopping trips and the escape to her upstairs den of disorder. Keckley orders would be carried out with excellence, and all her elegant details would be attended to, and Kay could resume her footing as the society matron she was raised to be, which suited her more than any marriage or career.

Emerald took her chair at the dinner table with a much lighter heart than lately. Not everyone was here yet, so she checked her phone messages while Kay and Nora placed steaming dishes on the table. No Louise was in sight.

The two ladies bustled to prepare everything, while Emerald's mind was on a vague message she had just read from a family friend. It was an offer of sympathy and help, but in such a way that confused rather than comforted her. Did this friend know information that she didn't? Was Mother worse, and Dad was afraid to inform her?

The table filled with people and food. Small talk and pleasantries went around, and the fiasco seemed forgotten. Just when Emerald was relaxing in conversation, she looked up and — with disbelief — saw Louise McSee bringing glasses as usual to the dinner table, in that irritating way of holding several in one hand by the rims, so that you had to drink right where her fingertips had been. Emerald glanced from her to Nora, and Kay, then back to Louise again. Not a word was said about the afternoon adventure, or about Louise "leaving us soon," or anything.

No matter: she had a notice to work out, Emerald told herself. Probably two weeks. Even the manner of her dismissal was marked by kindness by the Ashmont family.

Her mind went back to her Mother, though she mtried to keep it on her salmon. After a while it dawned on her that her aunts were whispering something secret. Their faces were important and solemn, and Kay's gestures, though busy with dinner, betrayed some type of inward distraction. At last they took their chairs, but kept glancing at one another as if in silent discussion.

Conversation was sporadic, mostly carried by Lars Franklin, who had slipped in as dinner began. Even he didn't pick up on anything amiss, enjoying his food and wine as much as ever, oblivious of Louise's recent scandal. Kay absent-mindedly played with her food, while Nora fidgeted and leaned over in a flurry of whispers to her sister. Kay was visibly shaking.

With a sudden icy feeling, Emerald wondered if Mother —

Mr. Saxon put down his knife and fork. "Ahem. No one else notices, I see; they are too appreciative of this fine cuisine set before us, and I too would like to go back to my communion with it without disturbance. But I am fine-tuned to the dynamics of this house, whether my desire or not, and cannot overlook when something is brewing between you two. Nora, I'll ask you, since – like Mt. Stromboli in Sicily, you're always erupting with information and cannot keep it in. Not like your sister, as sealed up as Mount Churchill. I climbed it once and nearly died from the cold. Out with it. I want to get back to my dinner."

Kay's shining eyes prefaced something big and exciting to be told. Nora smiled broadly. Emerald could breathe again.

Kay stood and announced, "The days of obscurity are over for Ashmont. There is an excellent chance that an event will soon take place here, which will put it on the map forever. An event – the most thrilling, because the sweetest and most sentimental, that people will remember for decades – a wedding."

Danny! He and Celia had set a date. How wonderful!

But the more Kay described it, it sounded very little like an event for mere locals. Anyway, Danny just now looked as wary as Saxon, as Kay overflowed with this great news.

"A little bird has informed me, through the grapevine you know, that this wedding is to be widely publicized, and the most notable names will be involved. Celebrities will be invited. Famous people from all over will grace these rooms with their charms, and will fill them with their grandeur." Famous people? What?

"Good heavens! Who is it? Who's going to be married here?" cried some from around the table.

But to that question Kay was absolutely dumb, and deaf to further entreaty.

"There's a chance, I say. This individual, along with her family, and I dare say an entourage of assistants, will be arriving tomorrow to see the place, and will discuss it. They are to decide by the end of the week."

What a flutter the ladies were in after this announcement, Nora especially, who fretted that the housework and laundry couldn't be done in time. The dryer was on its last legs, and the worst thing that could greet these illustrious people was a clothesline in the yard, with underwear flapping in the breeze.

"Louise will attend to that, Nora. You focus on the front rooms, especially the formal sitting room. Plan for evening coffee service. And pay attention to the sandwiches. Remember, crust on if bread and jam; crust off if chicken salad." Kay took her one and only bite of dinner without being aware of it; her eyes were dilated, and her thoughts wholly on this momentous opportunity. "It's a good thing it's a first marriage," she said, wiping her lips, "they will want it to be special." Emerald heard that with pain and looked up at Kay.

25

ASHMONT COMPETES

"Now," continued Kay. "Let's talk about the setup. The main staircase. The bride will be stunning with a long train, coming down that staircase. I'll paint the picture for them: 'Layers of magnolia garland entwined with the railing, and the intoxicating scent of orange blossoms and camellias attending the senses at every turn.' That's how it read in the Chronicle, last time there was a famous wedding here – 1978 I believe. The famous actress, Olivia Somebody – oh dear, I can't remember her last name; but I know she was in a film or two that we saw. Nora, we must have the newspaper clipping ready for them, out where we can show them. And we can present the library, or no – the formal dining room – as a place for the reception. The flow would be better there. But that leaves the problem of dancing. They'll want dancing, and an orchestra –"

"I hate to interrupt you," blurted Mr. Saxon, looking as if he had been longing to interrupt her, "But aren't you overlooking a few obstacles to hosting this affair? It's been so long since Ashmont has seen anything of that sort that you're forgetting what is required, I'm afraid. If you plan to use the dining room, that chandelier has got to be completely re-wired. And the cracked wallpaper, peeling paint, nicks in the furniture – these people aren't planning on a haunted house theme by chance?"

"Oh, you exaggerate as you typically do. Of course I thought of those things. Don't worry, between you, and Louise, and Danny, and us girls you know, we can take care of minor things like that. The important objective now is to win them over. Seal the deal. Ashmont needs something like this, an event of this magnitude. It shall restore, we shall restore, it to all its former glory – legendary glory." Tiny beads of sweat on her hairline gave her a glistening effect, and her eyes sparkled. She took a sip of wine.

"By the way, who is this famous person to be married here? Or has Olivia Somebody returned with her sixth or seventh husband?"

Kay shot him one long, victorious look, and spoke quietly. "The governor's daughter. Yes, the governor of our state, and his oldest daughter will be here within twenty-four hours. Lars, do pass the hollandaise, please."

"Oh!" breathed some, impressed. Inwardly, Emerald confessed she had expected a greater person than this. She had thought it would be a bona-fide celebrity, the way Kay had spoken of her. "Is she really that well-known?" she asked modestly.

"Well-known! Haven't you been reading the papers? Do you know whom she's marrying?"

Emerald didn't know; but Kay rapidly filled in her deficient information. The young woman's fiancé was a name she didn't recognize, but he was a professional baseball player who had made a name for himself on several teams.

"It will be all over social media, even the news networks. Celebrity talk shows, sports channels, magazines," gushed her aunt. "It will be the wedding of the year! Right here in our home."

"If they choose Ashmont, and I'm not saying I hope they won't," said Saxon, "you've got to make a stipulation or two. The lawn, the terrace – they're not fit for crowds like you're talking about. Maybe they could walk out on the grass and take a few photos, but that's it. No wedding out there, no reception out there. And the south wing will be off limits. We could never get those rooms cleaned out in time."

"Of course," said Kay, looking like an offended child. "Even I know very well that that wouldn't work. It's alright for my intimate gatherings, you know, my own friends, and the small numbers of guests we have, to be on the terrace; but the rest of it – the fountain, small pool, and the courtyard, especially the courtyard, need a complete overhaul. No, the house itself is what they're interested in, from what I understand. The interiors. Outside – well, that would be beyond our means, to try to get it ready in time."

The governor and his family came, not once – but twice over the next few days. Planners followed them from room to room, scribbling notes on clipboards, pointing, and speaking in low voices to one another. Kay wore long flowing dresses as she led them around, and looked every bit as imperious as the image she was trying to portray. Royalty, thought Emerald, admiring her from her vantage point as the silent observer. She could be a queen. She sighed watching her.

Yet Emerald could have gone out of her mind trying to figure out why Louise was still here! Sometimes she wanted to scream. She was the elephant in the room; except this elephant talked in an irritating accent and obtruded her presence with awkwardness at every turn. Had it not been so maddening, had Emerald only heard of this situation from a friend, or read about it in a book, it would have been hysterically funny! But she was in near proximity of it all, and felt the misery of it even more than the Keckleys, apparently. With horror she watched Louise in the middle of the governor's tour, bumbling, answering questions brusquely, and even treating the VIP's with aloofness and irritation. Emerald could only turn away, and groan inwardly.

The waiting began. Kay said they would make up their minds within a few days. There was a toss-up between Ashmont and another location, some historic home in Knoxville.

The two sisters were bundles of nerves, each in their own way. Nora was too shaky to work on her puzzle, so instead hovered near Saxon, asking him questions. That alone made him nervous, too; he cared little for the wedding itself, except as it would benefit Ashmont financially. He really did know the value of an event like that, and as he had invested so many years of his life at the mansion, wanted to see its importance augmented.

Kay was very quiet and pale. She walked back and forth, looking out windows. Sometimes she smoked; this habit had increased with the excitement and stress of the anticipation.

When Emerald got home late one evening, she turned into the driveway and her eye was caught by a brightness she had not expected. It was the uncovered windows of the Vienna Room, and someone had turned on all the lights inside. It was breathtaking.

When she went inside, she tossed her stuff down and went right to it. Saxon was patching wallpaper, and Nora was dusting. Emerald soon saw a third person in the room: Louise was fixing the leg of a chair.

"Wow! This room is gorgeous!" the girl exclaimed, testing the waters. "I could see it all the way from the street. Whose idea was it to take down those drapes?"

"Who do you think?" said Louise, looking directly at her.

"Isn't it divine?" cooed Nora. "I haven't seen those windows since I was your age! She had a wonderful idea, don't you think? Imagine the bride standing just there."

"So it was the bride's idea?"

"Oh no, it was Kay's."

Emerald was surprised into silence for a moment. Then she swallowed and said, "Aunt Kay thought of it? But I was under the impression" (glancing at Louise) "that she wished to keep it as it was."

"I had always thought so, too. But it just came into her head today, somehow. So she recruited Saxon to take them down, but I knew he would need me to help him."

Nora was in a tizzy all the next morning. She fretted herself into overdrive, looking over the arrangements Kay had scribbled on her note pad.

"'All the furniture moved'? Kay, how are we to manage that? Where is the furniture to go?"

"Relax, Nora. They've seen what they need to, in order to decide. From what I understand, it's a toss-up. The other place has better layout, but they prefer our natural lighting on the back lawn. Anyway, they told me they would send a letter – a certified letter – toward the end of next week. That leaves us at least six days to figure it out."

Nora read from the notepad again. "'Re-upholstery of window benches,' 'flower beds with bride's colors,' 'remove pecan tree from front' – how are we to pay for these? Even one is beyond our usual expenses."

"It will be recouped; all of it will be recouped, and double," Kay said several times during the discussion. "Just think of the prestige gained for Ashmont; think of the magazine articles, the photos that will be circulated. Why, I can envision prominent photos of us – of the house, that is – displayed in the governor's mansion. We'll be able to raise our rates, then, because of increased demand."

"Sister," said Nora, her voice dropped somewhat, "We need to speak to Louise about something. One of the guests from last week called to voice a complaint. It seems –"

They were interrupted by the front doorbell, and Louise's report that there was a special delivery. Kay froze, then suddenly smashed her cigarette into her unfinished oatmeal. The others followed her to the foyer, wondering if this was the Big Decision. Kay signed for the delivery and was handed an envelope. Then, ripping it open, she disemboweled it with trembling hands.

Everyone waited, breathless and silent, watching her face while she read.

"Well," she spoke quietly. Then she looked at her sister, and at Mr. Saxon. "It looks like we need to clear the calendar for the week of the twenty-fifth. We're going to have a wedding."

26

A SHOCKING CLAIM

Ashmont sprang to life with this new event on its horizon. Now, every day was filled with the racket of people working and making repairs. Designers arrived, helping Kay choose new upholstery and paint. Landscapers dug up the overgrown flower beds and cleared away brush. Everyone had some opinion to offer about how to make the mansion what it used to be; Kay listened to each suggestion, and then did everything the way she wanted it.

Having to renovate on a time schedule, the atmosphere at Ashmont was a kind of exhilarating madness. Emerald enjoyed seeing everyone so energized, so unified to accomplish this great goal. She admired her aunt's taste, room by room; but more than that, she loved seeing her completely filled with exuberance. To be around her was life-giving. She was the one carrying the most work and worry, but she was undaunted, meeting every challenge with upright courage. She relished the challenge, and loved being the one consulted at every turn.

The one cloud that darkened Emerald's outlook was money being spent. It was rather shocking, seeing the bolts of expensive material, the new plants, the extra workers hired (even Kay admitted it was beyond just the household's ability). In the only way she felt herself really useful, Emerald redoubled her efforts to slip into Kay's room as much as possible, and get control of the mess.

It was already in better order since that first day she had started. Neater stacks, anyway. She had cleared out trash and dirty laundry, and had dusted as much as she could, wondering if this is what it was like to be a mom of teenagers!

She dug deeper into the paperwork for lost money. It was fun, like finding hidden treasure, although the amounts she ran across wouldn't make a dent in the expenses being incurred just now. She thought of the conversation she and Nora had had weeks ago while working the puzzle. Antique jewelry – gems, royal gems, hidden somewhere here in the mansion. Why did they have to keep them a secret from Kay? Nora never had revealed it to her.

Kay had been in Europe many years before, in finishing school. What had happened there? Emerald's romantic brain easily imagined scenarios of princes begging for her hand in marriage, bribing her with jewels, sent to Ashmont after her return home. . . she would order them to be sent back. . . someone would pretend to do so, then hide them away, unable to part with such a precious commodity. . . Nora? Had Nora done this, possibly from jealousy?

When she thought of the youthful envy Nora had had toward Kay, who seemed to prosper much faster in worldliness and boyfriends, the matter seemed to unravel itself plainly to Emerald. Nora had taken it into her own hands to preserve and protect what would one day bring them lasting security.

Only one other person was aware of such valuables squirreled away around the house. The person who had frequent access to every nook and cranny, and had already shown herself to be of dubious character.

For the sake of the Keckleys and their home, Emerald must find those jewels – and soon.

To her personal disappointment, Emerald's main art class was canceled! It was the one she had looked forward to the most and from which she felt the most benefit. It met four times a week and was the reason she couldn't accept the job at Military Surplus. She couldn't believe her eyes, the day she ran up the stairwell of the art building, to Room 206, and saw the notice taped to the door. The class time wasn't moved; the whole thing was entirely done away with for the remainder of the semester.

Well, this situation was apparently the answer to the Sylvesters' prayers. With a resigned attitude, Emerald began reporting for work at their store that very day.

Gordon and Blanche were, needless to say, overjoyed. It was quite a contrast between their attention and going home to Ashmont, where she could slip in without notice. To be honest, the latter suited Emerald better. Still, their greetings warmed her to her very heart.

"Well, darlin', it's so good of you to come see us like this! We've missed you so!"

"I'm here to work, if you still need me."

"What's that? These old ears don't hear as good as they used to."

"She said she's back working here! Well I'll be! She came back to us! See Blanche? Aren't you glad you didn't ask that fat guy to come back? Emerald here is just what we need. The stars sent her back to us."

She resumed her duties without missing a beat, realizing how much she'd missed the entertainment of watching her employers interact. But today, they hadn't even indulged in an impromptu dance yet, before they began quizzing her about the upcoming wedding.

"Will they really have it there, do you think?"

"Yes. The Keckleys are going all out, renovating as much as they can. It's coming along really well. Everything looks beautiful, already." But she didn't mention the stripped off wallpaper or the uprooted flower beds she had seen that very morning.

"The Keckley ladies always knew the best way to do things," sighed Blanche. "I've been to one or two gatherings there, myself, years ago. It's a good thing they have some – some help."

"Oh yes, Mr. Saxon is a great help to them around the place."

"Well, yes, but what I meant was Louise McSee. I imagine she's a great help to Kay."

Emerald looked up, not knowing what to say.

Blanche's voice was lower now. "In fact, before Louise went to them, things were – well, let's just say Kay was nearing the brink. I know you know, sweet Emerald, seeing as you've been around her so much. There are – weaknesses. We all have them, of course. But Louise going there was the salvation of that household."

"She is a sharp one, Louise," interjected Gordon. "Really knows her stuff."

Emerald was bewildered. Were they talking about the same person? She couldn't help but mention her oddities. "I hate to say it out loud like this, but she will stick out like a sore thumb at the wedding! The way she dresses, like a – a farm hand. And always butting in at awkward times. It's embarrassing!" Emerald could have gone on and on about her. She wanted to tell them her suspicions of theft, and prove she had grounds for them. But both Sylvesters were looking directly at her, as if surprised by her concern.

"I know she's a bit – without grace – she's no sophisticate – but there would be no wedding if Louise weren't there. In fact, there probably wouldn't be any Ashmont Hall!"

The Invisible Door

27

FAMOUS WEDDING

Emerald came home as quietly as possible and slipped in a side door, stepping over debris, and – over Tiger John, who liked to unreasonably lie down in the middle of whatever commotion was occurring – sneaking past anybody who looked as if they might ask her to help. She had just scurried out of sight when she overheard: "Emerald Johnsey can help you with painting that molding, Saxon." It was Louise in her flesh-chilling northern twang. "She should be home soon. Don't strain yourself."

Safely upstairs, she looked down from her bedroom turret and observed various workings in the lawn down below. Surprisingly, she saw Kay and a few other people in discussion near the courtyard. Someone was pointing at it, squatting down to examine the floor, and the others were poking around it and surveying the ruins. Kay and the others talked back and forth. They seemed to be consulting her, and she was nodding in response. An outdoor project like this wouldn't be started so soon before the wedding, would it? Wasn't the interior only supposed to be used?

That little mystery was solved that very evening. Saxon had been hard at work all day and was eager to sit down to a spaghetti dinner. Just as he was beginning to enjoy his meal, something the ladies said made him cough and sputter red sauce from the north end of the white tablecloth, to the south.

Dr. Canter and Nora had been chatting with animation, discussing how much the event would do for Millcrest, how many out-of-towners would be likely to come, and the money it would generate for local businesses.

"The wedding of the year," sighed Nora. "Right here in our own backyard!"

"This is one time I agree with you," said Saxon, twirling his noodles around his fork. "Half of your opinion, at least. I, too, predict it to be the wedding of the year; but *not* in our backyard."

It was then – just as he had taken a man-sized bite – that Kay dropped the bomb on him.

"Actually, yes it will. I – I promised them."

"Promised? Promised what?"

"Well, in order to secure our illustrious clients, I had to comply. You see, they want a dance in the courtyard."

Nora sat there, staring at her sister. "The courtyard! We can't possibly have it done in time!"

"We can, and we must," said Kay, with iron in her voice.

This new development was now being discussed around the table. Wisely making no eye contact with anyone except her sister, she sidestepped all hints of opposition with dexterity that Emerald admired. She marveled at how her aunt managed to get her own way at all times.

Saxon, silently glaring at Kay for the past few minutes, now erupted with inevitable force. "Kay Keckley, do you know what is involved in all these plans and promises you so liberally dispense? Do you know that the courtyard isn't even in on par with a neglected dog cemetery? Do you understand the manpower needed, the money, the professional skills? Do you?"

"You don't have to shout!"

"I *do* have to shout! You don't listen to me unless I shout!"

This was in fact the one final stipulation that the governor's daughter had fought for – the one thing that Kay used to seal the deal. The wedding party wanted the ceremony inside, but they were concerned about the lack of flow for the after party. When the bride, having stepped outside to take a call on her cell phone, accidentally saw the courtyard, she was enchanted! A dance with her groom under the stars was to take place there. She insisted, and the governor reinforced her desires, leaving Kay no choice, as she explained, but to promise the impossible. She calmly gave every assurance that it would be a simple matter, and that it would only take a couple of weeks.

The overhaul began early the next day. A crew was hired to replace the stones and remove the cracked urns and statuary. Danny rented a monster of a machine for the overgrown patches of wilderness on the property, and Nora gazed longingly at it. "Oh, I want to be the one to drive that!" she sighed.

"Excuse me, ma'am, but what is your age again? And more importantly, have you had any experience in operating machinery of that nature?" grilled Saxon.

"I'm just as young as I feel, thank you, and I don't see why I couldn't be trusted to at least try it," she said with a little whine. "I'd love to get behind that wheel." Visions of Aunt Nora careening across the lawn in a bush hog made Emerald smile.

"Sorry, Nora, but I honestly don't think you can do it."

"I know that," she replied, frustrated. "What I want is a chance to *prove* that I can't."

One day when Emerald came home between classes to get more books, she was taking a peek at the progress when she heard the bubbling laughter of her cousin nearby.

Syb was coming down the hallway, looking very pretty in her old clothes, her hair in pigtails, and Julian right behind her.

"Stop it, I said. We're supposed to be helping, remember?"

"I am helping. I'm keeping you out of the way of the real work."

"Well, look, here's the only person who can help me manage you. Emerald, keep this nuisance out of my way, will you? Take him to school with you. He'll carry your stuff."

Accordingly, Julian did take the books from Emerald's arms, as well as her purse, phone, and sweater, leaving her empty-handed. "That I will," he said dutifully. "I will obey you, my regent."

"I can handle my own stuff, silly. Give them back. Besides, I don't want anybody to obey me."

"It's not your command, it's hers!" He said, nodding toward the blonde. "And you know she loves to be obeyed."

"Well," said Syb, "it's really Kay's orders that are paramount right now, and I promised her I would help all day since my play is finished. Get him out of here, will you, Em?"

Syb really seemed to want him to leave – and to leave with her. Emerald thought of the past jealous sparks that had flown from Syb, and was relieved that they seemed to be over. Perhaps she had met someone else, more to her taste. Emerald's heart fluttered as Julian walked her outside, not so much as letting her open her own car door.

"I told your aunts I would pick up all the new stones for them. I imagine they'll want you to help with the yard when you get home – all hands on deck, you know. You might want to take your time about coming back today, or they'll have you re-roofing the east wing."

"Not today," she laughed. "I already promised the rest of the day to the Military Surplus. It's a busy week for them, and they need to leave early for the dance hall tonight."

Julian lingered so long at her window that she had to actually start the car and pull away from him to get to class on time. The image of his twinkling eyes went with her the rest of the afternoon, and the scent of his cologne was still on her sweater when she put it on. The question was not whether she was attracted to him; that was a definite yes. It was whether there was anything deeper to his nature than what she had already seen of him. What were his drives, his goals? Anything more than flirting and being charming? She waited to find out, and realized how much she was enjoying the process. If she found him to be nothing more than inch deep, her attraction would evaporate; but if he showed depths of anything else to intrigue her – well, then she could see him in her future.

28

THE LECTURE

She was still thinking of Julian later while working. She didn't expect any more customers for the day, so she was busy putting out new stock and straightening shelves.

But the shop door burst open, the bell jingling merrily, and Emerald's heart gave a little lurch. Had he come to see her? She peered around the aisle to look. In walked Danny Grosch.

Danny was a somewhat frequent customer at Military Surplus. Actually, he almost never bought anything. He mostly browsed and just hung around, to leisurely chat with Emerald about odd topics, until a flow of real customers forced him out. The Sylvesters' considered him to be a close friend of hers, and good-naturedly overlooked his loitering about.

So well acquainted with the shop, he thought himself, that he would occasionally engage in selling items to other customers, and even correct Emerald's information when she was speaking with them.

Today he came in to look at wool socks, having Emerald double-check labels and boxes, and even go into the store room in search of a certain type – and then didn't buy any after she found what he was looking for. She picked up her clipboard and resumed counting stock, hoping he would leave after finding the socks unsatisfactory.

Instead, he strolled into the store room and got a soda from the drink machine. Then he sat on a stool and irreverently propped his feet on the Swiss Army Knife display, slurping his drink and stifling a burp.

He apparently felt it necessary to give Emerald a few words of advice about dating.

"You need to be careful about that Julian guy. He's not really right for you."

Her face became warm at the mention of his name, and she instantly felt defensive. Who did Danny think he was? Her brother?

She felt she'd better do something to deflect his suspicions. Toning down her indignance, she gave a little laugh. "Why would you think I was interested in him?" she returned coolly. "Anyway, he and Sybilla are more of an item. Haven't you noticed?"

"Well, you both need to be careful, then."

"I am plenty careful. You talk as if I go out on dates every night of the week. And as for Syb, she just enjoys being around him. He cheers her up; it's nothing serious, though. She might even still be in love with her ex-husband, for all I know."

"Falling in love is a myth," he said.

"Oh really?" she replied distantly, counting boot laces.

He slurped again, this time not masking the burp following.

"People talk about 'falling in love.' Falling in love," this time sarcastically lingering on the words, "as if they were talking about falling into a ditch. It's not real. It's a made-up sentiment found only in books, movies. What they are referring to," he went on significantly, authoritatively, "is allowing their feelings to lead their thinking."

"Oh." She counted the canvas watchbands, first black, then blue.

"You know Celia?" he asked her.

"The redhead I've seen you with? No. But she's cute."

"Yeah. She's just the right kind of girl, you know?"

No, Emerald did not know. Twenty-four blue, sixteen black. They needed to order more black.

Danny drank his soda and went on: "Lovely, put together. With all those little details that women like to take care of, like manicured nails."

Emerald was surprised to hear him talk in such a way. So he did notice the way women looked; perhaps he was surveying her, now, standing on a stepladder, trying to put packages on an upper shelf without falling. Her nails weren't painted. Not counting, of course, the flecks of paint from the portrait she'd been working on last night. She usually had that slightly messy look, like right now – hair in her eyes and having to be brushed back with her hand often; a hole in the cardigan sweater she wore; and jeans that frayed at the hem. Climbing down, she inadvertently met his eye, and the look confirmed to her that she had indeed been under his scrutiny for the past few moments.

Danny wasn't even aware of it himself, but he really had been comparing Emerald with Celia. It wasn't at all derogatory of Emerald. He mused that she was attractive, or could be – to the right man. She was interesting to look at. Her face had character; she had a nice smile. She was easy to talk to. That quality could help anyone overlook any faults in her appearance, or paint stains on her hands.

"Again," he continued, "what people mean by 'falling in love,' is that they were carried away with their emotions. It's a temporary wave of feeling. If they would just wait it out, like a virus, they would see such things don't last. People mustn't let their feelings dictate their actions. I can't help noticing at times, Emerald," he went on, crossing his legs comfortably and tapping the top of the soda can, "that you let little things get to you sometimes. Like being upset about those drapes someone put back up. There was no need to be so upset. You're not a child anymore, Emerald. Consider me in your life as an older brother, sort of – to help you. You need help, guidance. I'd like to be that for you, to guide you toward maturity." He stifled a burp.

She dodged him politely as she moved from shelf to shelf. Then she busied herself straightening the camping section, not much minding the harangue – and not even explaining to him about why the drapes had upset her. All this advice he was giving sounded suspiciously like a lecture; but she let him go on. It was helping to pass the time.

After a little silence, Emerald finished writing some numbers and said, "Well, that's great about you and Celia. Have you set the date?"

"Date? For what?"

"The wedding, stupid! The way you're talking, how that she's everything you want, and all that, why don't you go ahead and marry her?"

Yes, why didn't he? Danny tried to not seem irritated by the question, but he was. Crushing the can in his hands, he phoned in an answer to appease her curiosity. She wondered why he looked so uncomfortable.

The weather was beginning to sharpen into frosts at night, thrilling the heat-weary world and, at the same time, lulling it in preparation for a winter's sleep. Kay worried that it would be too chilly for the outdoor reception, but checking the weather forecast constantly, she convinced herself and the rest of the household that a window of warmth would be visiting their area right in time for the big event.

The house and grounds were greatly improved! For the standards sought by the wedding party, anyway. It made Emerald a little sad to see it so uncomfortably whipped into shape, like wearing a fancy costume and not being able to breathe freely. But she had to admit everything looked fresh and elegant, and the courtyard was coming along splendidly. Saxon continued to work doggedly at the courtyard; even Danny still joined him in the work, and the two could be heard late into the night, with their clinking of tools in the cool night air.

But one week before the wedding, disaster struck Ashmont – in the form of the flu. Every person came down with it, and suffered miserably through it, except for Kay. She seemed immune to whatever else the rest of the world was going through. This catastrophe looked like it would be the death knell of the celebrity wedding. Mr. Saxon was too sick to work on the courtyard, so Danny – weak also, but with a determination that was admirable – alternated between filling in holes, replacing bricks, and expunging weeds, sitting down to rest every little while. Emerald, from her room, standing at the window and munching crackers for her nausea, saw a bit of the work going on. She also saw Kay, still healthy, hovering around directing them; and Louise going back and forth with supplies.

After a few days, everyone was well enough to dread the wedding again. Linens were washed in the hottest water and every surface was wiped with disinfectant. Nora was just expressing her satisfaction that the period of contagion was over when Kay received a phone call. The bride was in bed with the same sickness! Her case was worse than others, as she had even been hospitalized. It was a waiting game, to see whether or not she would recover in time.

A lot of smoking, and much walking back and forth took place, over the next twenty-four hours or so. Emerald heard Kay say something about, surely somebody wouldn't be so idiotic as to catch a virus when they were about to get married; but she passed that off as her harried nerves talking. "If they don't get married Friday, surely they would just postpone it a day or two. Surely, after all this work has been done."

The eve of the wedding, after furniture had been moved and greenery had been hung, they found out the fate of the grand event. It had not been postponed. Nor was it going to take place on the original day.

Because the bride and groom were married in a private ceremony, in the hospital.

And apparently the bride thought it so romantic and impromptu that they weren't even going to have a reception at Ashmont, as Kay had assumed that "at least they would do that."

What a blow this was! In the hours after they got the news, Kay was as silent as stone, registering no emotion whatsoever. Nora fretted all the more over trivial daily things, and could be seen to wipe tears away every so often. Poor Saxon attempted to joke about being relieved it was cancelled; but anyone who knew him saw that he felt all the weight of the disappointment, monetarily at least. Solemn faces became the norm at the dinner table each night; no more talk of flowers, courtyards, or paparazzi.

The governor's daughter and her new husband lost no publicity by their hospital wedding; their fame was doubled by it, in fact. The Keckleys, and more importantly, Ashmont Hall, were the casualties in this disaster.

29

DISAPPOINTMENT

Since the wedding was called off, Emerald didn't like to be around the Keckleys. A morose silence blanketed the family; they scarcely tried to mask it even among the weekend guests. Breakfasts were now just thrown together by Nora, who went back to bed right after serving them. Syb didn't get out of bed at all for days – she had depended upon this opportunity to have her face appear on all the social media sites, with the magnetism these famous people would have generated.

Emerald still wrestled, alone, with the mess in Kay's room; most days it seemed she was just churning it up and rearranging it. How could Ashmont survive this great loss? Even with the generous consolation check they received from the governor, by way of apology, the renovation bills were mounting scarily high. She was certain they were headed for bankruptcy. Gone would be the legacy, the romantic mystery held by her family for so many generations; the house would fall into other hands, and would be probably purchased by a hotel chain or worse.

It was too bad, Emerald thought, that Danny seemed so reticent about his relationship with Celia to scarcely even acknowledge it. They could get married there, as the bride's family could probably afford such a place. Maybe she could talk him into it . . .?

The night before what would have been the Great Day, Emerald was about to go to bed when her aunt Kay stopped her, wanting to speak to her privately.

"I thought, if you're not too tired from your week, we could spend a little time together tomorrow afternoon."

Emerald couldn't believe her ears. What? Kay wanted to spend time with her? She was at a loss for words, so unexpected this was. Without waiting for an answer, her aunt continued.

"I thought you and I could go do some shopping and have lunch.

We haven't had much time to – well, just visit. Just talk."

This was the last thing Emerald had expected. Yet here was Kay, calm and composed, and looking forward to spending time with her. This was the day she had hungered for!

"I'll let Nora know," Kay said, as they walked arm-in-arm upstairs, "that there will be two fewer plates at lunch tomorrow."

This outing was not another opportunity snatched from Emerald's eager hands. She was not disappointed by a sudden remembrance that Kay had something else to do. Kay was not suddenly ill or in need of rest.

They set out early the next day in the champagne Lincoln and drove into town. They walked the sidewalks of Millcrest, so picturesque with its variegated building facades, old-fashioned lamp posts, and autumn flowers. They wandered in and out of interesting shops, coveting what was expensive, and making fun of what was tacky. Kay bought her something: a hair clip in the shape of a calla lily. "You look just like your mother," she said, smoothing Emerald's thick hair and fastening it on one side, "with your hair pulled back like this."

They chatted about things. Kay spoke low and intimately to her, drawing her away to herself, and the soft, feminine voice was like music to her ears. They went to an elegant restaurant, one that overlooked the crest of a mountain and took the breath away with its view. "Did you know your parents and I ate dinner here once?" asked Kay, as they sat at a linen-covered table. "Your father, and your mother – and I. We were very young."

Over pasta, they talked about Ashmont and what the wedding would have meant to it. "It would have been photographed for several publications," said Kay. "The wedding party had already received offers from the biggest magazines, and we had already signed the necessary papers giving our permission, as owners of Ashmont."

"What a shame that it fell through," commiserated Emerald. They were quiet for a little while.

"And when is your father coming to pay you a visit?" asked Kay, changing her tone. "I expected him to come see you, by now."

"Really? I'm surprised you ask. You know how much Mother needs him, with the illness." Emerald's voice cracked and she began talking faster, trying to gain control. "But I'll drive home at Christmas. He does write and call me often, though."

"But he needs a break, too, darling. I know how devoted he is to her; he always has been. I'm sure he can – I'm sure he can afford the finest care for her in his absence, can't he? Anyway, I want him to see how you're flourishing here, under my care. How pretty you are. You're coming out of your shell. No, we really do need to get him here, if for just a weekend. It would do him good, the change of scenery."

Emerald couldn't agree with her, but didn't say so. It would kill Dad to leave Mother right now! He as much as said those very words in his last letter.

The ride home was a little dismal, compared to the carefree afternoon. Kay said some things to sadden Emerald. Kay kept asking her about Mother's prognosis, and her quality of life, and whether the doctors had given her any hope at all.

"Not much, from what I understand," Emerald said, forcing the quiver out of her voice. "She might live several years longer though." Then there was silence between them, and Emerald's thoughts on this topic ran wild as they drove on the dark curvy roads. By the time they returned to Ashmont, she was convinced that Kay knew something she didn't. She had been talking to Dad, and Mother was worsening; this was Kay's way of preparing her. She was certain of it.

Late at night Emerald lay in bed, her thoughts miles away. But raised voices below her, and scuffling sounds, masked by the running of water in a tub, brought her back to the here and now. What was going on in Kay's room? Who was in there with her? She couldn't distinguish if the other voice was male or female, though it was firm.

The sounds transfixed and petrified Emerald. Suddenly she jumped up, hating the feeling of sitting atop a volcano rumbling beneath her. She didn't want to hear such sounds anymore.

She put on her slippers and housecoat and wondered where to go without being noticed. Silently she trekked her way downstairs, and decided to slip into the closet where the secret steps went down to the basement room. She would feel safe down there; or at least, safer.

The darkness of the room didn't bother her at all, because a harvest moon came right in through the window and made friends with her. It was so bright in one area that she could clearly read the book she had pulled from the shelf, intending to take it upstairs, but now sitting down and opening the cover.

She didn't even care which book it was, she just wanted to relish the feel and smell of something solid and antiquated. This was just an encyclopedia. But why wouldn't it open beyond the first few pages? It must have been untouched for twenty years, so stiff it was. Her fingers pried at it but was afraid of the pages tearing apart.

What was this, though? She opened the book to the last page that would turn, and found that something was wrong with it. Someone had cut a hole out, crudely with scissors, to make a little box in the center of the book; then had glued the pages around it together.

There was something inside the hole. She tilted it toward the moonlight and used her fingernail to edge it out. It was a tiny box.

And inside the box was a ruby ring.

30

KAY'S PLAN

Within a few days, something seemed to be brewing again among the sisters.

"I have had the most marvelous idea," Kay was saying. "You well know all the trouble and expense we've gone through, on account of that darn wedding. But look at Ashmont, look how it has been restored to its former glory!" She waved a hand for effect. "We haven't had a grand party here for years. A real dinner party, with white ties and tuxes, champagne and all the trimmings. We will plan one, and we will take that opportunity to photograph it for our new brochure. I've almost obtained a promise from one of the magazines for a feature spread."

Nora was almost crying through her smiles, and nervously picking fuzz off of Mr. Saxon's sweater. He shooed her away.

"Oh! It sounds dreamy! I have to invite my theater friends. And we must have the courtyard, a dance in the courtyard, just as we planned before," gushed Sybilla.

"We will use the large dining room just as we wanted to use. I'm so glad Saxon finished all the re-wiring in there. We will invite special guests to the dinner itself, and then many more to join us for drinks and dancing later. Just as our parents used to do, at least three or four times a year, back in the heyday. We will hire more help, and they will wear regular uniforms. We must finish out all the gravel outside, the small kind, that won't harm ladies' shoes." On she rambled, until she turned to Emerald.

"And you," she added, slipping her arm around her waist, "will help me. We must get your parents here for it."

What? How could Kay think this was possible? Mother was undergoing more treatments now, and could not bear a long car ride. Her appearance suffered; she was gaunt, and did not want to attend fancy parties. Kay talked on about it, about the change doing her good, and how she was longing to see her. There was something untethered about her, as she talked in excitement, almost to the point of mania.

As for Emerald, she not only wanted to shield her mother from an event such as this, she herself planned to escape it. She had missed the old, quiet Ashmont and was glad the stress of the wedding was removed. And the weekend Kay was planning it happened to be perfect for Emerald to drive back home. She tried to tell her aunt this, but was cut off. She found Kay to be tenacious about Nick and Charlotte being present, and pressed the topic to Emerald's frustration. She turned quietly away, and left the room.

At work the next day, to Emerald's great surprise, she found Kay's plans had been advancing with lightning speed. Blanche, today wearing a headband with rabbit ears, bustled up to her young employee and told her they had been invited to a Keckley gala at the end of the month.

"Truly thrilling!" She gushed, the bunny ears bobbing. "We haven't been there in years. I can't wait to see all those changes I've been hearing about. Even Gordon is getting a new suit for it."

"Because you're making me! We could look at the renovations at lower cost, if you ask me, if we rented a room there for the week. I thought you were going to save those for Easter, Blanche. Or will those be part of the new ensemble you'll be wearing for the Ashmont party?"

Emerald had counted on a closer friendship with her aunt, since the day they had spent together, but was confused as to why she seemed no nearer to her than before. The relationship seemed locked in ice. And what was more disturbing was that no amount of explaining to Kay could make a dent in her plans of inviting Nick and Charlotte. The fact that they lived four hours away, and were dealing with a major illness, were minor obstacles to be waved away as nothing.

Finally, after an impassioned plea from Emerald to her to please forego the invitation, on account of Mother's health, Kay suddenly turned to her with half a smile and demanded, "Then your father alone could come."

Now she was angry. For Dad to leave Mother's side was too much to ask right now! As she looked at her aunt, seeing the dilated eyes, the poise of her back in an upright, determined position, the phrase came back that Saxon had used: she has a will of iron. Emerald turned from her, unable to trust herself with what to say next.

Kay wasted no time in forging ahead with this plan. She was instantly on the phone, entreating Nick, chattering wildly. Her niece couldn't stay to listen. She ran upstairs to her room, formulating her own defense. She would not let Kay talk Dad into it. She paced her room, shaking. Why was this so upsetting to her? She wrestled with the thought. It must be in protection of her mother. She thought of the pale blue letter. Hadn't Kay and her mother been best friends once? Something like jealousy tainted this scenario – and yet why would Kay be jealous over just a cousin? She had plenty of dashing men friends to enhance Ashmont with their presence.

"Don't you dare leave Mother, just to come to her stupid party," she had gushed through tears, when she had a chance to call him. "She's going overboard with this thing, and is blinded to everything else but making it everything she wants it to be."

"I know, I know dear. Don't worry; I'm staying right here with your mom. I know Kay well, you forget. Calm down."

She decided to lay low until the weekend of the party, then just leave. She would make an excuse of why she was called home for a few days. She knew she could get off work then, and no projects were due for school. She said nothing, but just planned to slip out a day or two before, confident she wouldn't even be missed.

Still she watched, and wondered at her aunt's behavior. Kay still spoke of Nick's coming as certain as the sun's rising.

"Nora, get out that set of glasses from the bar, you know – the double old-fashioneds with the beveled edge. Nick always admired those. And be sure to make the divinity he always liked. We may need some more cream of tartar; I'll pick it up at the store."

Emerald said nothing to deter this delusion. Inwardly she had the comfort of assurance from Dad himself, that he was having no part of it.

Something happened, though, to compel her to speak up about her own plan to be absent.

Kay took great pride in following all the protocol of a social event of this nature. Details were meticulously planned far in advance, down to which candy dishes would be set on which tables. A mock dinner was set up in the dining room, with paper cutouts of each and every bowl, plate and saucer that would be used. Emerald, coming home from work, did not slip upstairs as usual; but being hungry went to look for a snack.

"Man, lady, man, lady, all the way across. I will sit here of course. Nora, that dish is too close to the corner. The mayor is sure to send it flying; you know his arms are always askew. Remember what happened last time." Emerald was intrigued by what they were doing and went in to see for herself.

She saw that sheets of paper were at every place setting with names scribbled on them. Conspicuously on two places nearest Kay were "Emerald" and "Nick."

Kay was now asking her what they would be wearing that night. "Ask your father if he can wear a tux. Rather, I'll do that; I was going to call him again anyway. But then you don't have a dinner gown, do you? You two must match. Maybe you can borrow one of Sybilla's."

Emerald steeled herself before saying it. "I won't be there, Aunt. Neither will Dad."

Kay did not acknowledge this at all.

"Her green one, with the sequins, would set off your eyes beautifully, Em. You'll wear it better than her, anyway. Sybilla always looked like a bridesmaid in it."

"But I said – I said I don't plan to – "

Nora began noisily asking her sister which napkin rings they would be using. They began a discussion about it, and Emerald turned to leave, her blood pressure rising. She was walking away when Kay called to her.

"Em, dear, Julian came to see you earlier today."

This made 'Em, dear' stop to listen.

"Come here while I finish this, and I'll tell you about it."

Kay was again re-arranging some of the fake plates. "He must be lonely. He waited for you for quite a while, but was getting antsy so I had Sybilla take him grocery shopping with her." Kay, for the moment satisfied with the table, pulled Emerald aside with her arm around her.

"I was going to let this be a surprise," she whispered, "but it looks like the truth just won't be held in. All the glorious little details of this dinner are falling together magically, it seems. You see, I am counting on you to be here. I must have you. Because – because we have arranged – well, we have a date for you. Now hush hush, no questions" (although Emerald had said nothing), "I will be mum on this subject. You will find out who it is, on the night in question. I must say, it won't be very hard for you to figure it out yourself. Nothing brightens a young lady's countenance so much as the anticipation of something pleasant, like dressing up for an evening with your *beau du jour*. I will only say, he admires you tremendously. He is forever dropping hints to us." She put emphasis on each of those last words she spoke, and looked at her so earnestly, that Emerald's heart fluttered in spite of herself.

Emerald wished her aunt had mentioned this before now, and tried to maintain an aura of subtle resentment of being manipulated into this situation; but the draw of an admirer caught her imagination and made her flush with pleasure. Of course she knew who it was.

31

FORCED TO STAY

merald struggled. She wanted the date with Julian; she even wanted to dress up and take her place among the other adults at Kay's sophisticated dinner party. But the pull of going home for the weekend, which she had already firmly communicated to her aunt, was the foremost in her desires. She hated being the object of shameless manipulation – in spite of Kay's assertion that she was only doing it to arrange a spectacular date for her.

So, she decided to skip the party and go home. Julian would be fine without her. He would understand. He would go stag, and probably get more sympathy and attention because of it. She would make it up to him later.

Thursday afternoon arrived. Work and school were done for the week, so she decided she'd better make a break for it then. She packed her bags and went out the back door, but was at a loss when she looked for her car. It was gone!

She tramped all the way around the yard and looked in Danny's garage, but her car was missing. Danny, wiping his hands on his coveralls, saw her searching and answered her question before she asked it. "Nora told me to take your car for new tires. She said Kay was worried about them. It will be ready next week."

Emerald dropped her bags to the gravel and groaned. She was stunned into silence for several minutes afterward. As Danny returned to his project, she thought of interrogating him, but knew that would be useless. This was all part of Kay's plan: getting her own way while masking it under concern for her. Worried about her tires – ha!

Emerald's thoughts burned within her as she acquiesced, with mixed feelings, to this trap. But at least Kay's maneuverings would stop with her. She didn't have to worry about Dad coming; he had assured her of his own defiance against Kay's wishes, however cunningly they were expressed. Emerald kept that one fact in her thoughts as her only consolation.

Even with some resentment, she couldn't help being amused by the swirl of exuberance around her as the party approached. Kay and her entourage were a wonder to behold. Emerald had only known a foretaste of her aunt's skills, until now, of engineering an event to the highest levels of taste and splendor. *Was a party really worth all this trouble and expense?* Emerald thought, as she watched her aunt. But it was hard-wired in her; she was a mastermind to command things like this, and Emerald observed her with awe. Time restraints, pressure, expectations – all these seemed to fuel her spirits to rise above every challenge. Emerald could have only crumpled under such stress!

It was the very morning of the event when it occurred to her: she didn't even know what to wear to it. As for the green sequined gown of Syb's, that was a no. She did not want to appear looking like a bridesmaid.

Since her car was still gone, she got a ride with Nora as she went for last-minute items. Nora dropped her off at a strip of shops, then left to get her groceries.

Two hours later, and having tried on at least a dozen dresses, long and short, each one more mortifying than the one before, she resigned herself to her silver emergency dress that was already hanging in her closet. Turning her attention to shoes and accessories, she bought some sky-high heels, and found a three-stranded necklace that she thought might work.

Nora picked her up and off they went back to Ashmont. But today, of all days, traffic was slowing to a stop all around them, and they realized they had happened upon a funeral procession.

"I've never seen so many cars in a funeral line! Who on earth died?" asked Nora.

"I don't know – maybe a city official? Looks like somebody important," replied the girl.

"Well, I hope it wasn't the mayor. Kay is counting on him to attend her dinner tonight. She would be so disappointed," said Nora. "But then, we would have heard of his death, by now."

With musings like these they passed the time, stretching out longer and longer, and feeding their fears of lateness. To change the subject, Emerald asked Nora something that had been on her mind.

"Aunt Nora, I found an old note from my mother to Kay, from when they were teenagers. They were very close, weren't they?"

"Oh yes! Inseparable! When I see you and Sybilla together, laughing, it reminds me of how Kay and your mother were. Where did you find that old note?"

"Well, the first page I found in an old box, and the second was in Kay's room. I was surprised to learn something, though. My mom had written – 'I saw you walking together – your blonde hair and his black.' That made me wonder, did Kay have a boyfriend with black hair? Who was the note talking about?"

"Oh, I wouldn't know. She had so many."

"My father had black hair."

"Oh yes, he did, I do remember that. But your mother wasn't smitten with him until much later, I believe. It seemed she was in love with one of the grounds-keepers when she was here."

"Really? Well, I'm a bit confused. I always thought it was Dad who was the Keckleys' cousin, but now I think it must have been Mother. Which one is it?"

But there was no time to continue this conversation, because the road was clearing at last and they were free to go. However, in her haste, Nora's foot accelerated so fast that she rear-ended the car in front of her! Both women lurched forward and screamed.

When the first moments of shock were over, and it was assured that everyone in both cars were okay, Emerald could breathe again. Nora and the other driver inspected the bumpers and decided no damage was done. While they were deliberating, though, Emerald's eye was caught by a very familiar car rolling past them slowly.

Was that who I think it was? She asked herself, but decided her eyes were playing tricks on her due to the shock of the wreck.

At last they reached home. With great relief she saw that none but the ordinary cars were parked in the Ashmont garage – no guests were here yet. Her heart beating fast, she gathered her things and slipped in at the side door and made for the back staircase. Passing the library, she noticed Danny sitting there with a book, and wearing a suit and tie. So, she would finally get to meet Celia tonight! And would be able to observe Danny's behavior toward her. This added another layer of interest to an evening that was already filling her with butterflies.

She actually heard the front doorbell ring as she gained the third story, and knew that the first guests were arriving. She needed to hurry.

Fastening her door lock with a click, she got ready. On went the silver-gray dress, the necklace, the frightening high-heeled shoes. She twirled like a little girl in front of the mirror, and looked at her image. Her legs did look more shapely, and her arms not so skinny as she was used to seeing them. The dress was lovely. But as she looked at her hair, her face, her glasses, she was worried. From the shoulders up, she could have been about fourteen! She would fix her hair differently, and the glasses – well, they would just have to stay behind on the vanity for this evening.

She brushed her hair into its default style, which was not much of a style at all, and wondered what to do with it. She pulled it straight back into a bun, with a tendril or two trailing against her cheeks. No. One or two more styles were attempted, but discarded. It looks like I'm playing dress-up, she thought with frustration. With alarm she realized that everyone had probably arrived by now, and looking down into the garden she saw several people being handed drinks and mingling with one another. Hastily she pulled one side back and fastened it with the calla lily that Kay had bought her.

One last touch: the ruby ring. She couldn't resist. She would wear it and would watch Louise's eyes, to see if they caught it or not. If she was smart enough to be looking for jewels, there was no way she could miss this rock. Luckily it fit her third finger; and Emerald felt like a regent, wearing such a stunner.

Please don't let me fall, please don't let me fall, she prayed, feeling like she was teetering on stilts as she carefully descended the stairs. Just as she was in sight of the front door, her heart skipped a beat to see it open, and Julian walk in, with a bouquet of flowers in his hand. Emerald swallowed and prepared to meet his eye.

But at that moment, Sybilla walked up to him, greeting him and taking the flowers. She said something inaudible, and latching herself onto his arm, she led him away, out of sight. She must be entertaining him until I make my appearance, thought Emerald, confused.

She watched them as long as she could, following them with her eyes, somewhat in a daze. It appeared that Sybilla was flirting just as much with him as ever – giving him frequent hugs, laughing at everything he said, sniffing the flowers she now carried. Was there some mistake?

Not knowing what else to do, Emerald walked right up to the couple. Syb's back was to her; but Julian greeted her with an admiring glance.

"Well!" he said. "I was wondering where you were." He gave her a wink.

"Really?" she answered, not knowing how to answer that.

"What is it about you that's different? You look, I don't know, taller or something. Let me see those shoes of yours. I don't see how girls wear those things."

Neither do I, Emerald could have added, wincing a little.

At last Syb turned to her and looked her over from head to toe – a little too purposefully. Emerald was embarrassed by it. "Em," crooned her cousin. "You look – so – where've you been? I have got to talk to you."

"But I was just going to ask her to have a drink with me," interjected Julian.

"Oh no you're not! I know you, monopolizing people. We have something very important to discuss. So you'll just have to talk to Mr. Saxon this time." She motioned to the other end of the room, where the old man was dressed up, but dozing as usual. Then, with a gesture characteristic of Kay, she slipped her arm around Emerald's waist and pulled her away.

Emerald wondered what this very important matter was. Maybe Syb's own date couldn't come, and she wanted to "share" Julian with her.

"It's Mother," whispered Syb. "She's in trouble!"

"Oh no! What's wrong, is she sick?"

"No, it's worse than that."

Emerald gazed at her, stunned. "What is it? Is there something I can do to help?"

"She – she's so upset. I've never seen her like this! The pastry for her quiches fell apart, and she doesn't know how to fix it. Can you go help her in the kitchen? She asked me, but I can't – the guests are arriving. I have to greet them. There's another car now." And she whirled from her.

Emerald suspiciously watched Sybilla now flouncing through the hall, checking her image in the mirror. Help with the quiche? Good grief! She took this mortification but it was sinking in to her that Sybilla was trying to keep her from Julian. But that didn't make sense. Sybilla must have known Kay had set her up with Julian, right? Who else could there possibly be?

She went to Aunt Nora anyway, finding the situation much less tragic than Syb had made out; however Nora was very happy to have another pair of hands.

"Why, aren't you pretty! Put on this apron, by all means. I'm glad you came instead of Syb because she's a bit of a scatter-brain when it comes to cooking. Although," said Nora, wiping flour from her ear and leaning toward Emerald, "she's perfectly capable. She pretends a little sometimes, you know. Bless her heart, she'd just rather be the one served, not on the other end."

Emerald nodded while tying her apron strings. Through the swinging kitchen door that Louise was frequently passing through, she caught glimpses of people she didn't know, wearing gowns and tuxedos, and she felt a little relieved to be hidden away in the kitchen, away from the unfamiliar. She did try to get a peek at Danny's date; he was standing in a corner, talking with someone, but a large, noisy man was standing directly in her line of vision. A time or two, she thought she saw Julian looking toward the kitchen, as if he were waiting for her to return to the party. Considering this, Emerald felt that her absence would work to her advantage after all, and so she was able to more readily whisk the salad dressing that Nora now handed her.

"Have you seen the dining room yet?" called Nora as she scraped asparagus into a dish. Emerald thought she meant the room they always took meals in, but Nora stopped her. "No, no. The formal one," she said, nodding in the other direction. "We rarely use it; you probably don't ever remember being in there before." Emerald went to the door indicated, and opened it; she took a deep breath.

32

DINNER PARTY

A magnificent room was before her. It was long, and oak-paneled, with not one – but two marble fireplaces, and several chandeliers – lit up like masses of diamond clouds. The lights made her think of the ring now on her finger, and she twirled it, wondering if her aunts, or Louise, would spot it sometime tonight.

How could such a room have been hidden away? Nora was right: Emerald somehow had never stepped foot in it, or known of its existence. She had probably assumed this doorway had led to a dusty storage room. So many of the other doors did.

With awe she surveyed the table, dressed as the belle of the ball. Snow white linens, flowers, place settings, chargers, finger bowls – no detail was overlooked; everything was styled exactly as in an era of Ashmont gone by, fifty years ago and more, when the ladies in chiffon would sail in and smile; and the gentlemen would hold their chairs out for them. All that was needed now was for the candles to be lit, and for elegant company to fill it once again.

There was something else she spotted, nestled beside each crystal goblet: the place cards. This was her chance to verify her mystery date as Julian. All it would take would be one walk around the table, and a glance at every name. Her heart lurched in fear and excitement. But Nora called her back. "Emerald, hurry! I'm about to drop this, it's hot. Grab a towel or something." She ran back to rescue her.

Between Emerald and Nora, at last the meal was completed; they double- and triple-checked each course and condiment. "Now. I think we're just about ready," said Nora, removing her apron and dabbing her moist brow.

Kay appeared, asking if the guests may be seated now. She wore a low-cut gown of plum velvet, and her hair was in a chignon. She was mesmerizing!

"Almost, give us one minute, then call them all in," said Nora, sighing with weariness and satisfaction. "It's all set. Look at the beautiful crust on this soufflé, sister. Mr. Saxon was right about the cognac." But Kay didn't stay to admire it; she was off to corral the company, and usher them into the readied room with grandeur. Emerald's heart now fluttered afresh, thinking of Julian. He had probably been looking for her, since she had been back here with Nora for so long; she entertained a modest notion that her scarcity would make him all the more eager to be with her.

"Oh, Emerald, we forgot the matches. Would you mind getting them? On the shelf above the toaster. And I must make a place at the table to set the fish mold. It has to stay in the fridge until the last moment." She bustled back into the dining room, but when she got to the doorway and saw the table, she froze.

"Oh my Lord!" her aunt shrieked. She wobbled, and seemed on the verge of fainting away.

Emerald rushed to her side, matches in hand. "What is it? What's wrong?" And then she saw the problem.

All the place settings and decor were perfectly arranged, as before, but now – as if he were the centerpiece – Tiger John the cat was enthroned in the very middle, having settled his kingly self in a supine position, fully relaxed and the picture of complacency. He lazily lifted a paw to bat at a stray piece of baby's breath, then lifted it to his mouth to gnaw on it. Emerald held a hand to her mouth, paralyzed.

Just then, the opposite door was opening: the guests were coming in, led by Kay. She, blissfully innocent of the horror awaiting her, had not looked at the table yet, since she was stationing herself to motion the rest of the company in.

"Do something!!" hissed Nora, grabbing Emerald's arm.

The girl rushed across the room, which was remarkable in itself because of the high heels, and desperately caught Kay's attention. What am I going to say to her? She thought wildly. She thought of something.

"Aunt Kay! Have you seen Sybilla? Where is she? I'm worried

about her," she lied, "because I haven't seen her all evening." From her peripheral vision she saw Nora retrieving the cat and sneaking him out of the room. Kay didn't notice this at all, because Emerald's ploy worked: Kay was instantly concerned, and back-tracked her steps to go locate her niece.

"I'm so sorry, dear people, but I must find our Sybilla, she's here somewhere, isn't she? I was worried that she didn't know dinner was ready. We simply couldn't start without her, bless her heart."

With a hasty lighting of candles, and flicking away of a few cat hairs, Emerald prepared the table as footsteps were once again heard approaching. Kay was seating herself at the head of the table just as Nora placed the hideous fish mold in the empty place – now cleared of any felines. Everyone *ooh'd* and *aah'd* over the impressive display before them.

One by one the seats were taken and the long table was filling up. Still standing aloof, Emerald gracefully placed herself somewhat near Julian so that he could come claim her. He, however, after another admiring glance at her dress, took the chair next to Sybilla.

Emerald felt a stab into her heart. She just kept standing there, glaring at the back of Sybilla's updo.

A hand touched her arm; it was Nora. "Over there, dear," she said, indicating a chair a few feet away.

Kay was also directing her, with a nod of her head toward the other end of the table. "Yes, Emerald, over there. Take your seat, next to your date."

But the only seat not taken was on the other side of a bald town councilman, and he had brought his wife with him. Her eye traveled from his fat back, to the vacant chair, to the man just seating himself on the other side of it – and it was ... Danny Grosch!

What? What about Celia? But there was no Celia there, as a desperate glance around the room attested. She robotically walked to the chair, halfway expecting to be corrected and called back – but sure enough, she read her own named swirled on the place card next to him. She sat down, numb.

"That's right," said Kay, giving her a nod and a smile.

For the next few minutes Emerald fitted herself into the form of propriety called for at a dinner party. She smiled, she passed the dishes cheerfully, she did everything to blend in to the scene and not cause any more attention to be drawn toward her than already was. She saw that Mr. Saxon glanced at her and Danny from the opposite end of the table, and that Aunt Nora was frequently smiling at them.

The red ring glittered on her finger, and she thought it had attracted the notice of a few eyes. But when she realized she had forgotten to scrape paint off her hands from her most recent project, she folded them in her lap in embarrassment. She must eat, though, and did so with as little attention to herself as possible.

After a few minutes in this way, settling into the atmosphere of conversation and tinkling of crystal, Emerald began – by osmosis – to appraise what Danny himself thought of this little setup.

For one thing, he was totally silent. Verbally silent, that is; because little by little she became more keenly aware of every smack, chew and swallow of his hearty appetite. She wondered if he was even conscious of her. He seemed to sit there and eat just as if it were any other night of the week; except that they were dressed up and using the good china.

Louise now re-appeared – Emerald had wondered what had happened to her, while she and Nora had finished all the work – and she saw the reason for her absence. She was dressed as a real maid. Complete with trim black dress and white apron, she brought in the serving platters and made her way from guest to guest. She even wore a maid's cap, but unfortunately had forgotten to remove the feather earrings, now swinging back and forth and in ridiculous contrast to her attire. She looked as stiff and uncomfortable as Emerald felt.

After a while nobody was eyeing them anymore, so she concentrated on dinner and not being bumped too much by Danny's elbow. Once or twice he said 'excuse me' but those seemed to be the only exchange they would have all evening. She couldn't think of a single thing to say to him; anyway, she didn't want to. She intended to look as aloof and icy as possible for the sake of Sybilla and Julian, who were on the opposite side of the table, a little way down, laughing and flirting as much as possible. How could Syb do this to her? What did she intend by it? She saw Syb making a face and doing an imitation, probably of one of the other guests, and Julian was near choking on suppressed laughter.

Kay was most purely in her element tonight. She relished giving and receiving attention like common currency. Emerald couldn't help watching her as much as possible. Every movement was polished without appearing formal. Every interaction with her guests was friendly. She spoke with propriety, ease, and humor. How did she learn to do all that? Emerald confessed to herself that much of this was an act, since she had sometimes seen her sullen and wrapped up in herself, especially among family. She admired her no less, though. It was an art.

No one spoke to Emerald the whole dinner, except for Rita Canter and the bald man on her other side. They were trying to draw her into their friendly argument about Millcrest economics, and asking her opinion of the re-zoning of the industrial district. Rita mentioned that Emerald drove there every day for work, at Military Surplus, and the councilman was surprised.

"Oh, so you know the Sylvesters!" he exclaimed. "Why, I frequent their establishment myself at times. Fine people. In fact, I'm surprised they were not invited here tonight."

"Oh, but they were invited," interjected Kay, picking up on their topic. "They will be joining us after dinner, with a few more friends. They had something come up and told me they would be late." This was a surprise to Emerald, knowing how much Blanche was looking forward to dining here. She wondered what had happened to prevent their attendance on time?

Dessert was being handed around by Louise now. Aunt Nora seemed to be in a coughing fit, and people were suggesting she drink some water, when Emerald realized Nora was staring directly at her with wide eyes. She was trying to communicate something.

Emerald glanced around to see what was the matter; then, she saw it. The cat had come back! He had slipped in while Louise was bringing in the trays of cheesecake. She saw his tail now floating upright behind the backs of the guests, and she knew he would try the same trick as before.

Quickly, the girl slipped from her chair to scoop Tiger up just as he was about to jump on the lap of a senator. She deftly got him out of the room and was taking him to the back door to lock him out for good. Depositing him in the grassy area, she almost jumped out of her skin to nearly bump into a man who was standing there! She had to look at him for a long moment to realize who he was.

"Dad!"

33

THE KISS

Was she looking at a ghost? Hardly, as Dad's all-too-real chuckle was heard by her own ears, and his arm was around her in a hug. "Careful now! You're going to trip, with those shoes you've got on. Or have you grown that much in these past few months since you've been here?"

"But – you told Kay you and Mother wouldn't be coming! Is she here too?"

"No, no, she's at the medical home, and her best friend is with her. They're probably watching their favorite TV show right now. She has been feeling better, and wanted me to come. To see how things are going here."

Emerald tried to be angry at Kay for achieving her desire, against her own protestations, but it was hard to when she realized how good it was to have Dad's arm around her again.

"When did you get here?"

"This afternoon."

"But – why weren't you at dinner?"

"I've been catching up with some old friends of mine!"

And he nodded toward Blanche and Gordon Sylvester, seated in the courtyard, who had been watching the reunion in quiet delight. Blanche now laughed.

"I don't know why I never made the 'Johnsey' connection before tonight! What an idiot I am!"

"She's quite an asset to our little business, Nick. I do believe our commerce has increased, with such a charming young lady to help," added Gordon.

Emerald now remembered that Dad had said something about knowing her employers. They had been acquaintances for many years.

"You two were missed at dinner," she told them. "But I'm glad you got to visit with Dad. I'll make sure you get something to eat later."

"Oh it wasn't the dinner we were looking forward to so much, although it was fine I'm sure! It was —" and the two immediately stood to their feet and twirled on the courtyard floor, arms clasped, and Blanche's sequined gown catching the reflection of lights strung overhead. Kay was so right about this courtyard! It was a wonderful spot. She left them to enjoy their soundless dance, and Dad settled down into a lounge chair to watch them with twinkling eyes.

Emerald rejoined dinner just in time for Kay to bring it to its conclusion. She observed the tradition of Ashmont's former years: "Ladies, we shall remove ourselves to the 'drawing room,' as Mother Ann says, while the men sit here and finish their coffee. And," she announced, "I have a token of appreciation from us here at Ashmont. A party favor, if you will." With these words she opened a box of Cuban cigars, and began to offer them to the gentlemen. Even Danny took one, noted Emerald as she placed her napkin on her plate and prepared to stand. Some of the men were pulling out chairs for the ladies, but not Danny; he was fumbling with the plastic wrapper on his cigar, and acted as if he forgot about her existence.

More guests arrived for the after-dinner party. It was now that Kay triumphantly brought Nick Johnsey in, holding him by the hand, and told Emerald she had a grand surprise for her. Emerald, perfectly composed, was thankful to have been prepared beforehand.

Within a short time the whole company were mixing together and filtering through the house, noisy, merry, and hot. By ten o'clock Emerald was yawning, but Kay was just getting started. The wine was flowing freely at her insistence and she was laughing and flirting more with every half hour. Her daring dress was, by default, the focal point of the room, and Emerald was a little embarrassed for her.

She had thought the party would be winding down by now, but

to her surprise she saw headlights from cars outside; fresh arrivals were here. The dignified dinner gathering was now being augmented, and the party was just beginning.

Emerald was pulled into a dull conversation with the senator's wife but was distracted by the frequent laughter and shrieks from Sybilla and her theater friends. After declining joining in a game of Rook, she snaked her way through the guests and escaped the room. On her way out she got a glimpse of Kay sitting on the senator's lap – yes – and calling for Mr. Saxon to tell another funny joke.

She went to the kitchen for a glass of water, then placed it in the sink as usual. She turned around to see Louise looking at her.

"Are you holding something?" she asked Emerald.

"Not anymore. Just the glass I was drinking from."

"Is there something in your hand?" Louise demanded. And she grabbed both the girl's hands and turned them over, looking at both sides. Of course, Emerald knew this was an excuse to look at the ruby ring.

"Kay didn't ask for anything, did she? Did she ask you to bring her something?"

"No she did not! And if she did, why should I tell you?" With that, Emerald turned away from the woman.

To get some fresh air, she stepped outside onto the terrace. She saw that Julian was out here too, among a few couples now joining the Sylvesters in the courtyard. The music had started, creating an enchanting scene! Gazing at the dancers, her eyes fell on Julian's profile; something inside her fluttered as she admired him dressed so well. He was laughing heartily at a story someone told, so she didn't think he noticed her appearance, but to her surprise he met her eyes and let them linger long enough for her to blush.

She broke away, thankful to be a free agent for the moment, and enjoy the liberty of walking in the cool grass while she regained her composure. Sitting down on the tree bench, she distanced herself far enough to view the house as a panorama. Laughter and music, perfume and heat were at a distance now, and she was able to survey it with a calm eye. Ever since she was little, she had felt a need to step away and process whatever she was experiencing.

And then there was Dad. She felt better about him leaving Mother with a friend, but it still unnerved her to be under such manipulation from Kay. And Kay was too frequently near Dad, too touchy, too possessive of him tonight, in front of her friends. There she was now, with her arm around his waist, parading him around the terrace and chattering away. He was only her cousin, and there she was acting as if she were introducing a brand new husband.

She was so focused on watching Dad and Kay that she had not noticed someone was approaching her. The shadowy figure came nearer but she could not recognize him at first, so unaccustomed to seeing him in formal attire: it was Danny.

He did not sit on the bench with her, but picked up a pear from the ground and began munching on it. Now was her chance to ask him why Celia wasn't here.

"I was looking forward to meeting your girlfriend tonight," she said. "By the way, I hope you don't think I asked to be fixed up with you tonight. Because I didn't."

He didn't answer at first, still chewing on his pear. "I guess it was Kay's idea. She already knew about me and Celia. We broke it off a few weeks ago."

Hmm! *Interesting,* she thought. She was tempted to ask why, since he had held her up as a model of perfection; then she realized he might have been dumped and didn't want to embarrass him. Instead she tried to change topics. A scant conversation between them was carried on, as well as could be with his pear-eating, but he seemed to gravitate toward the concert they had been working so hard on. *I guess that's heavy on his mind – he's worried about it,* she thought.

They were slowly making their way back to the house, and Emerald noticed the eyes of a few people upon them. It must look like they were taking a romantic stroll together. However, Danny was now telling her about the next piece they would be tackling in orchestra, and his critique of the way she played the lower notes. "Jut your chin out more, it might help you not to sound so raspy," was this romantic comment, under the Ashmont moon.

It seemed like he would say something complimentary to her, about her dress, anything. But he had not even noticed. She caught a couple of triumphant glances from Kay, and felt insulted by her presumption! Talking about her musical faults was not her idea of sentimental conversation. Danny was now finishing the pear all the way down to a nub, and digging something out of his teeth afterward. Gross.

As a sort of protest, she let him walk on before her, and she gradually fell away, not wanting to be coupled with him in the eyes of the others any longer. She took the herringbone path out a little farther away in the opposite direction and bided her time in returning to the party.

The few sips of wine she had taken were worn off now, and she walked very steadily, but the toe of her shoe caught on one of the bricks and – splat – down she went!

Absurd! Just as if she were that little girl again, tripping in the same exact spot. She mostly landed in the soft lawn, but it was dewy moist and she sat up with bits of grass stuck to her. She wasn't hurt, but the most important thing was – had anyone seen her fall?

Trying to get up on her feet as gracefully as possible, she felt a hand – two hands – upon her, helping her with their firm but kind grasp. Had Danny come to help her? She was too embarrassed to look into his face for a moment. She heard a voice with an accent.

"There you go, there you go, Em. You got it? Did you hurt yourself?"

"No, I'm fine. Thank you, Julian."

He walked next to her, his hand steadying her, and she tried to regain her composure. She was glad he couldn't see how her face flushed.

Before they approached the greater light of the terrace, while they were still in the shadow of the fruit trees, he stopped her gently and leaned close to her.

"You're so beautiful tonight. I had to tell you." And with his hand he tilted up her chin, and kissed her lips.

Emerald's head was swimming with this sudden action; she

wilted in his arms. Opening her eyes, she saw Julian gazing at her. Unable to speak, she rested her head upon his shoulder a moment, feeling the smooth tuxedo fabric against her cheek, and intoxicated with his nearness, and the manly scent he wore.

34

AVOIDANCE

As exuberant as Sybilla had been the evening before, with enough glee and vivacity to spill over the next two weeks at least, she exhibited the very opposite of it the next morning. If last night's effervescence was the bubbling up of fresh springs, today was the stagnant dregs from the bottom of a slough.

Emerald took one look at her stony countenance and refrained from saying a word. She wanted to escape as soon as she could from the toxic force now plopped down at the table, arrayed in a chenille robe. There was no cream for her coffee.

"How many times have I told Louise that I cannot do milk. I cannot do half-and-half. I cannot do the powdered crap. I need cream, actual cream in the morning. What do we pay her for? I guess I'm going to have to draw her a picture. I know," she continued sarcastically, slicing the tender morning atmosphere with her words, "I'll draw a picture of a cow and put it right on the refrigerator for her to see. She can take it down and tape it to her chest, to remind her and everybody else, if need be, that she is a forgetful old hag and cannot remember the most basic needs of the family she was hired to serve."

Emerald swallowed her meal fast, and was able to slip out unscathed. *Had Syb seen Julian kiss her last night?* she wondered. It would perfectly explain an acid mood like this. Also, she totally ignored Emerald at breakfast, and the rest of the day.

But she really didn't think anyone had seen them. They had been well screened by trees and darkness. Anyway, bad moods were pretty common for Syb, especially in the morning.

She found Dad on the terrace, hands in his pockets, shuffling about and inspecting the plants. She smiled to see him in his signature unworried state, drawn in to whatever objects were at hand, to observe with his engineer's mind.

He was going to stay at Ashmont a couple more days. He enjoyed getting a load of Louise, he told her, as she was exactly as Emerald had described her.

"A very eccentric character, I agree. But the world would be so boring without such people. She means no harm, Emerald. She's just an odd bird."

"You've only seen a few hours of her, Dad. I'm telling you, she is up to something. I know for a fact. Even Lars Franklin has an eye on her." It was at that very moment that Emerald realized Lars wasn't at the party – and couldn't figure out why not. He and Kay, especially when dressed fine, looked like a matched set. She had been so intent on finding dates for everyone else that she forgot herself, it seemed. Maybe he had had a previous engagement.

"Anyway, I'm glad to have you in my vicinity, Dad, but I have a feeling I won't see much of you," she said, getting up from her patio chair.

"And why not? Are you that busy? Are the Sylvesters monopolizing your time that much? You don't have school today, you know."

"Oh no, that's not what I mean at all. But if you think about it," she said, her voice softening, "you'll figure out what I mean." She cut her eyes toward Kay who was now making her appearance, looking regal in her morning caftan, bringing a plate of fruit outside. Sure enough, she settled herself as close as possible to Nick and began to supply him with goods. Her attentions and monopolizing of him were not just for last night, but apparently for his whole stay.

The party had had its interesting moments but, for the most part, had wearied Emerald. She wondered at Kay's fresh looks and spirits so soon after it. When the soiree had ended, scarcely six hours ago, Emerald had mounted the stairs and gained her little third story nest and looked forward to sleep. Alas, when finally shedding her glamour for her favorite cotton pajamas, she was still so tightly wound up that her eyes would not close.

She could not think about Julian's kiss without thrill upon thrill.

She replayed the scene in her mind countless times. He was so tall, and so near her at that moment; so tender – devastatingly tender. And to whisper to her of her beauty, after a long night of being painfully dressed up, with no compliments from anyone, even from her own date.

It occurred to her that Julian was really the only person she could have unguarded conversations with. She could really be herself with him. She didn't have to be afraid of what he thought of her, when she got mad or irritable; in fact it made him smile when that happened. She could ramble, cry, or pout, and he never thought her unreasonable. At Ashmont she seemed to be watched for such behavior, and then accused of being offended, to be blamed for not being predictable.

Julian did not leave her thoughts at all that day. She seemed immersed in him, his voice, his manner. She felt safe in such indulgences because she knew him to be gone right now: he had left early this morning to fly back home to New Zealand for three weeks. She had overheard him telling someone last night.

As for Danny, she was embarrassed to pieces that people might actually think they were a couple! She remembered the glances of interest and approval that had been cast toward them. Even worse, the photographer Kay had hired captured a shot of them during the few minutes they were actually standing together, and Syb had posted it on several social media sites already. A false illusion of them splashed to the world. She would have to undo this tangle by distancing herself from him, as fast as she could.

Outside of her job and orchestra practice, avoidance of him was pretty easy to accomplish. He wasn't often in the house. If they did meet indoors or out, she did not make eye contact with him, and he didn't seem to have any reason to speak to her.

She almost skipped the next rehearsal because of it; but it was the last one before the big concert. Anyway, she didn't want to be a coward. So she went about it in a businesslike manner. No one would have ever known they had been on a "date." It was good that the awkward experiment of romance was over; it got it out of the way; now they were inoculated against such a condition occurring again between them.

But tonight he seemed to have some sort of axe to grind. Nothing they played sounded good to him, and it was frustrating to be stopped after only a few moments, over and over again. The song they were doing now seemed a hopeless case.

Measure by measure Danny dissected it, making everyone play their parts alone, slowly, then adding instruments one by one; until the song itself was totally devoid of meaning. Each section of horns played what was before them, repeatedly and slowly, to the point of slicing every note apart and laid bare to his critical ear. While the trumpets were in surgery, a frustrated sigh was heard just behind Emerald. She turned around sideways in her seat to look at the tuba player.

"I've got to be at work at nine," he groaned quietly. Phillip was a tall, burly young man with thick hair and a deep voice. His instrument suited his dimensions exactly. He shifted it on his lap and rolled his eyes. "When is he gonna let us outta here? Last time I was late my boss didn't believe me. 'Orchestra rehearsal. Yeah right,'" he imitated, making her laugh.

Emerald shook her head in commiseration. "Why is he so severe tonight? Are his nerves getting to him? You've played in his concerts before, haven't you?"

"Yeah, it's always like this right before a performance, but I've never seen him so wound up as he is now."

Danny was whacking the baton against his metal stand, adjusting his glasses, having trouble finding the right place on the score. Emerald wondered why he still hadn't gone to the eye doctor for a new pair. Now he was straining to look at the flutist's music, scribbling something on it, and having her do her solo again and again. More vibrato here, less strength there; this measure was falling flat, that part didn't crescendo enough. Emerald felt for the poor lady who had to carry it alone, under such scrutiny.

After another half hour, they were released at last. Emerald rapidly packed away her oboe and hurried to her car; she didn't want to bump into him as they left, as sometimes happened. With a sigh of relief she drove off, thankful that no one seemed to view them as a dating couple, most of all, Danny himself. They could now go back to the way it was before – whatever that was.

She beat him home and slipped upstairs without wanting anyone to notice. She didn't even want to be with Dad, since Kay was likely still at his elbow being charming. Sure enough, the sounds she heard in the front room confirmed the ringing voices of her aunts, high in entertainment, and she was glad she was able to escape them just in time.

But Dad, instead of being held captive below, was up on the third floor, looking around. "Why did they put you way up here?" he demanded. "You mean you have to climb those stairs every night? I passed at least six rooms that you could have had, on the way up here."

His daughter was surprised that he found fault with it; she had loved her little nook from the first night she was there. It made her feel – out of everyone's reach. Dad looked around and shook his head at the cracked ceiling and the faded wallpaper. "No wonder she doesn't charge you anything. This might as well be servant's quarters."

Emerald suddenly thought of the many hours she had spent weeding through the wilderness of Kay's hoard. A servant. Yes, Dad was right. If he only knew the innumerable afternoons of "helping" poor Kay from floundering in her sea of possessions and trash. Something in Emerald snapped into place with this realization.

"Dad, tell me about Mother. And how Kay got you to come here. Sometimes Aunt Kay – well, she goes overboard with certain ideas –"

He chuckled. "You don't have to tell me that! Remember, I grew up knowing her pretty well. She can get manipulative. Some women like to feel they have power over others. Take it in your stride. And don't worry about Mom; Brenda is with her, and anyway I think I was getting on her nerves. She was actually glad to see me go."

35

THE VIOLIN

Dad's suitcase was sitting by the front door and Emerald was relieved. She was anxious for him to be out of this vortex of a house, where everything seemed to revolve around a mysterious nucleus of which Emerald was still trying to figure out.

She had to hunt him down just to tell him goodbye, but at last she found him sitting in the library. The aunts had descended upon him there, during his last chat (and a cigar – don't tell Mother, he warned her with a glance) with Mr. Saxon. She joined him quietly on the sofa, absorbing the pleasing aroma of leather and tobacco, but wincing at the flowery presence of Kay's expensive perfume, so out of place here.

Before Emerald knew it, Kay was modeling some new shoes for Dad, demanding his opinion, and Nora was spreading something to eat on the credenza so they could "lunch early – to keep Nick on schedule." To keep Nick on schedule would mean he would need to leave within ten minutes, which they were obviously trying to avoid at all costs. What did they want from him, so desperately? Maybe Dad didn't see the desperation – he was happily accepting a plate from Nora – but Emerald was about to burst with indignation at such a scene. When Kay asked her to be a darling and run upstairs to get the other pair of shoes to show him, she knew she had to escape.

"Actually, I have to go. I have to go – practice my music. I was just about to get my oboe and leave. Danny wants me right away. Bye, Dad," she said, with a hasty hug and avoiding eye contact with her aunts.

His rental car was parked in the half-circle drive, so she depended on that as proof that he would soon be gone.

Danny really had sent her a text that he needed to talk to her about the concert. At first her heart had fallen, knowing that her limited skills were unsatisfactory to his high level of performance, and that he was probably going to ask her to bow out. Either that, or make her practice an extra two hours today! In any case, she was so enveloped in her concern for Dad, it faded in importance and she was just glad to get out of the big house.

As soon as she saw music in Danny's hand, she knew she was in for a rigorous practice. She resigned herself to it, moving some stuff out of a chair and getting her horn ready. But he had a surprise for her.

"You're going to have to play the solo for the concert."

"What?"

"Joyce broke her arm last night. There's no way she can play her flute now."

"Are you kidding me?"

"I brought the music for you. Let's start . . ."

"What about the clarinet, won't that work for a solo? I can't do it! I mean, really, I don't think I'm up to par on your standards, Danny."

"You'll do fine. I promise. Ethan squeaks when he's under pressure."

"So do I."

But he was clothes-pinning her music to a lampshade and rolling up his sleeves, so she sighed and complied. As daunting as this situation was, though, it actually helped her tense nerves by giving them another outlet besides enduring the doings of Kay.

She practiced. Her mouth and fingers became sore, and she still hadn't shaken the headache from last night. Danny paced back and forth as he directed, causing her to have to turn to keep him in her line of vision.

It was an awkward way to play, but it served a purpose: it gave her a chance to see if Dad's car was still in front of the mansion or not.

"No, no, no!" insisted Danny, stopping her for the third time. "There's something wrong there. F sharp, remember?"

"F natural," she insisted back. "It says it right here." She pointed to the sheet of music dangling from the shade. Danny stared at the paper and then turned away, still with a vexed look. "Well then, make it a sharp. Here's a pencil," he barked, nearly stabbing her hand with it.

She smirked in spite of this rough treatment. He couldn't scare her. If they were with twenty other people she would have crimsoned and stayed quiet; but when alone with him, something strong in her shot to the surface and met his challenge with equanimity. It happened so naturally, and gave her pleasure; as well as to himself, she thought she detected. He seemed to appreciate the douse of cooling aplomb on his intense moods from time to time. Nora's flutterings about him were maddening, and Sybilla turned him utterly perplexed, then indifferent. Emerald had observed him – when with the orchestra – mostly nettled, at either the limping performance or something in his own head; it was hard to tell.

"And who do you keep looking for out there?" he demanded. "Your foreign boyfriend?"

"He doesn't come back till next week," she returned, not correcting the boyfriend part. "Look, I'm doing the best I can with this. But the way you're pacing, and so antsy, it's making me nervous."

He didn't answer, but did stop his pacing. She played from the beginning again, and he stopped her at the usual place. Then, walking to his desk and opening a case, he took out a violin and bow. She stared at him with wide eyes. Danny played an instrument? He adjusted the strings tenderly, then positioning the bow on them, proceeded to play her solo part.

The violin! She had no idea he could play it. She forgot all about her headache while he played; she just sat, gazing, with her heart swelling with his song. How masterful it sounded under his touch! And it was all from memory; not once did he look at the sheet music. She was drawn in, forgetting Dad, forgetting the Keckleys, and that she was sitting in Danny's apartment. The notes wound around her senses and carried her thoughts far off – the same feeling she got, sometimes, when wandering the lawn overlooking the Millcrest valley.

This was it! This was the music she'd been hearing randomly outside, ever since she'd arrived. She stared at Danny, processing this realization. The soulful melody was completed now, and he was cleaning a smudge off the instrument. The only thing he said was, after a moment, "Maybe it is supposed to be an F natural after all."

Suddenly shy, and not knowing what else to say, she said, "Well, I'm too hungry to practice anymore."

He rummaged around in his mini-fridge for a long time, then looked through the cabinets, and at last procured a repast. "Here, let's have some lunch," he invited, placing it on the table. She bit her lip to keep from smiling at what he apparently considered a sufficient meal: tuna and crackers, canned fruit cocktail, and a bag of pork skins. After washing his only two plates, they ate.

"Thanks, I appreciate this, Danny," she said. "It's cold in here – do you have a jacket or something?" He brought her one, along with a box of tissues. "Your nose is running," he commented.

She sat wrapped in his jacket, but still shivering. There was a black stove in the corner of the room; he lit it for her and she moved closer to it.

"How long have you played the violin, Danny? I had no idea."

"To be honest, I'm not sure. Somebody gave one to me when I was two or three, so they tell me."

"You never had lessons?"

He half munched on a pork skin, half chuckled. "No. No lessons."

"That's amazing, that you taught yourself. It's really beautiful."

They were quiet a while; she thought he must be thinking of something else, but found his thoughts were still on the music. "I found it was the only way I could cope with – with everything. It was like the only language I could speak, and be understood."

She thought of the times she'd heard his music outside, and agreed with him silently on his description. It was like a voice within another realm, calling out to be heard by another with ears to hear it. Not just notes made by strings and wood, but another language altogether. That's exactly how her paintings were, to her. The strokes made by her brush were so much more than colored liquid on canvas. They were her soul's voice.

As she listened to the popping embers, her thoughts went again to Mother, then to Dad. He would be gone by now, surely, she thought.

"How long is your father staying?" asked Danny. "I thought he was leaving today." She saw that he was looking out the window.

She went to the window too. "Why are they keeping him here?!" she cried, and tears now stinging her eyes. Danny was now looking surprised at her outburst, and thoughtfully turning his gaze from her to the mansion.

"You really think they're doing that?" He only asked the question by way of assistance to her, but she took it as sarcasm, and she grabbed her stuff to go.

Walking into the big house, she found her aunts busily preparing dinner. "Oh, your father is staying one more night with us, aren't you glad?" asked Nora when Emerald appeared in the kitchen doorway.

"But — but my mother was expecting him home today!" Her voice cracked.

"Darling, now dearest Emerald, don't you worry about a thing," said Kay, with that disarming action of slipping her arm around her niece's waist — which she now recoiled at. "He'll leave first thing in the morning. He told us he would. Oh, my, you're burning up, dear. Have you caught a cold?"

36

ILLNESS

"**D**ad, what in the world are you doing?!"

Emerald found him in the Vienna Room, the next morning, disemboweling the broken grandfather clock and examining some pieces in his hand.

"Just fixing the clock. You know I can't resist a challenge of this sort. Neither can my helper here, you see; he brought his workshop to me when I couldn't move this ancient monster to his place." He nodded toward Danny, who was getting out some tools and was preparing to assist in the surgery. "This thing hasn't worked since the 1980s, Kay said. Now that she's fixed this room up so nice, she wants to show it off. I told her what a great idea it was to uncover those windows. Don't you think?"

"But you could be home by now . . ."

But Dad didn't hear her, as he was now deep inside the clock tower and mumbling something about all the dust. He re-emerged, at last, with a sputter or two. "No wonder Saxon never went near this thing. He said it was because it was so noisy that everybody was glad it was broken, but it's really because he doesn't care for spiders any more than Kay or Nora." He brushed a cobweb from his shoulder.

"Tiger, what's under you?" said Emerald, seeing the cat lying on bits of metal pieces that were scattered on the carpet nearby. She pushed him out of the way and ran her hand over the odds and ends, wondering how Dad was going to replace all these parts, when she realized a small, flat box was among them. Was this one of the hidden jewels? Didn't Mother mention in her teenage note, that a clock was one of the secret places?

She opened it and smiled. Yes, here was a necklace and earring set with mint-blue stones in silver settings. But there was something else: a folded piece of paper – another note. This time it was from Kay to Mother. The handwriting looked much the same as Kay's did today. It was dated twenty-five years ago.

> To my 'cousin'. I will tell you a secret. I am in love with him. I know we will be one, someday. And when we have a baby girl, I will name her Emerald Ann.

Emerald sank down in a nearby chair, reading this over and over. After a while, since Dad and Danny were still busy fixing that stupid clock, she left the room. She had the jewelry box and note in her pocket, knowing no one would notice they were gone.

Kay met Emerald in the hall. A look of victory was on Kay's face, since she had been so successful in keeping Dad here. Emerald's irritation increased twofold and she turned to walk away.

But Kay exclaimed about how ill Emerald looked.

"How feverish you feel! And your color isn't good. Now, you need to go to bed, dearest Emerald. Nora will bring you a tray. Here, I want you to take this – it will do wonders." She shook pills from an unlabeled bottle and put them in the girl's hand. "They will help you rest. That's right, gulp them down, this juice is good for you too. Why don't you take a warm bath?"

Emerald broke away from her, not trusting the emotions that were rising to the surface and ready to flow hot from her tongue. She fled to another part of the house and tried to think. This house. . . this house seemed to be swallowing her up, and now her father too. But he didn't seem to mind, or perhaps – he was blind to it. Kay's maneuverings were so subtle yet effectual that it was no wonder Nick didn't recognize them. Kay was trying to bind her and Nick to her side; and was succeeding.

She wandered the recesses of the house; pacing helped to settle her nerves. But the medicine was taking hold and dulling her thoughts.

She checked on Dad one more time, with the hope that he was leaving tonight after all. However, she had to relinquish any thought of the kind. The women were setting up a room for card-playing.

"Nora, let's use the padded chairs. And make sure Saxon is your partner. Nick will want to play across me, like we did years ago. I know how to watch him for all his tricks," she said, and both ladies laughed. Emerald slipped upstairs without saying goodnight.

She reached her room with leaden legs but didn't even make it to her bed. She sank down into a chair in the corner, and was out cold.

She awoke in complete darkness. Her body was stiff from being curled up in the chair for so long. What was this rough blanket around her? She didn't recognize it. After a moment or two, she realized she was still wearing Danny's jacket from her practice session.

Totally disoriented in the dark, she had no idea what part of the night it was, or if she had just gone blind, or what. But she heard distant voices from down on the terrace, so after a minute she stumbled to the window and looked down.

Was she dreaming? Was she watching a movie? What was this enchanted scene she was looking at, far below?

She beheld a scene in the courtyard. A table, dripping with linen, was covered with candles and china. A bowl of flowers – big, heavy peonies – sat in the middle, anchoring it. Music was playing; they had moved the phonograph outside, and Emerald felt a little violated. She thought she was the only one who appreciated that relic, and did not want to see it moved from its place. But the voice of Sinatra was on, and made the whole scene seem airborne, from another realm.

There were people. Her head swam as she tried to focus on them in the dim light. Ladies and gentlemen. Her dad was among them. Nora, Kay. Kay was dressed in all black. It seemed odd that she would wear that color – it did not blend with the ethereal appearance of the courtyard. But after a moment Emerald knew why, because she could not take her eyes off her. The contrast was irresistible, and thus she made herself the centerpiece.

She shivered. *I have to go to bed, I'm so tired.* The courtyard began to look like an amusement park. Floating, spinning like one. With watery eyes she tried to focus on their faces and exactly who was there. A few, she had never seen before. Was that Lars Franklin? Yes, his looks were distinguished among the other men, with his dark skin and glowing teeth, now apparent in a laugh.

Two people were separated from the others, walking along the herringbone path. They held hands. She easily could tell the lady was Kay, in her gown of velvet midnight. But who was the gentleman? He was rather short and walked pigeon-toed. It looked like – it looked like Dad. Emerald's eyes held them in an iron gaze. What were they doing? It looked as if – it appeared as if Kay and Dad were – *embracing.*

Nick left early the next morning, but his daughter did not know it.

Someone told him Emerald wanted to sleep in today, and did not want to be disturbed. Someone forgot to mention that she had been ill; so he left Ashmont with the satisfaction of believing her in comfortable rest and well-taken care of by her hostesses. Since Nick Johnsey would have noticed if she were missing a screw in her eyeglasses, but not if she looked pale or run-down, or had a runny nose, he returned home with only good reports of her happiness and well-being.

But Emerald lay in bed up on the third story all day, and no one knew that she was so sick she couldn't stand up. A fever raged in her body and she needed water, but could only get a little out of her bathroom faucet. She could not find her phone and did not have strength to go searching.

At four o'clock a visitor mounted Ashmont's steps between the stone dragons and rang the doorbell. It was Blanche Sylvester.

"I didn't know what happened to Emerald Johnsey – she didn't show up for work this afternoon. Is she alright? I tried to call her but no one answered."

Within a few minutes a group of concerned ladies – led by Nora and Blanche – bustled up to the attic room and opened the door. There sat Emerald in the corner, barefoot, with her head on her knees; pale and quivering.

"Do we need to call a doctor?" cried Blanche, as Kay got her in bed and Nora brought socks.

"What time is it? I'm so thirsty. . . "

"Now, now, we won't call any doctors if you don't want us to," cooed Kay. "Nora, bring her some soup and toast. Poor darling, she's clammy – but at least the fever must have broken."

Emerald really felt better within a short time, and in fact felt absolutely beloved by the group now hovering over her and bringing her things. Blanche offered to stay the evening hours with her.

"I have my Sudoku with me, so I'll just sit here and work," she told the girl. Nora brought a tray of food, and Kay covered her with the softest of blankets. Emerald wanted to ask Kay about the note from the clock, but just then the dry toast filled her mouth and she could not speak before Kay disappeared.

When all was quiet, and she and Blanche were alone, Emerald asked her questions about the day.

"Was it a good afternoon at the store?"

"Oh, a normal enough Thursday. We had spent a few weeks in the mid-sixties but decided to go back a few years. That was my favorite time, the fifties. We picked 'Singin' in the Rain.'"

Emerald smiled when she saw the drift of Blanche's thoughts. "What I meant was – did you have a lot of customers? I hope it wasn't too busy for y'all to handle alone."

"Ah! No, not that many. Mr. Gunn still has skunks. He's tried everything we've got, though. I told him to go to the market and get garlic bulbs."

After a silence, during which nothing was heard except Blanche's pencil marks and the frequent squeak of an eraser, the topic of Kay's big dinner party came up.

"It was the talk of the town for days afterward," Blanche said. "There was a big feature in the paper about it."

"Yes, I know. I always meant to ask you – someone mentioned to me that night, that you and Mr. Sylvester were once on the board of something, here?"

"Trustees. Yes. Do you think this four is in the right place?"

"So you must know a lot about the house, the Keckleys, and – everything."

"Yes, I suppose so."

"Do you know much about Louise McSee? And why she was hired here?"

"Yes," was her only answer. But after a moment, she added, "It was a good thing she took the job. No one else would have done it."

"Tell me what you mean. How was she so important here?"

Blanche's face clouded a little, but she answered her with, "Kay Keckley has a – problem. Louise is the only one they've ever found, who can keep it in control. Without Louise, Kay would have succumbed again, and Ashmont would have – " She did not finish the sentence, but only shook her head. "Especially since the Keckleys have no other relatives to step in."

She had said the phrase while looking down, focusing on her puzzle. But was it just an unthinking remark? Didn't she remember that right here in this room was a relative? Emerald decided to prod gently at this comment to see if it would correct itself.

"Are you sure? No cousins, aunts or uncles? Nieces?"

"Oh, I'm positive! There, I think I've got this whole block done. I'm going to learn this game yet." Her glasses were balanced on the very tip of her nose until Emerald thought they would fall right off.

"Back to the Keckleys. Yes, we knew their family from the time their grandfather was hired to take care of the house and grounds. He married a sweet country girl, the old lady who is still alive and kicking. They had had no siblings, though. When Kay and Nora grew up, they had plenty of society friends, but no cousins to romp with. I always thought what a shame. A few rowdy cousins would have leveled out some of that uppity-ness that crept in from time to time." She kept her voice low. The glasses held on without falling.

Emerald stared at the cracks in the ceiling, trying to process what was just said. Why then, had she grown up believing she was the niece of the Keckleys?

She searched her memory, weakly, for evidence to the contrary. It's true that Mother and Dad had always called them Aunts Kay and Nora. And even Cousin Sybilla. But where was the proof?

Her family's connection with the Keckleys had always been murky. She remembered explaining to others where she imagined the bloodlines fell, that Dad was their cousin, but in vain she ransacked her memory for that account actually coming from her parents' mouths.

And the note from the clock: Kay wanted to name her daughter Emerald Ann.

Her lack of siblings had always nibbled at Emerald; she had never heard any explanation from her parents as to why they had no other children.

She thought of the many times Sybilla had called her "cousin," as if she knew more about the matter than herself. Emerald bore no physical resemblance to Kay or Nora. She did, however, have several of the same traits as Mother Ann. Sometimes the old lady made observations that Emerald could have spoken, herself. The most striking thing was that they both preferred simplicity over splendor. Emerald thought of the times Mother Ann would place daisies in mugs or soda bottles, and set them about the house; but that later would be whisked away and replaced with elaborate bouquets.

Her thoughts fell silent for a moment, then they crept a little further.

Was it possible that Kay gave birth to her, then Mother and Dad adopted her?

Blanche was using the squeaky eraser again, and Emerald thought grimly – that someone was using an eraser on *her*, and wiping out a central portion of her identity.

37

DANNY

Danny stood on his balcony, coffee in hand, not caring that the quick falling rain was occasionally dripping off the eaves and making little splashes into his mug. Being outside on an ugly day, with clouds of charcoal threatening angrier, fiercer things to come, suited his mood. He was brimming with frustration and wanted to punch something, or fire a rifle, or shove something off a cliff. What would those gentle ladies in the big house say to thoughts such as these, if they knew? Nora especially was always accusing him of having nothing but innocent intentions and the purest thoughts. But she wasn't here, and so he felt free to think them without alarming anyone.

For the last several years, his life had been grindingly coming to a dead end. Not a single cherished dream had materialized; in fact each one seemed to be unraveling before his eyes.

He had envisioned himself, by this time – age 32 – an established engineer, or maybe an architect, or some type of civil planning authority. Instead he wasn't much more than an errand boy who still didn't have his own home.

He was excellent with his hands and learned all kinds of trade work in his spare time. Automotive, electrical, woodworking, plumbing: he had a knack for learning how something worked just by looking at it, almost; and he relished whatever tasks came his way. In his early twenties he figured the blue-collar life was best suited for him, as his father before him, and relinquished the burden of college he couldn't afford anyway. But with passing years he began to hunger for higher things, bigger projects, and a larger salary.

He took a few classes at Finley, working his way through slowly, alongside much younger athletes, intellectuals, and Greeks. In the meantime he took on the job of hired hand at Ashmont Hall, fitting in his studies as best he could, and being grateful that his room and board were included. In his garage shop he listened to the local classical radio station, and in between chores would play his violin. Those moments gave him the expressive outlet that was so soothing to him.

But his collegiate progress was painfully slow. He was still helping his dad pay off some family debts, and could only afford to take a college course every now and again.

About a year ago, Nora Keckley had come home from church, spinning gravel and parking below his apartment with her signature screech of a tire. With her purse still on her arm, she knocked on his door and blurted out some exciting news that she knew was meant for him to hear. The church needed a music director. A paying job.

He almost laughed outright.

"Now, don't tell me you can't do it, Danny. I know how talented your mother was, and you learned so much from her. She held her own among the big names down at that college, teaching classes and taking over when the Millcrest symphony needed a director. She didn't have a chance to do it for long, bless her soul, but she fired up the critics plenty in her heyday."

That was true. His mother, for many years, had supplemented the family income by giving music lessons, and ended up blazing a men-only trail later in life when her talents became more widely known. Growing up, Danny's older brother had picked up some piano knowledge, and he himself the violin, but the two boys were more often needed in their dad's busy repair shop where they had the most hope of future security for themselves.

But Danny had started young enough for music to take a deep root in his soul. He remembered his first faltering notes, and the thrill of improving them, then weaving them together into songs, long before any boyhood memories of fishing or exploring. He would occasionally go to the college with his mother while she worked, and humor his curiosity by playing around on any available instruments or watching any rehearsals that might be going on.

He would imagine himself in the place of the director – that place of honor and esteem, with the sea of glimmering horns beneath him. Having the whole orchestra's power within scope of his two hands, felt like the time he held a half-grown eaglet that he'd found in the woods. The movement, the struggle, the striving for release, the aspects both delicate and full of strength – weakness and power blending together in one entity – was exhilarating to him.

But he had only been a child then, and never really had any formal training. What if he didn't need training for this job? Would anyone be able to tell?

He decided to apply. The day he was interviewed, he had on an outdated suit, shiny shoes, and well behaved hair, but he appeared before the church board with everything but what he needed most. He had no resume.

He remembered the looks on their faces; the half smiles with a touch of pity. Foolishly he had brought his violin with him, packed in its tattered case, which he nudged under his chair while he spoke with them. It was never opened that day. He answered their questions, and then got out as fast as he could. Then he drove back to Ashmont to his part-chauffeur, part-handyman position, appreciating at least the reclusiveness of it.

To his great surprise, after a month, the church called him back. They wanted to know if he was still interested. He would direct all the music and he was to begin the next Sunday. The fact was, that no one else had applied for the job, and they needed it filled right away.

He stepped into this role with shy joy, being surprised they would hire him, but even more so at the new-found exhilaration in being entrusted with it. He was just like those symphony directors he admired from afar. Well, sort of.

Because, added to the embarrassment of having almost zero formal training, there was a deeper one that was becoming harder and harder to hide. He could not even read music.

He had tried, again and again. Something gripped him with strangling anxiety when staring at the pages of printed notes. The ink on the paper, the tiny symbols and sticks and dots, were like death by a thousand cuts to him! This was not music. Music was flight and excitement, a naturally-flowing river of living expression. The black marks on the page were as restrictive as the bars of a cell.

He never could bring himself to admit this to anyone. Therefore he faked it, and stared at his orchestra scores with glazed eyes and rising blood pressure. He memorized everything by listening to the recordings. So far, though, it worked. The little choir of gray-haired people followed right along, noticing nothing amiss. The orchestra was made up of college students and they were more keen, however. He knew they whispered about him sometimes.

For example, Emerald Johnsey had often glanced at him with a look of concern. She could tell he was pretending to read the music. Why had he insisted she join the orchestra? Her clear eyes had sometimes settled on him, unnerving him, and he regretted exposing his ignorance before her. Maybe that was just his ego bristling; she added a sophisticated sound to the group, so he swallowed what he could of his pride and acquiesced to the situation.

When he heard Joyce had broken her arm and could not play the solo, his heart gave a lurch of gratitude. What luck, this chance to exchange a poor performer for a skilled one! Joyce's airy sound and flat notes had grated on him to the point beyond irritability; and he quietly rejoiced that Emerald's superior performance would be the crown of the concert.

But Emerald had problems. For one thing, she was sick. He had overheard Nora telling Saxon about it – that she almost had to go to the hospital and was still not out of the woods yet. But there was something else. Danny thought of the times she had seemed gripped with an inner unrest. And her claims that the women were manipulating her and her father: he began to realize those were more than just bursts of emotion or suspicious jealousy. So, he watched them himself.

He had thought it odd one day, right after Emerald first moved in, that Kay Keckley had taken down a photograph from the wall and told her sister to hide it. He saw the entire scene – they didn't know he was watching them from behind his newspaper. Kay had made sure the girl was upstairs, then said something about "she still thinks Nick and I are cousins! Oh, if she only knew. We'd better hide this, Nora."

Emerald's outbursts only validated what he himself had seen: the little tricks and performances they would manufacture, to achieve their desired results. Using her to get something they – Kay, rather – wanted. What was that thing?

To walk off his perplexities, he went to the big house in search of Saxon. He wanted to ask his opinion about a carburetor for his truck, anyway. Walking in through the kitchen, he was reluctantly soothed by a smell of something cooking on the stovetop. He almost passed it by, but decided to just look and see what it was – it was coming from that big humming pot. He lifted the lid; it was soup, homemade chicken soup with noodles? No, rice. It smelled good. But who was cooking it, since the women of the house were gone, and Louise had the day off? Old Fred Saxon, cooking lunch? He doubted it. But there was no one else here.

The steam from the soup had fogged his glasses up, so he took them off, wiping them with his shirt, as he walked through the house glancing in the rooms – all empty. Wasn't that music he was hearing, though? He saw a light coming from the library. Saxon was in there, then, indulging in solitude and a smoke. He walked toward it.

"Hey, since when did you become a chef?" asked Danny, standing in the room's doorway. But no fragrant tobacco greeted him there, no stodgy form filling the fireside chair. Where the heck was he? Danny cast a glance around the room and turned away – and then back again, this time replacing his glasses.

The liquefied sounds of Chopin mingled with the rain outside, dripping notes as fast as the pattering rain. The sounds of rain, and fire, and music, blended together and wound around his senses, drawing him back into the room. It was magic, audible magic, and he was paralyzed by it as he glanced around the room; he almost overlooked her.

Emerald was supine in the window seat, wearing flannel

pajamas, with tissues in each hand – and fast asleep. Her nose was red; she had a cold. She shivered. Quietly he took a throw blanket from the sofa and spread it over her, and placed a pillow next to the cold window glass to preserve her warmth. Then he remained there, gazing at her.

From nowhere, a gush of compassion welled in him as he looked down at her. She could have been a little child, the way she was curled up, hands clasped together. How vulnerable she seemed. He thought of Kay and Sybilla, and how they used her, ran her ragged. They had her on a never-ending treadmill of fulfilling their own wishes. He suddenly remembered and realized her weariness of the last few weeks, her concern for her mother, and anxiety for her Dad staying here too long. Add the stress of the concert to that: no wonder she was sick. She snored a little, and he smiled.

38

EVENING QUEST

Emerald was weak for a few more days, but gradually felt well enough to resume her classes and work; she was glad to get out of the house. Just a few more weeks, and she could go home for good.

She had decided to end her studies at Finley after this semester. There was no other way to disentangle herself from the feminine whirlwind that she lived in, here at Ashmont; though she hated to leave such an intriguing house and grounds. The thrilling mystery, when she first arrived, had turned to something twisted, and she was sinking into it like sucking mud. Questions that could never get answered, puzzles that were never solved, like Nora's partly finished thousand-piece that was spread out in the Vienna Room right now.

She practiced her solo and gave Danny her best, though she doubted his opinion of her skills. Knowing she was Plan B, she saw that his standards had been necessarily lowered, and she wanted to disappoint him as little as possible. But gone was the joy of playing; now she was just trying to get through it.

In the midst of everything, Emerald's oasis of pleasure was thinking of Julian's return. She had had three weeks to decipher what she felt for him, three weeks to interpret his kiss: as a transient bubble of pleasure? Or something deeper?

Knowing him was cotton-candy sweet. By the same token she wondered, reluctantly, if there could be any substance under it. But the very fact that he talked with her, considered her feelings by letting her speak her mind, went a long way with Emerald in a house where everything must be pre-approved before being verbalized.

She wondered what he was doing in New Zealand, whom he was seeing. His absence created an eagerness in her that the most attentive behavior, on his part, could never have. He would be back in two more days.

Tonight was the very last rehearsal before the concert. She had not even had a chance to play the solo with the rest of the group. Since she was closing at Military Surplus, she told Danny she would be a little late, and he barely even acknowledged that as a reason! She would have to go through a drive-thru for a bite to eat, then go straight to the church.

At six o'clock she grabbed her stuff and locked the heavy door behind her. Getting into her car, she was startled to see a vehicle rapidly pull into the spot next to hers. It was a golf cart, of all things. Inside, Julian was behind the wheel, sporting a summer outfit and loafers with no socks. He must have just arrived in the States wearing hot-weather clothes of his native land.

"Hey! Like my new ride? Come on, let me take ya for a spin," he grinned charmingly.

Emerald laughed at him. "What are you doing in that thing? They're not allowed on the road, are they?"

"As usual, you're right," he said. "Which is why you need to hurry and get in. The longer I sit here persuading you, the bigger chance I have of getting caught."

"But I'm already in a hurry. I have to get a quick dinner – "

"Let me treat ya! Let's go down the road to that new taco place. I've missed American food."

She was going to resist but a police car was seen around the corner, and he hollered for her to jump in. Oh well, it would take about the same amount of time as her first plan anyway. She got in, and they zoomed away.

Shyly taking note of his bare, tan knees, she scolded him for dressing so lightly. "It's near freezing tonight! Aren't you cold?"

"Ah, it feels good compared to the heat wave I've come from! I had a chance to take an earlier flight, so I threw my stuff in a bag and jumped on it. Don't worry about me. Say, aren't you looking a little thin? You haven't been pining for me, have ya?" And he winked.

"I've been sick, and I didn't eat much for a few days," she admitted. "Which is why I'm so hungry tonight. Look, there's the place, let's pull in there. By the way, why are you driving this thing?"

"Just borrowing it from my old job at the golf course. They don't mind. My car had a flat tire, and lucky I thought of getting this so I could run up and see you before you left work."

But to her dismay, the new taco joint was overrun with customers. Long lines filled the place and Emerald gazed with despair at the decadent-looking photos plastered all over the windows. She didn't have time to wait.

"Julian, I have to hurry. I have to get to my practice. Danny's gonna be really mad at me."

"No worries, just sit tight – I know where to go. Not far, I promise." And he sped out into traffic, weaving in and out between cars. "Good ole American barbecue, that's for us tonight. See the smoke ahead? Hot and ready for us. Won't have to wait at all."

But when the cart started puttering and slowing down, Emerald's anxiety returned.

"Ah! She's running short on power!" grunted Julian, pumping the pedal with telltale results: the cart came to a decided stop. "I must've run her too long." They barely made it to the restaurant parking lot, but since they were there, Emerald was relieved to at least be able to eat.

They stood in line at the counter, salivating over the smells of pork and chicken. "How are we going to get back to my car, Julian?" She asked, while not taking her eyes off a platter of corn on the cob.

"I'll go get it for you. I can run the distance in no time. Give me your keys and I'll be back in a flash." She was grateful for this solution, and off he flew, with his white loafers looking like wings on his feet.

But after placing her order and hearing the amount owed, an icy feeling seeped over her when she realized she had no way to pay! Her wristlet and phone case were attached to her keys and they were racing down Main Street right now in the hands of her "rescuer."

"Oh!" She groaned. Other customers were waiting at her elbow and she had no choice – she had to relinquish her place in line to them while she waited for Julian's return.

She sat at a naked table, kicking the leg in frustration, watching the wall clock as the minutes marched on. There was no way she would make it to rehearsal, even half of it. Where was he?! He'd had plenty of time to get back by now.

At last she saw her car lights and heard the familiar horn. Her hope for his delay was that he bought them something else to eat. She no longer cared what it was.

But no, he said he had "met a friend" on the way, and had chatted for not more than a few seconds, he swore, with him; and that he had gotten a phone call and needed to answer it; but that now they would have a cozy supper together and get to the church in plenty of time. "What did you order for me?" He had the gall to ask.

"Nothing! Zero! You had my money the whole time. And just forget about the rehearsal. I'm way too late. I should have gone right there." Her words felt like razors coming off her tongue, she was so angry, but he wasn't at all affected, and even smothered a laugh.

They went a second time to the counter and placed their orders. She handed a credit card to the employee, but he didn't take it. Instead he pointed to a sign: CASH ONLY. "Our card machine is down," he told her.

Before Emerald had time to vent her utter despair, Julian grabbed her hand and pulled her out of the eatery. She was almost in tears by this time.

"Now, now, don't fret! I have a friend who works at Chez Martine. He told me to put something on his tab anytime I want. Come, get in, don't worry about it," he coaxed.

"Chez Martine?! I'm not dressed well enough to take out their trash. Neither are you. You know they have a dress code." The tears were now streaming down her cheeks, so weak and hungry she was, and livid, at this suave idiot driving her around. He was having a great time. Using a car and gas that didn't belong to him, and no money to procure any dinner for either of them.

What would Danny say to her tomorrow? She would try to come up with a decent explanation, but she dreaded those blank glasses and pained expression. And, no doubt, her performance would suffer, since the concert was tomorrow night and she hadn't practiced in over a week.

They came to the entrance of an elegant façade. *Chez Martine* was painted on the sign above the door, written in script so fancy it was barely legible. They stood there a minute trying to decide what to do.

"I'll just go in and explain the circumstances. They'll understand."

"They'll understand we're a couple of hoboes looking for a handout!"

"A place like this is too civil to damage their reputation. When they know we're students at Finley, they won't turn us away. Just you watch." And he disappeared through the revolving door.

Emerald stood at the restaurant window, longingly eyeing the plush room and glinting dinnerware. She found herself practically pressing her nose against the glass – like a street urchin.

A laden tray carried by a waiter caught her eye, and she followed it as he served a couple dining in the corner. She could barely make out the salt-and-pepper hair of a gentleman, as he was screened by his companion, a lovely woman with blonde hair very similar to Aunt Kay, at least from the back. If she hadn't known Kay to be home entertaining some new boarders, she could have sworn that was her.

Her stomach growled again, and she impatiently turned to the door to see if she could glimpse Julian. She was just debating whether or not she should go in search of him, when she saw him triumphantly striding toward the door, with a successful look on his face.

"You'll never guess. Check it out." And he gestured toward the window she had been peering in for the last fifteen minutes.

"You mean they're going to *feed* us here?" Her faith in Julian and his talent for charming people was instantly restored.

But her clothing, that she could see more clearly under the lobby lights, was worse than she thought. And – tennis shoes! She reached for her hair which was a wild mess. "Oh, I look so – please tell me they're going to let us eat in a back room somewhere."

He took her by the hand and led her straight into the restaurant. Did he already obtain a table for them? Why was he pulling her so fast?

They walked past the hostess stand, through the labyrinth of tables and glancing eyes. "Julian!" she hissed. "I don't think they meant for us to be so visible!"

His destination was a particular table in a cozy corner. But it already had people sitting at it.

In fact, it was the very table she had observed from outside, with the attractive older couple. They were Aunt Kay – and Emerald's father.

39

CRISIS

Emerald's eyes required a moment to process who was before her. She went from Dad's plaid tie, to his graying hair, to his smile; then to Kay's shimmering appearance and that same look of victory she had worn before. Then Emerald looked down at the table. At that moment, Kay reached across to her companion, and clasped his hand.

Apparently, with Mother being ill at home, Kay naturally was trying to resume her place in Nick's life and secure herself some funding in the process. Emerald remembered what Syb had said, that Kay would get her hooks into Lars if she could. That was a dead end, it seems, so she went for the nearest other source within her reach.

Was Kay really that desperate? Could she find no other object of romance than her old beau Nick Johnsey, a married man? Emerald sickened to think of how Kay was probably looking forward to her mother's death, and was priming the pump for herself before such an event even happened.

The girl turned and fled. She didn't know where to go, she just ran. Somehow she ended up in the ladies' room. She wept.

She wept out of confusion and pain. Things began to click into place: what Mrs. Sylvester had revealed to her – about the Keckleys having no other family at all. The possibility that Kay was her birth mother. And just now, when she saw the two holding hands, there was an electrifying thought that they may have had an affair long ago! And was she a result of that affair?

At this thought, Emerald threw up in the sink, and wept all the more.

She felt two hands, a lady's hands, upon her shoulders. She felt a cold wet cloth wiping her forehead. Kay had come to check on her and was now trying to console her. Emerald broke away in disgust.

But when she opened her eyes and blinked them clearer, it was not Kay she beheld. It was a darker lady, wearing a flowered dress and glasses and a look of sympathy. It was – it was Emerald's mother.

Her mother! Her mother was now embracing her. Emerald – too bewildered to figure out how she was here – collapsed into her arms with relief.

"I thought – I thought that Kay and Dad were – were – "

"Were what, sweetheart? That Kay was trying to take him away from me?" Emerald saw that Mother was half-smiling.

"Yes! I did! I've seen the way she has acted around him, hanging on to him, claiming him for herself. It made me sick! How could she do that?" Emerald demanded, and at which Mother just held her tighter.

"You forget that I've known Kay most of my life. I know what she's like. Don't worry about your dad. He knows her too, you know. You should hear how he's been laughing about her behavior – how we both have laughed. Poor dear, I'm so sorry you weren't in on the joke."

"And then when I found out we're not even related to the Keckleys!" Cried Emerald afresh. "Mother, I have been telling everyone I'm their niece, or at least cousin!"

Her mother looked truly sorrowful at this. "I guess we've said 'Aunt Kay and Aunt Nora' so long that you never heard any different! No, sweetie, there is no blood relation. I can't believe I never thought to clarify it to you. And I guess Kay never did, either."

"But Mother – there's something else. Something that I just began to think of tonight. Please don't think I'm crazy. I want you to tell me the truth: you are my real mom, right? You gave birth to me, and you and Dad are both my parents? Right?"

She was wrapped in Mother's arms before the questions had stopped, being reassured of the truth.

"I don't think you're crazy. I'm not laughing," said Mother, although there might have been a tiny twinkle of humor she was hiding in her eye. "Yes, you are our natural child. Don't you remember the picture of me dressed as a pumpkin when I was pregnant with you?"

Emerald laughed through her sobs and kept hanging on to her embrace. Next she told her about the note in the clock.

"I think *I* wrote that note, Emerald! I remember telling her over and over, what I wanted to name a little girl. Although she may have been jealous and copy-catted me; she did that sometimes. We did call each other cousins but that was just make believe. And yes, I knew that she had a tremendous crush on your dad at the time. She has always been a helpless flirt. But no, your dad never fell for her charms. You should ask him about that, yourself."

They went together to the corner table where Nick, Kay, and Julian were seated.

"I was keeping this a surprise for you," Dad said as his daughter sat next to him. "I knew it had been months since you'd seen your mom."

"You poor thing," exclaimed Kay, seeing her red eyes. "Nick, you should have told her! You see she wasn't prepared for such a beautiful sight, Charlotte here, looking so healthy and splendid!" Kay slipped her arm around her mother's waist as she had so often done with Emerald.

"I've been so much better lately, that I just had to come see you," Mother said. "We only decided at lunch today, to make the drive. It took a little help from Kay, and from your friend Julian here, to pull it off." She nodded toward the young man, who grinned, then handed Emerald a hot roll.

"I thought she was gonna bean me! I've never seen her look so mad, when I finally showed up with her pocketbook again. Poor girl was about to faint away from hunger."

Emerald ate her dinner with immense relief, though she was still disconcerted about the whole run-around of earlier. She kept gazing at her mother, who had never looked more lovely, even sitting next to the illustrious Kay Keckley.

Her parents stayed for the weekend. They were able to go to the much-dreaded concert. Emerald sat in the orchestra pit with sweaty palms as the people filed into the church, with a hum of quiet anticipation, and the darkening of lights. She looked at Danny – only when assured he would not meet her glance – and thought he looked well in his gray suit. In her joy in her mother's presence, Emerald had not remembered to explain to him about why she wasn't at the final practice. In the meantime, he knew nothing of her parents being here. He had only heard that Emerald and Julian had gone out for a fancy dinner, and didn't come home till after midnight, according to Sybilla's reliable information.

In an effort to make it up to him, Emerald called to mind all of Danny's careful instructions about the solo: right down to exactly when to take a breath. She did her very best for him. Yet while he directed her, he did not look at her at all. That must be a negative sign. She was crestfallen.

She received her parents' praise afterward, but her satisfaction was diminished in knowing she had disappointed Danny. She glanced around the room in search of him, thinking for sure he would be mingling with the audience and receiving their compliments, but he seemed to have vanished. She had wanted to introduce him to her parents and explain their sudden arrival in town, and thus her missing the final practice.

But out in the parking lot, she spotted him. He was with a very pretty girl, the very Celia that Emerald had almost forgotten about. Something inside Emerald was silenced and humbled at this sight. She had to halt her instinct to rush forward to talk to him; instead she made her way slowly to her car. She heard the sweet tones of Celia's voice carrying across the empty lot, and Danny continued there in conversation with her.

She saw him glance up and take notice, for the first time, that Emerald was about to leave. He broke away from Celia and jogged toward the blue car, trying to catch her before she left. Emerald tarried a bit so he could do so. A sudden shyness washed over her and she was afraid of what he would say. She imagined him telling her "Why didn't you crescendo more during the bridge?" Or "You should have held out that D longer, like I told you to."

But when he actually reached the car, as prepared as she was for reprimands, he caught her off guard by not mentioning the concert at all.

"Was your dad here tonight? I wish I had known, I would have said hello to him."

"Uh – yes. Yes, he was here, and my mother too."

"Your mom? That's great! So she's better? I would have liked to meet her."

Emerald was so surprised at the normally tacit Danny Grosch, inquiring about her parents and wanting to talk to them, that words failed her at the moment. She had to struggle to think of how to respond.

"Yes. Well, thank you. They, uh, they're driving back tonight. But maybe they'll come again."

"That's good." He dawdled at her car door longer, as if trying to come up with something further to talk about.

"I think the concert went well, don't you? Are you glad it's over?" Emerald commented.

He seemed to have to remind himself of what she was talking about. "The concert? Yes, it went fine." It was as if he were describing a routine dental check-up.

She was just working up her courage to ask him what he thought of her performance. Half the words came out – "I hope I did okay…" when Celia's car pulled up next to them.

"Danny, aren't you coming?" Said the sweet voice.

"In a minute," he told her.

An awkward moment ensued with all three silently waiting for – no one knew. It all hinged on Danny. Emerald tried to help him along by returning to her question. "I hope the solo came out okay."

He paused then answered, without looking at her, "beautiful." The word stunned her and she kept looking at him, waiting for more. Finally he said "I'll see you later," and turned away to Celia's car.

40

EMERALD HAS PROOF

After a fitful night's sleep, during which Emerald dreamed of a gray metal lock box filled with sheets of music, carried by a red-haired girl, with Danny following behind in pursuit of her, and the strains of Chopin getting louder and softer the whole time, she wasn't quite ready for the visitor that entered her room at six the next morning.

Through her window.

Sleepy, she had heard a rustling and was turning over to yell at Tiger John to stop messing with the blinds, when in came the leg of a man who had climbed up the outside of the house and was now bodily in her room.

"Are you insane?" cried Emerald, blinking at the figure standing over her. "You can't do that!"

"I knew there was a way up here, so I didn't have to announce myself to the gatekeepers! Sybilla told me she used to do it, and I accepted that as a challenge for myself. She showed me the way up one time. I guess she never thought I'd remember it, though."

"Julian, get out! I'm not dressed!"

"I've been texting you for two hours! Why didn't you answer?" They both looked around but couldn't find her phone. "Oh no," she groaned. "I must have left it in the orchestra pit last night."

"Do you have golf clubs? I got us a couple of passes today."

"I've been sick! And no, I don't have any."

"Ah, well, no worries. Let's go, so we start ahead of the other players. The weather will be especially fine today! Fresh air, sunshine, and a pleasant companion are just what you need to restore your health."

To make him get out, she promised to go to the greens with him but not play. "I'll sit in the cart and watch. No! Not through the door! Are you kidding me? You'll have to leave the same way you came in. If you fall to your death, that's on you."

Ugh, she just wanted to sleep! But knowing further rest wouldn't help, not with those recurring dreams, she got up and threw on some clothes. Being away from Ashmont today would probably help her state of mind, anyway. She wanted to sort out her plans for the next few weeks before school ended.

Julian turned out to be right, partly. Emerald did enjoy the fresh air and sunshine, but the pleasant companion did not do as much to restore her health as he had promised. She sat in the cart and watched him play, admiring his athleticism and handsome profile beneath his visor, but that's where her appreciation ended. Their talks together (which couldn't be called conversation) were indicative of every other interaction with him from that first day. Cotton candy sweet, fluffy, and as satisfying as trying to eat air.

Even his talent at making her laugh had waned, as he was saying the same stuff he had said several times before. And his accent, oh, his accent! What used to enchant her now pained her to hear! She was frankly tired of trying to interpret his words back into something native, so that she could understand him properly. On top of that, the deep tones that formerly gave her butterflies, now sounded so guttural it's as if he was burping repeatedly. She tried to hide her grimaces by squinting in the bright sunshine.

When she finally got home that afternoon, frustrated that she didn't know where her phone was and therefore couldn't hear any news from her parents, she at least felt relieved of the burden of caring anything about Julian. Today did it for her. His charms had come to an end, and she no longer felt obligated to see him as any different than a brother who needed a good scolding sometimes. He had so many admirers that she didn't worry one bit that this turn of feeling would bring about loneliness for him.

Tea for guests was over, but Emerald was just in time to see Kay leading her visitors out to the courtyard, chattering away to them. She liked to watch Kay working her magic from behind a screen of some sort, where she would be unnoticed. Just now there was no one in the laundry room, which had a small window with a peek outside, so she decided to watch from there.

But her foot bumped against something, and it made a clatter. It was that metal lock box she had seen in Kay's room! Covered over by dirty laundry, so as to hide it.

So! *Proof* of Louise's thefts. Emerald wouldn't move it – and Kay was too busy to go and tell her about it. But she could take a picture of it to show Kay later.

But she didn't have her phone!

She joined the rest at the supper table, a little late, but before anyone could ask where she was. The only one missing tonight was Danny, who had to drive some guests into town.

"We'll have a quiet Thanksgiving here next week, just us, apparently," said Kay. "Emerald, will you be going home?"

"No, I'll just stay here. I'm supposed to help the Sylvesters with the store on Friday." She didn't mention that she had arranged with her professors to work ahead so as to finish her classes as early as possible.

"My play opens the week after that," said Sybilla. "You must all come see me in it. I am the antagonist. I'm the selfish, worldly divorcee who gets her own way all the time."

"Where on Earth did you get experience enough to know how to play that?" asked Saxon in an innocent tone.

Louise was placing a hot casserole on the table just now. When she left, Emerald saw her chance to lean over to Kay and mention the box, quietly, as the others were passing food.

Kay heard the revelation with veiled eagerness. Her wide eyes were turned to Emerald as she told her the exact location and how she found it. But she didn't expect what Kay did next: she jumped up from the table, before Louise could reappear, and told the others, "I'll be back in a moment!"

Emerald trembled for this upcoming crisis, this long-awaited exposure of Louise and her crimes. After a while, Kay returned to the table, composed, and with an affirming glance toward Emerald -- a glance of camaraderie and appreciation. Emerald glowed inside, gratified.

She couldn't help but notice Syb's eyes turned toward her several times during the meal. *She wonders what secret Kay and I share,* thought Emerald. But what Syb said next sent an electric shock through her.

"Emerald, has Mother or Kay ever told you? We have a policy here about overnight visitors. One of our guests told us about a young man climbing out of your room in the early morning hours today."

"I didn't want you to say anything," fretted Nora, "until after dinner was over. And not at the table!"

Emerald, stunned and quiet at first, finally blurted out, "He had only been there five minutes! He had climbed in to wake me up and ask me to play golf!"

"Climbed in? As in climbed in the window? On the third story?"

"Yes!"

"And how did he know exactly how to get to your room?"

"Ask Sybilla! She knows."

"I don't know what you're talking about!"

All eyes were turned on her. Even Louise had stopped mid-stride to glare at her, bowl of hot rolls in hand.

Nora, who really did consider this situation as a simmering scandal that might threaten their livelihood, went on in her trembling voice. "I had to call Nick and Charlotte today about the robe they accidentally left. I went ahead and mentioned it. I knew they would want to be aware."

Emerald's stomach turned to stone.

41

THE BOX IS OPENED

A silence hung heavy in the air, as Emerald sat paralyzed. She was just about to repeat the truth, but then why wouldn't they believe it the first time she told it?

They heard the front door open, then shut, and a man's boots were heard approaching the dining room. It was Danny.

"Sorry I'm late. Is it too late to get a bite to eat? That looks good." Then he handed something to Emerald. "Here," he said, meeting her eye, "I found your phone at the church last night. Not to be nosy, but I couldn't help but notice all those texts you were getting. It looks like he started at 5:00 this morning, asking you to go somewhere today?"

She could have thrown her arms around him in gratitude! Oh, how sweet to be justified in the presence of her accusers.

By way of extending grace, Emerald helped Nora clear the table and wash the dishes. Louise had gone off to do something else, and Kay was probably entertaining their guests as she usually did in the evenings.

After all was clean, Emerald dried her hands and went up to Kay's room. Now would be a good time, while it was vacant, to sort through the last stacks of papers and other odds and ends. She was halfway up the stairs when she realized Kay had most likely retrieved the lock box (when she had excused herself during dinner) and maybe Emerald could take a peek in it.

But Kay was in her room, not downstairs as Emerald had counted on. She greeted the girl with welcome, though, and insisted she work as if Kay weren't there. "Don't mind me, dear, I'm just about to leave. Just finishing up. I must go downstairs to be with our guests, and to show them the true hospitality of an established Southern home." Emerald thought she must be very tired; her words were a little slurred.

However, she didn't leave. She sat on the bed; she walked to the bathroom; she brushed her hair; she went back to the bed; she got up and went to the window and tried to do something with her curtains. And the whole time, she chattered to Emerald.

"I don't know what I would have done had you not come here, my darling. You have made a wonder of this space. Look how clean and organized everything is. You know, I will always call you my niece. I know there is no blood relation, but you are nearer to my heart than any relative I could have."

At first, Emerald enjoyed these endearing words, coming from a woman she had long admired, but something seemed amiss. They were too plentiful, too fawning. And there was something else. Kay's eyes shone unnaturally. She had that untethered look that made Emerald want to escape.

Then she spotted it: the gray metal box. And it was open. Sitting on a small table near the bed.

Kay kept fidgeting with things and talking non-stop. Little by little, Emerald worked her way closer to the box. She just had to see what was in it.

While Kay was bent down, doing something with her shoes, Emerald took a peek.

There were small, brightly colored things.

Jewels?

No, she didn't think so. They were too uniform. And they were scattered among several small plastic bottles. They were prescription bottles. The colored things were pills.

Kay saw her looking into the box. Their eyes met.

"Don't tell her! Emerald, don't tell her! Please! *This must be our secret!*"

Emerald didn't know who Kay was referring to. The look on Kay's face made her struck with terror. She controlled her voice very carefully and replied, "No, I won't tell her."

In her room, alone, she finally had a chance to finish her latest painting: it was the completion of the sketch she had begun while listening to Danny's violin outside, all those weeks ago, and not knowing where it was coming from. The music was sweeping a small girl up through an invisible door, beyond the façade of cold, hard reality and into the realm beyond.

To capture the abstract, on canvas, was harder and more satisfying than anything to Emerald. She didn't know if anyone would comprehend this painting or not, but it fulfilled something deep inside her.

She found a suitable frame but the corner was broken, so she would ask Danny to fix it. She had to get outside, anyway. Most everyone had gone to bed, but the house was hot and she longed to get her lungs full of chilly mountain air. She needed solitude to process what she had witnessed earlier. Kay was involved in something she didn't want her sister to know about.

Poor Nora, who was always innocently busy about linens, meals, and puzzles, had no idea that Kay was obtaining medication and keeping it hidden away. Where did she get them? Emerald knew very little of narcotics or anything addictive, but even before completing the thought, she felt she was close to hitting upon the truth she had tried to unearth all these months.

Was Louise getting them for her?

That would explain Kay's keeping her here.

42

THE PEPPERMINT PONY

Now Emerald was counting down the *hours* when she could leave. The week passed slowly, being a holiday, with everyone having an altered schedule. Her room was no longer a haven, after Julian's intrusion through the window, and knowing that Louise and others took liberties looking around in there.

As uncomfortable as she was, she was still watching for an opportunity to alert someone to the problem of Kay's addiction. But who was the right person? She was torn between Nora and Lars Franklin.

One other matter weighed upon her: she had never told anyone about the jewels. The ring she had found in the cellar bookcase, and the necklace set in the grandfather clock, were in her own jewelry case on her dresser. But she decided she would put them back where she found them. She certainly did not want such items to be found in her possession, in this house that was ever-encroaching upon her very soul!

Danny asked her to meet him for lunch the next day. He said there was something he wanted to show her. The invitation was unexpected, and she was surprised at the shy little flutter she felt. She thought of the times she had been repelled by him when she first knew him, so superficially. The months of practicing with him for the concert changed her; but more than that, he had shown himself to be her ally – quietly, but firmly – in her unsure relationship with the Keckleys.

She arrived at The Peppermint Pony as he asked, in between classes. He wasn't in his normal work clothes, but had on a green checked shirt with khakis.

"I just have to tell you what I found out, Danny, I'm about to burst!" She told him of the episode with Kay in her room, and the bottles of pills at her disposal. He listened with concern and agreed that all things pointed to Louise McSee as the supplier.

"How can it be, that with all those people living there, no one seems to know what's going on? I've seen her tipsy quite a few times, and I thought it was just the wine she likes to serve her guests, but this explains her extremes so much better."

"What about Lars Franklin? Do you think he's aware of it?" Danny asked.

"I have no idea, but he seems to be the only one who can do anything about such a situation."

They ate in silence, deep in thought, but after a while she realized he was looking at her with a smile in his eyes.

"Try not to worry about it. That situation with Kay has you really torn up. Now for the reason I asked you here. I can't believe you haven't noticed."

She was bewildered at what he meant, until she followed his eye to the wall nearest them. On it hung her painting of 'The Invisible Door,' the one she had given to him to fix the frame. Beneath it was a sign with the artist's name, and that she was a student at Finley.

"Ever since I brought it here, they said they've had people asking about you. They want to see more of your work."

Emerald quietly started packing. She replaced the jewelry in their hiding places without anyone noticing. She gathered her stray art supplies and school projects. She cleaned out her closet and put everything into her suitcase. Then, she went downstairs as if it were just another ordinary day, asking the sisters if she could help with housework.

Kay had that exhilarated look again, as if she were teetering on the edge of a precipice and no one knew how to control her. She said she was excited about Syb's play opening tomorrow, and the assembly of people she was planning to have over afterward.

This state of her personality always made her talk a lot, but it silenced Emerald. Especially since she knew about the lockbox of pills.

She looked at the woman with discomfort mixed with pity, and saw her as one grasping at fleeting glory, unwilling to relinquish anything life had ever offered her. Was there no one to help her? What would become of her, left to her devices with no one to intervene?

Nora, in her typical bustling about, complimented her sister on her arrangement of the furniture. "I will never have the gift you have, Kay! You can look at something and know just the right touch. No wonder we have so many repeat guests."

"Ah, you're sweet! I can always count on you to boost my spirits, dear Nora!" exclaimed Kay, whose spirits, if anything, needed restraint just now, thought Emerald.

"Sometimes one looks for a true friend, a soul mate, to share one's life. Here at Ashmont is the nearest I've ever come to being my true self, among those I love. I trust they will feel the same about me."

Nora piped up. "Oh, I agree! You are the best friend I've ever had. And I will always trust you, my dear sister. I know you would never keep anything from me."

Pity for both women made Emerald speak up. She turned to Nora and placed her hand on her arm, signifying the seriousness of this question:

"Nora, did you know that Kay is hiding something from you? Ask her. Ask her what she's hiding." Nora's bewildered eyes went from one face to another. "Kay, tell her about the lockbox," Emerald continued.

After a moment Kay laughed outright. "Why would I hide that from Nora? What does she have to do with anything?"

"You told me we were keeping it a secret from her!" cried Emerald.

"No, not from her! What do you mean? No need to hide anything from Nora; Saxon could hide a giraffe in the kitchen and she wouldn't see it."

"But Nora was the one to tell me she thought there were hiding places in this house! Months ago. She said valuables had to be hidden away so Louise wouldn't find them. I've caught Louise, myself, snooping around plenty of times."

"Hiding places! And you say you've found some?"

"Yes! Come with me – I'll prove it to you." She led them to the Vienna Room, no longer the tomb it used to be, and opened the base of the grandfather clock. She felt for the flat box and drew it out, opening to show the necklace set.

"See? It's only one, but they're all over. In the cellar, too, I know. There are books with the middles cut out. These are what Louise is on the hunt for! She is trying to steal these from you."

Both ladies stared at the open case in silence.

"They're the antique jewels that belong to this house, to this family. No telling how much they're worth. Nora herself told me about them."

Now Kay threw her head back and laughed, and this time there was something vicious in the sound. Emerald backed away from her a little.

It took Kay a minute to gain composure. Emerald was deeply alarmed.

"These are *replicas*, Emerald dear, that Nora has been buying off infomercials for years! She's hidden them all over the house with the idea that I am out to find them for myself." She paused to breathe deeply and corral her words again.

"As *children* we created hiding places for fun; we made those cutouts in the books. She even had that old basement library sealed off, last summer, thinking I would find that fake ruby ring Emerald has worn lately. I guess somebody showed her how to get down there through the foyer closet. Ooh, it was such a *secret*," she said sarcastically. "We don't want any guests finding the spiders and fake jewels we keep down there. *Ha!*"

Poor Nora looked bewildered and embarrassed, and Emerald felt so, herself. Now Kay was jabbing a folded piece of paper toward the girl.

"See? Look at the 'certificate.' Nora probably still thinks these are royal gems, or some nonsense."

Emerald opened the vellum-lined paper. She read:

Royal Regalia Incorporated
Jewellery inspired by pieces owned by royalty of
England, Russia, Spain and more.
Our collection of stunning parures includes Element of
Emerald, Pearlesque, Essence of Ruby, and
Diamondette.
Royal Regalia, Inc. is owned by descendants of
genuine royalty of European descent, and designs are
reflective of crown jewels, brooches worn by queens, and
adornments of royal blood for generations unnumbered.
This certificate guarantees this is a genuine inspired piece
created by skilled craftsmen and produced by a special license.
Enclosed please find a genuine inspired keychain,
complimentary gift for purchasing this one-of-a-kind
creation at the low price of $19.95 per month.

43

SUN AND STORM

Sun and storm were at war all day, wrestling for dominion over one another. When Emerald worked her last shift at Military Surplus, the light poured through the antique windows; but on the way home a charcoal sky threatened the landscape with fury. Then, just as she parked, the sun gained victory again and spread its glory about the mansion in a pool of gold.

She went upstairs to finish packing and to change. Tonight was Syb's opening night and the whole household was to attend the play, storm or no storm. She wanted to go ahead and load her car with as much as she could, so she could be on the road in the morning.

Kay caught her before she went up.

"Fasten this, will you dear?" She asked, holding her arm out with a dangling bracelet. She smelled slightly stronger of perfume than usual, but otherwise was her normal self. "Lars will be driving me tonight, and Saxon will take the others. I'm sure they have room for you. Anyway, will you let Lars in when he arrives?"

"Actually, I need to be getting ready, myself. Could Louise answer the door?"

"Louise is not here," she said in a low voice. "And she won't be coming back." She met Emerald's eye with a significant look.

Well! What could have happened? Thought Emerald wildly. She didn't dare ask her, but carried this bit of knowledge away to chew on silently. Kay hurried off, and Emerald was left downstairs with no one but the cat.

Before she began to worry about getting ready in time, an alarming round of thunder and lightning descended upon the vicinity of Ashmont. No rain was heard yet, but a fearsome display of wind was going on – and the trees all around were bowing and swaying further every moment.

Shortly thereafter, Saxon, Nora, and Mother Ann assembled themselves in the foyer, armed with coats and umbrellas. As bad as the weather appeared, no one said anything about staying home – not on Sybilla's grand evening. She must not be disappointed.

"Let's all wait in the car. Sybilla will be ready in a moment," said Nora. "I'm sure she'll be right down, and we'll be ready to drive off. Won't you go with us, Emerald? We have room."

"I believe I'll ride with Kay and Mr. Franklin. I still have to get ready," she answered.

So, with some slow bustling, and a few grumbles from Saxon, the three got settled in the Lincoln and were waiting in the driveway, ready to receive the star when she came down.

Emerald was standing there, watching the moving sky, when there was a loud crack. A tree limb was falling toward the car that held Saxon and the ladies!

He saw it too, and stepped on the gas with enough force to move out of its way within a few feet. Poor Mother Ann looked thoroughly traumatized – Emerald had seen her flowered hat tip backward with the sudden movement of the car, and now she was trying to set it straight.

Though safe, they were now entirely divided from the house and those who remained. The tree's massive limb blocked the entire driveway. Even the other cars – Emerald's and Sybilla's, being in the garage – could not get out.

Kay heard the story and debated about what to do, but at last she ventured out in the wind to instruct Saxon to go ahead to the theater. Lars would bring the rest and meet them there.

Sybilla was finally ready and came downstairs, decked out in her costume and heavy makeup. When she learned she had missed her ride, she paced like a tiger.

"Oh, when will he get here?" She demanded. "I'm about to start Aunt Kay's smoking habit if I can't get on the road soon. He'd better show up in five minutes, or I'll have to hire Danny to take me," she said.

"You can't. He's still in town. He said he wouldn't be back till late tonight," Emerald told her.

"Fine. I'll call Julian," she said with a sideways glance, which didn't affect Emerald in the least.

Even after Emerald was ready, there was still no Lars, and Kay began pacing with Syb. High winds were howling and rain had started; but Kay said they were to pass over soon, and all would be clear. There was still half an hour until curtain, so they had just enough time to make it – if Lars arrived soon.

Now Emerald noticed that Kay was drinking something and talking more. First about the weather forecast, then of her gratitude for Lars coming at any moment; then random unconnected remarks about the house, and Louise, and plans for next week. She said something about Louise being not far away, and that she would be able to call her as soon as she needed her again.

These latter thoughts set off an alarm inside Emerald. She looked at the woman and saw that glazed and exhilarated look again. It was as if she were teetering on a ledge, about to topple off. Someone had to help her. Emerald no longer cared if she looked like a meddler. Kay was a slave to her addictions, and Louise was her supplier. And she was the only one who knew this.

She was so deep in thought that she didn't notice the flash of headlights that were seen coming down the driveway: Lars had come at last. Kay and Syb flew out the door, running toward him; but he got out of the car and told them to go back inside, that the play was postponed, that almost the whole town was shutting down due to severe storms.

44

ELECTRIC WORDS

"This would happen to *me!*" Syb cried, knocking Tiger John off a chair so she could take it.

The four of them were gathered in the Vienna Room, where Lars was building a fire.

"Saxon will take care of Nora and Mother Ann," he said, brushing debris from his hands. "Thank God he is with them, but I wish one of them had a phone so we could contact them."

"Do you think they'll be able to come home?" asked Emerald.

"I doubt it. Too much damage already. Limbs were falling like matchsticks on my way here – I almost didn't make it at all," answered Lars. "He'll probably secure a hotel for them, and come home tomorrow."

"This was the best night for an opener," moaned Syb. "It won't be the same to start next week. A famous producer was supposed to be there tonight."

While she was wallowing, Kay left the room. *Now's my chance,* thought Emerald. She went to help Lars with the fire, and began to speak to him in a low voice. She told him about the recent scene in Kay's room, and that she had seen Louise with the pill box open in the laundry area. Talking fast while she had the opportunity, she confided her suspicions of, at the least, dishonesty, and the greatest, outright theft.

"Kay told me Louise is gone for good!" she whispered. "Did you know anything about that?"

Before Lars could answer, Kay stood in the doorway and began shrieking!

"What happened? Who did it? What are they trying to do to me?!" She came right up to Emerald's side and demanded answers. "You did it, didn't you? You did it so your parents could find out!"

Totally mystified, Emerald stared at her, then at Lars for help. "I don't know what you're talking about!"

"The picture! The photograph! It was removed, and now it's back! How dare you alter arrangements I myself make! Who do you think you are?! My intention was to display it in his own room when he visited us. To remind him of past fun, the times we had together. When I went to retrieve it, it was gone! You did that! And now you've hung it back up, just to taunt me!"

Lars was physically steering Kay to be seated and calm herself, but she went on: "He was supposed to marry me! Charlotte was never good enough for him!"

This declaration pierced through Emerald.

"Kay!" said Emerald, sinking into a chair out of weakness. "What are you saying?"

Lars looked at Emerald and shook his head. "She gets like this sometimes, you know. Don't let it worry you. Sometimes she's still – stuck in the past."

"She never deserved him! She had never been to finishing school, had not had the advantage of wealth, of political footing, and friends. Real friends who could represent you to the world properly. I used to sit and watch her, knowing how inferior she was – and yet Nick liked her better. Her sweet disposition, her kindness" — she said the words sarcastically – "fitted her to be a *nun* or something, not the wife of a professional man with money!"

"Money! *Now* it comes out!" cried Mr. Saxon, who now stood in the doorway in a dripping coat. He and the ladies had come home after all, and had walked inside the house without the others hearing them.

He was gazing at Kay with fury in his eyes. "I knew you couldn't say many more words before you so lovingly referred to your true love, your idol." Saxon was ever the only one with a voice strong enough to subdue Kay, when he wanted to, with his laser-like truths and indifference to her tactics.

Nora had heard enough to throw her fretting into overdrive. She bustled up to her sister, begging her to be calm and to consider what she was saying. "Dear Emerald mustn't hear you talk this way; she doesn't know you don't really mean it," she cried.

"Mean it? Of course I mean it! Didn't anyone see plainly that Nick still prefers me, even after all these years? Did you not see us laugh and dance together? I saw the way he looked around at this house, remembering our old fun times, sighing over what could have been."

At this speech Emerald looked at Kay narrowly. She no longer felt angry, because Kay was thoroughly deluded. Her mouth was running and her eyes glittered, but it's as if the words were being issued from some mischievous spirit within, equally without compunction or meaning. Nora and Lars looked at one another, then at Emerald, and she felt their pity and embarrassment.

"I'm sorry you had to hear these things, Emerald," apologized Nora. "Kay is fragile. She's, oh, what's the word . . ."

"I think the word you're searching for is 'unbalanced,'" said Saxon drily.

A new round of storm-blast was beating down upon them, with flying debris and hail now heard with the wind and rain. In an effort to stabilize the mood of the room, Saxon lit a pipe and settled into the biggest chair he could find.

"Actually, I love a good storm. It makes the fire burn brighter. Makes me all the more thankful for this dry place and a solid roof. It'll blow over soon, and we'll feel silly for all our worrying."

"I'm just relieved we have no guests! Dr. Canter is the only one upstairs right now. She told me she was working on some college forms and was glad for the obligation to stay home tonight," said Nora.

Just as those words left her mouth, lightning flashed, accompanied by an explosion of thunder, and then a tremendous crack. Then – the lights went out.

"Oh!!" screamed Sybilla, which did everybody's nerves good to hear.

Their world was black. Every unsettling sound from inside and outside was magnified, as if being fed through a microphone.

"Nora," said Saxon, groping in the dark for a dish to tap out his ashes, "looks like you'll finally get your cruise. Look at the ocean coming to meet us in the front yard."

Now Dr. Canter made her way into the room, and the group stared at the fire as their only anchor, helpless and waiting.

"What's that sound?" asked Lars, moving to the window. It took a moment, but others also recognized the sound of a machine of some sort. A whirring of a motor, and cracking of wood.

"If it's a car, it's probably Julian," asserted Sybilla. "He was supposed to be here."

"No, not a car. It's a man outside – I could see him while the lightning flashed. A man holding something."

45

CRASH AND COMPANY

"Who is that?" and "What could he be doing?" began to circulate among the ladies. They could make nothing out in the blackness except an overcoat and hat, and that he was operating something in his hands.

"Why, that's Danny! He is actually out in that mess with a chainsaw, cutting up the limbs," said Saxon, re-lighting his pipe. "That one is worth far more than he gets paid, to be sure."

They settled back down and awaited the return of electricity, with Nora saying something about dinner. "We haven't eaten in hours! I will go make us some sandwiches. I am sure something will do you good, Kay," but even as the words left her mouth she noticed Kay was not in the room.

Back to her secret stash, thought Emerald. *The next time we see her, she'll be higher than that chandelier.*

"I imagine she will return very soon. Lars, may I borrow that flashlight?" And off Nora went to be useful, the activity that had saved her sanity thousands of times in this house.

It was so hard to hear one another, with the ebbing winds and rain, that at first no one heard Sybilla exclaim about something else she was seeing outside: Kay's Lincoln was alit and revving, and the driver was speeding away down the now-cleared driveway.

"Kay's gone! Where could she be going?" she cried.

"Foolish woman! She knows better than to go out into that," commented Saxon.

"Fortunately, or not," spoke Lars, "I think I know where we can find her." His voice was low, but Emerald, standing near him, heard it as clear as a bell.

When Nora heard this news she nearly fainted. She set her tray of food down and sank onto the couch, being consoled by Lars. "If there's anyone who can take care of herself, it's Kay," he told her, with a sideways glance at Saxon that meant the opposite was true.

Danny now came inside and found everyone. He said he tried to stop Kay, but she ignored him.

"She just jumped into her car and sped away," he said. "I wouldn't have cleared the limbs if I'd known what she would do. But I thought it would help the utility crews when they repair the lines."

Everybody felt that the room was peaceful again (with the exception of Sybilla, who was looking irritable and rapidly texting someone). The fire crackled and the rain slowed to a drizzle. Emerald stared at the flames with the remembrance that her last night here, like her first, was in a storm. She had felt there would be mysteries to unravel on that first night, and now – she wished some things had stayed hidden away.

A familiar sound was heard coming down the hallway: the squeaky tea-cart that was used every afternoon for the guests. The rumble of the wheels made everyone look up and around, wondering who would be getting it just now. Before Emerald could complete the thought – *Where is Mother Ann?* – she nearly jumped out of her skin to hear a crash, many crashes, of many items, exploding in the doorway!

They whirled to see the poor old lady, who had been wheeling the cart with a mighty collection of the best china they owned. It had tipped over as she was trying to cross the threshold. Teapot, cups, saucers, sugar and cream bowls, were all represented by the pile of shards at her little slippered feet. She trembled and began to cry.

"Mother Ann! Are you alright?" rang out in echoes as they rushed toward her.

"You brought that all the way from the other part of the house? With no light?" was the astonished cry of Rita. "You should have called for help."

"Yes, Grandmother, why did you think we needed these?" asked Nora. "I had already brought the brown mugs."

"I – I didn't think those were good enough. I thought – we needed to use the good ones. For our guests."

"But we have no real guests tonight, Dear! Lars is our old friend," Nora replied.

Since everyone was crouched down, picking up the shattered pieces, they didn't expect the next voice they heard – almost directly over them.

"Poor Mother Ann," said Kay, coldly. "They shouldn't have let you do such a thing. Who sent you for those?" and her icy eye glanced around at each person – unluckily almost in a bowing position at her feet.

"I know," Kay continued. "Emerald probably did. Things around here usually aren't *good enough* for her."

The girl's face burned. It was typical that she could not think of how to rebuff such an unfair accusation. She bent lower, grabbing at the broken china, her fingertips bleeding. She saw that the floor where Kay stood was wet, and that she seemed unaware that her clothes were soaked.

Kay carelessly stepped on the broken china, crunching some of it into bits, and made her way to the fireplace.

"We noticed you had left, Kay, but I must admit we didn't think to see you again so soon," said Lars, trying to change the tone.

Kay walked to a small cabinet and opened it, revealing glasses and bottles. Emerald had had no idea it was there. She poured herself something and took a swig. "I did leave, yes, but there was a small accident. Just at the end of the driveway. Someone hit me. He's still talking to the police about it."

"Julian!" said Syb, jumping to her feet. "Is he okay? I was wondering what was taking him so long! Was he hurt?"

"The man in question was not hurt, no. They were taking too long to discuss it, so I came back to the house without them noticing."

Emerald became aware that Danny was quietly trying to get her attention. He came nearer and said, though staring at Kay, "The reason I cleared the driveway was so you could get out. You need to go home. But I want to drive you, myself. You've got an oil leak."

She opened her mouth to resist, but he said, "I've already moved all your stuff to my truck. You want to get out of here, don't you?"

"Yes," she answered quietly, still bending down.

The four-hour drive would put her back home by midnight: her heart rejoiced.

"Sister, I can't imagine where you would be going in that weather," Nora almost shouted, re-filling mugs of tea and trying to dissolve the tension in the room. Her nerves were raw and required constant action. "Mother Ann, do continue to work on your newest afghan. The zigzags are quite arresting to the eye. Don't you agree, Lars?"

Kay maintained her station in the center of the room, freezing anyone under her glance.

She began talking again, and freer. "Did I tell everyone," she stopped to hiccup, "Did I tell you all what Emerald found in our cellar? Where we used to play, as children, Nora?" Everyone was quiet. "She found priceless gems! Belonging to royalty!" her voice was exaggerated. "She's been looking for them ever since she's been here. I suppose she was going to find them and keep them for herself. That's probably the only reason she moved in with us."

This was too ludicrous to be angry at, but Kay's theatrics kept Emerald's – and everyone's – eyes glued on her.

Kay was far from being done. "She was going to keep them, sell them, and take the money back home to her mommy and daddy. And they would have everything they wanted. Isn't that funny, Nora? Our pretend niece was going to take the jewels – our *family jewels* – and make a profit off them, when her daddy is already rolling in money." And she laughed drunkenly.

"Now I don't really think that –" began Nora.

"Kay, you're talking crazy now," said Saxon.

Emerald was still stuck on the "rolling in money" part. What was she talking about?

"I said, isn't it funny?" Kay went on, "That she was going to take the money home to Daddy, who is a millionaire already, and the funniest part is – "

She stopped to catch her breath.

"The funniest part is – *she isn't even our niece!* She's not related at all! And she thought she was the whole time!"

Kay collapsed into the chair in tipsy glee, kicking up her leg and swinging it wildly. Her hair was still wet and clung to her checks in small globs. She had the look of having gained complete victory in battle. She went on:

"I believe we can call it a night, we're all safe from the big bad storm, aren't we? No, no – no one needs to accompany me upstairs. I'm quite alright." She turned to Lars and spoke to him as if confidentially, without at all lowering her voice. "Oh, I forgot, my room is not quite presentable for others' eyes just now. Emerald has been working in there, and she has left stuff everywhere. You cannot even walk. Dirty laundry, trash, a real mess. She said she would help me organize it, and she has been in the room many times, but just between us, it's worse than when she first started. She seems to just churn it up and then leave. She always goes up to her own little room, where it's all so neat, the way I would like my room to be. I thought she understood that. I'll just say, I'm glad we gave her that old maid's room and not one of the nice ones. We need to save those for our guests, our important guests. The ones who actually pay for their rooms."

The taunting flame had been brandished. It had waved in front of the dynamite over and over. At last it came close enough to make it spark and catch fire. Emerald shot up and went to her, with hot words springing from her tongue.

"How dare you! How dare you tell such lies! How can you say such things about my family! Of course you don't want anyone in your room, because you're a *filthy, drunken slob!*"

She was shaking. Danny came up and put his arm around her, gently guiding her back to her chair, just as she had seen Lars do with Kay. Nora sniffled and looked for a tissue.

The electricity came back on. They all blinked in the light and looked around.

Emerald was still too angry to regret any of her words, but in the naked glare she thought of all the other ears who had heard them. As for Kay, she was steadying herself by holding onto the mantle, patting her hair with her other hand, and not making eye contact with anyone.

The front door was opened, and footsteps advanced down the hallway toward them. Sybilla said something about Julian being here, and was running toward the doorway asking him questions about the wreck.

But the man who appeared was not Julian; it was a man Emerald had never seen before.

Syb stopped in her tracks and stared at him. She gasped, then passed out cold.

46

HOME

Danny was driving. Emerald sat next to him, sipping the coffee they had just gotten from a drive-through. They had made it through the clouds, and a few stars could be seen in the velvet sky, now that they were beyond the hilly country. Only a little further to go.

The first hour they had traveled silently, but both felt a sense of escape and relief. The events of the evening had emotionally worn Emerald out. Danny told her to get some sleep, but her eyes wouldn't close. She couldn't stop thinking about the scenes that had unfolded before her.

Sybilla's opening night had been cancelled, but there could have scarcely been any more theatrics on that stage than what had been performed in the Vienna Room at Ashmont Hall.

She thought of her outburst in Kay's face. That moment of mutiny had forever seared their relationship, and it could not be undone. Her sense of justice had come to a boiling point and her anger had rushed forth, stamping everyone's memories with the hot branding iron of her words. The price was that Emerald would now be hated by Kay, but at least she could breathe the fresh air of honesty.

It was the others that she worried about. She imagined the horror that Nora had felt by hearing such a description applied to her sister. And even Mother Ann's feeble ears had heard them too, as forcefully as they had torn through the air.

Dr. Canter – what did she think? There had been several times over the past few months when she had worn a pensive look around Emerald, which could be interpreted as either on the verge of reprimanding her, or warning her about something. Emerald never could decide which.

The angry explosion could not be diminished, but it was

curtailed, thankfully, by the entrance of Sybilla's ex-husband.

For the Keckleys, the shock was great at such a moment, and after so many years. From what Emerald could remember through her tears and elevated emotions, the man was slim and handsome, balding a little, but with eyes filled with fervor for Sybilla. She had fallen flat on the floor in her shock! So hard that her theater makeup was smeared on the carpet afterward. But she had been helped up and tenderly attended to – the first person to her aid was in fact, Kay. Emerald wasn't surprised. Her inebriation had not affected her reflexes in the moment of Sybilla's distress.

When Syb came to, her former husband was kneeling by her and holding her hands. Words and tears were exchanged. The whole evening Syb had been wrapped in her own cares, not even being frightened by the storm; but this finale left her trembling as a kitten. The last Emerald saw of her, Frederick was wiping Syb's tears and holding her like a child.

Mother and Dad were asleep when they got home, so Emerald made a bed for Danny on the couch. The next morning, though, he left early.

"Wasn't I surprised to see your old unicorn blanket on the couch, with a body under it!" said Mother, putting a plate of French toast in front of Emerald. "Danny apologized for bringing you here so late, but he said your car needed fixing, and that you were determined to come home."

"I had to," she answered. "I had to get out of that house."

Dad now joined them in the kitchen. "I would have rather you waited till daylight to come home, but no harm done," he said. "Your mother kept asking if you were okay at Ashmont – I guess she didn't quite believe me when I said you were fine. A woman's intuition trumps bare facts, I see."

Emerald told them all about Kay's hoarded room and how she was blamed for it. She told them about the bills and disorganization. "How can Ashmont keep running in that state? How can Lars let Kay operate the house in such chaos?"

"He doesn't. Kay doesn't have anything to do with the finances."

"What? Who does? Who pays the bills, who collects the money?"

"That professor, Dr. Canter, does. Lars hired her a few years ago. He needed someone on the premises and who could intercept the income before Kay could get her paws on it. She keeps all the books, and gives Kay an allowance every month, and keeps her on as strict a budget as she can. Although that might be an impossible task, even for a college professor. I did some checking up, you see, after your mother pestered me to. Found out a few things."

Emerald's clouded mind was clearing up after hearing this. Why hadn't she realized it on her own? Of course Dr. Canter was in charge of the money! The random checks and cash and invoices were only peripheral items. The real business was accounted for on Dr. Canter's laptop.

Now Emerald broached the subject that had weighed heaviest on her.

"Dad, Kay is – an addict. She has to be. You should have seen the pills at her disposal. And the drinking, on top of it. No wonder she seems to go haywire at times. And I found out something. Louise McSee is her supplier. She's been fired now, thank goodness, but Kay won't let her get too far away. She'll always know how to reach her. I had always wondered why she was tolerated at such an elegant house, and now I know."

"But didn't you tell us about the Sylvesters' knowing her, and that they thought highly of her? They said she saved Ashmont, or something to that effect?"

"They must have been blind, like I was, Mother. They're pretty eccentric themselves and may not see beyond Ashmont needing employees, and her being strong enough to work there. That's the only thing I can think of."

"Well, in spite of all the drama you've endured, it's too bad you didn't stay to finish your year at Finley. Maybe you could go and rent an apartment?"

"I don't know. I'm not sure I want to be seen anywhere in Millcrest anymore! The people who know me still think I'm the Keckleys' niece! I'm embarrassed to be connected with them. And after I blew up at Kay, no telling how she'll smear my reputation everywhere she goes."

Emerald had been disappointed that Danny had left without saying goodbye. She supposed he had brought her home as a kind gesture, as a sort of finale to their friendship. Then, he left soon after, as if not wanting to be thanked.

Now he would be released to go back to Celia and resume his relationship with her without any restrictions. There was a very real possibility Emerald would never even see him again! Before she could chicken out, she called him to thank him for bringing her home.

There was no answer. She left a voicemail.

No return calls, no texts, nothing from Danny came that day, nor the next. This was his way of signaling to her that he wasn't interested.

Emerald decided to call the Sylvesters. She half-expected them to have heard she had flown into a rage in front of a crowd of people, then hang up on her, but they had not even learned that she'd left town.

"Why, we were just talking about you, hoping that you would drop by today! Is it true that the young lady's ex has come back? And that they are together again? It's all over town!"

She found out some things from that conversation, mainly that life was same as ever at Ashmont, as far as they knew. But then Blanche mentioned something that sent a chill through Emerald.

"We heard that Danny Grosch is moving out. He stopped in this morning and mentioned it. Said he's had a job offer somewhere, and is making plans of some kind." That's all they knew.

47

UNEXPECTED GUEST

Charlotte Johnsey's health was much better, but she was not out of the woods yet. Some tests had been run recently that gave her doctors concern. Emerald – though a bit numb from her ruptured exit from Ashmont, and from Danny's total silence – was thankful to be at home and help where needed.

But when she would wake in the mornings, she found herself a little disappointed that there wasn't a cracked ceiling, a mothball-scented room, or vines with pink roses swirled across the walls. There was no window opening to a mountain view that pulled the breath from her lungs, and left her with a thrill of anticipation for the day. Here, the only thing to be seen from her bedroom was the outer edge of their subdivision and the backside of a Friendly's Market.

She would wait one month. Four weeks would pass away before she attempted to call Danny again. Evidently he didn't want communication with her right now, for reasons that – wondering what they were, kept her awake in the night – so she would respect his wishes and try not to think too much about it. But she would definitely try once more.

And anyway, she needed her car back! Her parents said they would drive her to Millcrest and leave her with the Sylvesters, who had urged her to come visit, for a weekend or so. She would look in on the Keckleys and say hello. She wanted to see how Sybilla and Frederick were doing. She wanted to hug Nora and Mother Ann, and gauge Kay to see the level of rage still against her.

But she would wait until sometime after New Year's Day.

Danny would be gone by then, packed up and moved to his new job. Maybe she could learn some clue as to where he was. He had bought a house, probably, with his new salary and was preparing for a wedding to Celia. She wouldn't try to re-establish their friendship, but she still wanted to thank him. So she decided to learn his address, and send a thank you note with combined well-wishes for his future.

She was extremely depressed.

She and Dad were decorating the tree; Mother was going through the Christmas cards. Emerald saw that Dad's eyes held a sparkle she had never noticed before, and that his eyes were often upon his wife. Her illness and especially her poor prognosis had made time precious, and every new day of strength was a fountain of delight and gratitude.

"Oh, that looks awful, Nick! Don't bunch them up so much. Let Emerald show you how to do it."

"Hey, what about her side? With all those ribbons sticking straight out? It looks like a porcupine."

"But I'm not done yet! And this is the latest style. Just wait till it's finished. And don't worry, Mother, I'll fix Dad's side."

"Heavens!" She replied, staring at a card she had just opened. "This is unexpected, even from Kay."

"Oh, she never fails to send Christmas cards. I've heard her say it a dozen times."

"But from South America?"

"What??"

Sure enough, included with a traditional "Seasons Greetings" was a postcard with a rather racy Latin American image. They were in Rio de Janeiro.

Emerald burst out laughing. "Nora got her cruise! I never thought she would. Good for them! I wonder if it's just the two sisters?"

"Kay, Nora, Mother Ann, and – brace yourself – Mr. Saxon! They're all four there. I don't think Saxon would have been able to let them go alone. He's been tied up caring for them most of his life."

"Either that, or he has a taste for exotic travel just as much as Nora. He probably engineered a pitstop in Cuba for fresh tobacco," said Dad.

"The thought of him lying on a cruise ship deck – with his pipe! This gets funnier and funnier," Emerald said, repairing the damage her father had caused to his side of the tree. "Does it say anything about Sybilla?"

"Not a word. I assume that's a good sign, for her and her ex."

"No telling," said Emerald thoughtfully.

The days crawled by and Christmas was coming up. When it was over, she would firm up her plans for visiting Millcrest and doing her detective work.

She paid attention to every social media outlet, stalking Celia. She couldn't help it; no matter how much she lectured herself against it. There were no engagement photos posted, but vague hints of something exciting around the corner that she would be sharing soon.

Emerald was wrapping presents and hearing the buzz of conversation between her parents, who were in the kitchen cooking sugared pecans on the stovetop. The scent was heavenly.

Suddenly, though, the smoke alarm went off and Dad hollered that they were on fire! He fanned the smoke away, but didn't realize he was projecting it right where Emerald was. She ran toward the front door, half laughing, half coughing. Opening the door, she darted out into the fresh air, but someone was standing there and she ran smack into him. It was Danny.

When he heard about the fire he rushed in to lend a hand, but fortunately Dad had gotten it under control. Still, the burnt pecan smell singed their noses and everyone wore a grimace while opening all the windows.

"Young man, you arrived just in time to see this family as we really are," said Dad, plugging up a fan and positioning it to blow through the kitchen. "Thank you for not being so polite as to leave us to burn down our house. Others would have said sorry they were disturbing us."

Emerald was trying to act naturally, but was thrilled to the core that Danny was there. She found it difficult to look him full in the face, but stole shy glances at him, noticing his hair was neatly combed and that he wore a tweed jacket she'd never seen before.

He had brought her car back, hitched to the back of his truck. He also said he had a Christmas present for her and wanted "to see how everyone was doing." She saw Mother and Dad glance at one another with a certain look.

"Grab your coats, everybody, we're going out for pizza. That'll give the house a chance to air out. Danny, you got here at just the right time! You are about to discover the very best oven-fired pizza south of New York."

48

CHRISTMAS GIFTS

Danny spent the holiday with them. He had no choice, once Charlotte found out he would only be going back to his garage apartment and not even the Keckleys would be at Ashmont as usual.

"After I took you home and drove all the way back, I realized I had lost my phone," he told Emerald. "I still have no idea where it is, probably at some gas station."

"No wonder you wouldn't text me back! I thought it was because – never mind."

They were sitting on the back-porch swing, and should have been shivering, but neither felt the cold air at all.

"I have to ask," she began, "what has Kay said about me? I'm still shocked I yelled at her like that, but she had pushed me too far. I couldn't take it anymore. Has my image been tarred and feathered all over Millcrest?"

"Emerald, it's like that stormy night never happened. She doesn't acknowledge it at all, whatsoever. My guess is that you told her the truth so directly that she had no option but to deny those words were ever spoken. She talks about you fondly. She even asked me to come get you and bring you back. That was before Lars made her leave."

"Oh, tell me about that!" she cried, gobbling this information up like a delicacy.

"Well, first let me tell you about Sybilla. Would you believe she and her ex-husband were remarried the very weekend he came back, and that Kay and Nora were actually planning to go on their honeymoon with them. Lars Franklin recognized what was going on and maneuvered the Rio trip instead."

"Are you kidding!" she cried, her eyes shining with amusement.

"I discovered several more things, also. I was the only one who could help Lars get the women ready for their trip in time, what with all their luggage, and in closing up the house, so we had time to discuss lots of things I never fully understood."

Ashmont Hall, he told her, made much more money than people realized, but most of it had been hidden away in view of Kay's outrageous spending habits.

"I found out Dr. Canter was in charge of the books," she said.

"Yes. They had to have someone on the premises who could keep tabs of everything. They installed her as a boarder two years ago. Before that, the money was like water through a sieve. Creditors were beginning to sue. And Kay was ignoring everything, going on shopping trips and running up debt like crazy. But, It wasn't only that."

"I knew it wasn't," she said in a low voice.

"Kay had a couple of minor surgeries a few years ago. Since then she's known every doctor in the area by their first name, and had juggled them and some others to get prescriptions she wanted. When it started to come to light, Lars hired Louise McSee, because she had previously worked in a jail and had experience with that type of thing. She knew which pills were harmless, which ones were dangerous when combined, and kept them locked away to ration them out to Kay while her case was being investigated."

"Seriously?!" Emerald couldn't believe her ears, and felt her mind being stretched further trying to grasp this. Louise, rather than being a drug dealer, was actually in control of Kay's medicine and keeping a tight rein on her.

Danny went on. "Lars told me he knew Louise could handle her, when Kay threw a glass pitcher at her and Louise put her in a headlock afterward," he smirked. "They needed someone with nerves of steel. Kay's in the habit of throwing things, breakable things, to get her way. Out of the public eye, that is."

"I remember finding a box of Kay's pills by accident," Emerald told him. "She scared me to death, how fierce she was, protecting them."

"It's because she knew Louise would take them and hide them. Lars told me Louise had to get very creative, finding new hiding places."

"Hiding places! Yes, Kay always perked up anytime a hiding place was mentioned. That old house sure provides a lot of secret spots. Poor Nora. She knew Kay was always on the hunt for something; she was just mistaken in what she was looking *for*."

This new information, which solved many smaller mysteries for Emerald, awed her and made her quiet.

They sat in silence for awhile, Emerald processing her thoughts, and Danny watching her change of expression under the winter moon. The movement of the swing helped ease any nervousness they might have felt, as his hand brushed against hers and she responded in a clasp. The electric moment did not last long, as Charlotte called for them to refrain from freezing to death and come in for cocoa; but the sensation stayed with both of them for long afterward, and bound them together in sweet remembrance of it.

Emerald fretted that they wouldn't have anything for Danny to open on Christmas morning. "I don't even know his sizes," she moaned, "or we could run to the mall and get something."

"Never mind, don't you worry," said Dad. "Your mother has something up her sleeve."

Accordingly, the next morning, after they ate a massive breakfast and took their coffee into the den, the largest package under the tree had Danny's name on it.

"What is this?" he asked Emerald, but she had no idea. He opened the box, pulled away the tissue paper, and peered inside. Everyone watched as he took out a blue and white afghan, hand-crocheted, and with a gingham design. It was Mother Ann's work.

"She sent several," explained Charlotte, "one of each member of the family, plus some. They arrived last week. She wanted to pass them on before their cruise. I had so much fun figuring out which one to give to each person!"

Emerald and Nick both found theirs under the tree: the pink and yellow that Emerald had seen her at work on, and a green one for Dad.

Danny found more in his big box: Charlotte had baked some

cookies for him, and there was a jar of sugared pecans. "In honor of your first night here," she explained, "and don't worry, those aren't black."

He shyly passed something to Emerald: the gift he had promised her. She unwrapped it and saw that it was a CD set of Chopin, the very same arrangement she had enjoyed on the Keckley record-player on that rainy day. How could he have known how much she loved it? He wasn't even in the house then – or was he?

"Here's something else. Not from me, but from – a mutual friend of ours. I guess." It was in somewhat extravagant, thick paper, and had a disproportionate bow that had been smashed (rather irreverently). Who could it be from? The Keckleys? Sybilla?

They watched as she pulled away the paper; she groaned at the absurdity. It was from Julian, and contained a framed photo of himself.

"He brought it to Ashmont the day after you left," explained Danny. "I told him I would give it to you; he has no idea I delivered it personally, though."

Emerald was wiping tears and shaking, and for a moment everyone thought she was weeping. It was only when she lifted her head that they saw the now-uncontrollable laughter. "I'm sorry," she gasped. "Julian. . . he's so . . .ridiculous. I just never realized it as much as this moment."

With relief, Danny was able to relax and enjoy the rest of the holiday. He had to go back home, though, he told them; he must leave first thing in the morning. "I have a new job, you know," he said.

Too quickly (she thought, and scolded herself later for), Emerald expressed her dismay. "Does this mean you're moving off somewhere?"

"No," he responded with a guarded smile, "but instead of telling you about it, I'd rather show it to you. When are you coming back to Millcrest to visit?"

"As soon as you want me to," she answered.

The Sylvesters were delighted to have their guest, although she did not spend much time with them. Danny selfishly kept her all to himself, Blanche and Gordon told each other, with a smile of remembrance of their own youth; which led of course into a twirl and a two-step, in time with inaudible music, no matter where they were.

Danny took her to a part of the Finley campus she had never seen: the performing arts center. It was where she was to see Sybilla's play but never got to.

"This is what Celia really wanted me for," he told her, sitting down at the piano. "To accompany her on an album. She's a jazz singer."

He played a few strains and then seemed to become self-conscious under Emerald's eye, so he closed it up again.

"I had no idea, but that's not what surprises me. Danny, you mean you play the piano too? I didn't know you as well as I thought I did."

He smiled. "And you still don't, because I haven't told you yet my big secret. I can't read music. I never could. If I play, or direct, or sing 'Happy Birthday to You,' I could never read or write a note of it. Anyway, I'm off the hook with Celia, because some Nashville label heard her sing at the Peppermint Pony and offered her a recording contract."

"But I know you and she dated for a while. You really liked her, didn't you?"

He waited a minute before answering, which Emerald was used to. She waited patiently, knowing whatever he said would be all the more potent and truthful.

"About a year ago, I thought I loved her. That is, I diagnosed myself as loving her, because I valued everything about her. Technically, she was everything I was looking for in a girl. She fit my ideas about love neatly, and she seemed to like me too. But I found myself forgetting about her for hours at a time. I finally admitted all that perfection was kind of boring."

Emerald saw that he didn't meet her eye while talking, and that he spoke a little fast. She wondered if her own faults (although he would have never called them that) were seen as attractions to him; and she took courage.

He had to clear his throat to keep talking. "Anyway, faking reading music all this time has worn me out, so I decided I'd better learn. So I'm a new student here at Finley."

"But what about the new job? Where is it?"

"Well, it's this," he said, tapping the piano. "I accompany singers, or actors, or provide backup on any number of solos. Piano or violin, either one. And it's a trade-off. They let me take classes for free. So I'm no richer than I was, in money anyway. But I feel I have a new start."

He took her back to his garage apartment, where he still lived while keeping an eye on Ashmont Hall.

"Not much for you to do with the others gone, huh? When are they getting home?" Emerald asked, while tidying up the sitting area.

"Lars said they were staying at least two months. I might as well stay on here as long as they let me, as cheap as it is. Have you seen my glasses? I can't remember where I put them."

"Here they are," said Emerald, finding them on the protruding brick that made a little shelf. It's where he had left Syb's note about finding a job for her, weeks ago. "And there's something else! I had wondered what had happened with this!"

She picked up a framed cross-stitch picture of a robin, showing it to him. "This hung on the wall in the place of that picture of Kay and my parents. What's it doing here?"

"Oh yeah. I swapped them out, just to mess with Kay. She sure went off about it, didn't she?"

"Yes, and I got the blame for it!"

Danny told her the history of the picture, and how he had witnessed Kay removing it when Emerald first arrived. "I wondered why she did it, but forgot about it until you told me about her weird behavior. So when I found the first one, I put it back just to see what she would do. It's like with those curtains you took down. She comes unglued when anybody touches her stuff without telling them first."

They were standing close together, and Emerald was wondering if the next moment would bring them even nearer. Her heart beat faster, and so loud that she thought he could hear it! She looked up at him and their eyes met. But just then he saw something outside and his look was torn away from her.

"Stupid cat! He's running around like crazy out there! I'm supposed to keep him inside. That was the one strict order I was given, and they're paying me for it, so I'd better go get him. Wanna help?"

So the next twenty minutes had Danny and Emerald chasing Tiger John across the lawn, laughing and yelling, cornering him, seeing him escape, and cornering him again. At last Danny got him out of a tree and handed him to Emerald with one hand, while he brushed himself off.

They were near the old bench between two tree trunks. She sat down, catching her breath, and holding the cat on her lap. Danny came over to her and plucked a leaf from her hair, then his hand lingered, caressing her cheek for a shy moment. She smiled at him, and he sat down next to her.

"When you took me all the way home, and then left early the next day, I was disappointed," she said quietly. "And then when I couldn't reach you, I thought you didn't want to hear from me again."

"I was an idiot to lose my phone like I did. It tormented me to wonder whether or not you were trying to contact me. That's why I got your car fixed and brought it back to you as soon as I could."

They were silent. She was absorbing the strength of his words, fully realizing his feelings for her were all that she felt for him. He spoke again:

"I thought you had probably forgotten me."

"That's the last thing I could do, Danny." She unloosed her hand from the cat's belly, and reached out to him. He took it and kissed it, then kissed her lips.

Tiger jumped down and ran off again.

J. Z. Richardson

Made in the USA
Coppell, TX
08 December 2021

67508948R00152